WELL PLAYED

NEW YORK TIMES BESTSELLING AUTHORS

J.S. SCOTT
RUTH CARDELLO

Well Played

Cover by LoriJacksonDesign
http://www.lorijacksondesign.com

ISBN: 978-1-946660-55-8 (E-Book)
ISBN: 978-1-946660-48-0 (Print)

DEDICATION

There is no way I could do this project and not dedicate this book to my amazing writing partner, Ruth Cardello. Ruthie, thank you for making Graham and Lauren's book a journey instead of a project. Not only are you an incredible author and writing partner, but you are such an amazing friend. Thank you for always being there for me.

Xxxxxxx Jan (J.S. Scott)

I knew Jan and I would be friends from the first time we spoke.

Jan, I was already a fan of your writing, but I soon became a fan of you as a person as well. You are generous beyond what you let most people see and I am grateful to count you as one of my closest friends. Some friends come into our lives for a short time while others become a part of us. I now cannot imagine my life without you in it. Thank you for inviting me to write with you. This book will forever have a special place in my heart—as you do.

XOXO Ruthie (Ruth Cardello)

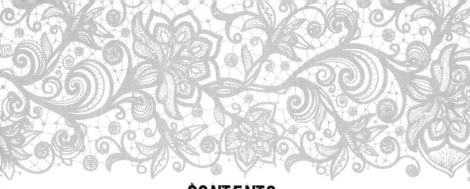

CONTENTS

CHAPTER 1

Lauren

S pecific moments tend to embed onto your psyche. They are so traumatic, so painful, they instantly imprint onto your long-term memory.

This was destined to be one of *those* moments. If I survived. If my ability to breathe returned.

I clenched the doorknob as my brother scrambled to cover his naked ass with a pillow. He swore and told me to get out.

I froze.

Holy shit, nothing will ever be the same.

Hope, the woman whose mouth was inhaling my brother's cock, scrambled to retrieve her clothing from the floor. Her face was tomato-red. It should be. *She's engaged to Graham Morgan, my brother's best friend.*

Or she was.

"My lesson was canceled." My voice was strangled as were my insides.

"You should have said something," Jack said in a tone he'd used once when we were much younger and I'd caught him downloading porn on my computer.

That memory was also embedded.

I'm not a prude, but certain societal codes of behavior should be adhered to. *One:* Not violating my computer or—ew—my room because you're grounded from the Internet.

Two: This!

"I'm sorry—" I stopped; I wasn't sorry. I was numb. I waited for Jack to break out in a smile. It had to be a prank. Graham and Hope's wedding invitation had arrived two days ago. Mine was secured on the refrigerator at Dad's place with a heart magnet. We were in Aspen to celebrate the pending nuptials as well as my graduation and Jack's promotion. "What are you doing, Jack?"

He shook his head without answering, and I pitied him. He usually wasn't an asshole, at least not as assholey as he appeared with a pillow clutched to his genitals as if his nudity was the big issue.

Clothing in hand, Hope dashed from the living room, down the hall, and into the master bedroom. I wanted to escape, too, so no judgment on my behalf.

"Hope," Jack bellowed.

She didn't stop.

He grabbed his clothing and charged after her.

A cold burst of air brought a flurry of snow through the opened door. It instantly melted on the dark wooden floor of the luxury chalet Graham had rented.

We had spent weekends in Aspen, although never in a place so nice. During high school, Jack and I had scraped our pennies and rented the best discounted rooms we could afford. Graham had joined us, but we'd refused his money. He'd never talked much about his home life, but we knew it wasn't good. Eventually, he'd stopped arguing and simply swore he'd get a huge NFL contract and repay us someday.

He finally had, and the expense of this chalet probably balanced the account.

On autopilot, I closed the door, unzipped my jacket, and hung it in the closet. I peeled off my boots and neatly placed them on the mat. I should have sought the warmth of the blazing fire in the stone hearth, but I still had the visual of my brother and Hope sprawled in front of it.

I shook my head.

That's an image that can't be unseen.

The kitchen seemed like a safe destination. I poured a glass of Merlot, and even though I wasn't a drinker, I finished it off in one long gulp.

This can't be happening. I gripped the counter behind me. Graham had trust issues. Jack and I were the only family he had. *Jack, how could you do something this stupid? This cruel?*

I poured another glass and downed half. My stomach churned in warning.

Voices in the living room forced me to abandon my wine and walk toward them. Although I couldn't make out what they were saying at first, they were obviously arguing.

Hope dropped her luggage in the foyer and retrieved her coat from the closet. I stood, silently observing. "I have to get out of here," she said desperately. When she realized I was there, she said, "I'm sorry. Graham is on his way. I should tell him not to come, but—" She covered her face with her hands. "This wasn't supposed to happen."

I might have felt sorry for her if I weren't still trying to erase a certain image from my mind. It was still disgustingly vivid. Jack wrapped his arms around her, an act that angered me.

"You're upset. You can't drive like this," Jack pleaded.

"I have to. I need to think. This isn't me. I don't do things like this." She looked for confirmation from me, but I looked away. I hadn't known her long enough to refute or support her claim, nor did I want to be put in that position.

"It's going to be okay. I'll drive you," Jack said, as he cupped her face between his hands.

My voice finally functioned. "What about Graham?"

Jack turned to acknowledge my presence. I expected him to be angry with me, but his face held a pained expression instead. "I'll drive Hope to the airport then come back. He's still a few hours out."

"I should be the one to tell him," Hope said, although she didn't look or sound convinced.

"No, we've been friends our whole lives. I'll tell him," Jack said firmly.

How noble of him. I wanted to slap him. His declaration had the opposite effect on Hope. She melted against him, and I wanted to vomit. There were many words I could have let fly, but none would have helped the situation.

I turned to walk away.

"Lauren," Jack said as he approached me. Whispering to keep Hope from hearing, he said, "Don't say anything to Graham if he beats me here. Tell him we were out when you arrived."

"I won't lie to him," I said forcefully, brave from my wine buzz.

"Then drive home now."

My mouth gaped. I didn't know this Jack. "What if Graham gets here before you? Don't you think he'll worry if no one is here or answering his calls?"

The door opened, and Hope slipped out.

I started to tell him what I thought of his plan, but he walked away.

He grabbed his coat and swung the door open. "Listen, I fucked up. You don't need to tell me how badly. Don't say anything to Graham, okay? I'll make this right. I swear."

He slammed the door before I had a chance to agree or tell him to go to hell.

I grabbed my cell and brought up Graham's number. He deserved to know what had happened. He deserved a chance to talk it out with Hope if that was what he wanted.

I stopped in front of the fire without calling him. I paused, trying to understand my feelings. My anger had dissolved; I felt relieved—almost happy.

That was as unnerving as seeing Jack and Hope together. Graham was my honorary brother from another mother, my protector, and even my confidant. Jack's betrayal would cut Graham deeply, and my heart *should* be breaking for him.

Leaving my phone on the mantel, I went to my room to pack. No matter who told Graham, chances were he would hate all of us, including me, simply for bearing witness. He'd cut members of his family out of his life for that very crime.

I tried imagining my life without Graham but couldn't.

Confused and disgusted with myself, I transferred my belongings into my luggage, pausing when I saw my reflection in the bureau mirror. I told myself my feelings were irrelevant. Graham had never looked at me the way he looked at Hope.

I wasn't in her league. On my best day, I was cute. On my worst, I was a slightly overweight, bespectacled nerd with awkward social skills.

Many people spend their entire lives trying to stand out. I only wanted to blend in. Strategically, I had learned to keep the majority of my thoughts to myself. Sharing them had never made my life better.

At age four I pinpointed the error in a cartoon character's attempt at Fermat's Last Theorem, a problem that had taken mathematicians until 1994 to solve, and sought to discuss it. Not having the mathematical vocabulary to properly express how I would have solved it, I'd asked my teacher, and was instantly transferred to a school for the gifted.

I graduated from high school at fourteen, had an undergraduate degree in applied mathematics by seventeen, and my PhD in condensed matter physics by twenty. Whether it was what I wanted or what I was told I should want, I was still unsure. When I requested a year off to find myself, I was directed to therapy.

Some good came from that experience. I learned to value my emotions even when they didn't match the expected. Feelings weren't wrong, actions were.

I also met my best friend, Kelley. She was interning at the practice where I paid for two sessions, debated the basic principles of psychology for two more, then on my clinician's prodding, went on to formally study it.

In retrospect, the suggestion to get my own degree if I thought I knew so much might have been sarcastic, but I wrote a dissertation to support my views and had an additional diploma a year later. Unlike my clinician, Kelley found my questions invigorating. She defined friendship as two people bringing out the best in each other. We were still close even though she had gone off to college in California to finish her studies, leaving us to communicate only by phone for now. Besides Graham, she was the only person who accepted me as I was.

On impulse, I retrieved my phone from the mantel and called her. No answer. I checked the time. It was early enough that she might be in class. I left her a voice message—a long, detailed update that included a trip to the kitchen for another glass of Merlot.

CHAPTER 2

Lauren

"Wake up, Peanut. It's too beautiful of a day to sleep away."

I opened my eyes cautiously but didn't sit up from where I'd fallen asleep on the couch. My short-lived buzz was gone and my head was throbbing. Graham Morgan, all six feet five inches of gorgeous muscle, was standing above me—smiling.

Could the whole thing with Jack have been a bad dream?

Graham lifted my legs, sat on the couch, and lowered them back onto his thighs. He was comfortable with me because I had never so much as hinted I might have feelings for him. He would never know how I savored his touch or how I'd never dated anyone who made my stomach flutter the way it did every time he looked at me.

He ran his hand up and down the shin of one of my legs. "So, where is everyone? Still out on the slopes? Did you stay behind to meet me?" His smile was easy and pleased, the kind someone gave a dog who greeted them with a wagging tail.

I sat up and removed myself from his confusing touch. My head spun and I groaned.

He leaned closer and took a whiff of my breath. "You've been drinking." He placed a hand over his heart. "My little Lauren, all grown up, drunk and passed out before dinner."

"I'm not drunk," I croaked, sitting cross-legged facing him.

"Worse, hungover." Graham attempted a sympathetic look then laughed. "Do you feel like shit? Because you look like you do."

"Thanks." I shoved him with my foot. It's what he expected and what I would have done if this were a normal day.

He grabbed my foot and held it. "So grumpy. I'll have to cheer you up. How long has it been since someone tickled you until you peed yourself?"

He was joking. Not only had he never done that, but he would have never allowed Jack to go that far either. No one hurt me. No one embarrassed me—not when he was around. Off the football field, Graham was a gentle giant to me. Still, the mischief in his eyes told me I wasn't going to completely escape.

"Don't even try it." I attempted to yank my foot free even though a part of me was loving having his full attention.

"Come on, Peanut, smile just a little," he said as he slightly tickled the bottom of my foot.

I squirmed and let out an involuntary laugh. "Stop." It felt good to see him again, too good. He hadn't made it home for the holidays, so it had been over a year since I'd seen him in person. I felt guilty enjoying myself when he was about to receive devastating news.

He squeezed my foot gently before releasing it. "No frowning. I missed you and I'm in a really good mood."

"I missed you, too," I said. It wasn't exactly witty exchange but it was honest. My mind was racing with everything I wanted to but couldn't say. Was Jack right? Would the truth be best received from him?

I shivered and glanced at the hearth. The fire had burned out, leaving only smoking ashes. An omen that nothing was forever?

"Did you eat yet?" I asked because if I didn't find something to distract myself I was going to start vomiting the truth. It was killing me to keep it from him.

"No. I'm starving. The fridge should be stocked. You hungry?"

"I could eat something," I said.

"First one to the kitchen makes the sandwiches. Last one cleans up." He stood and bent in the stance of a runner waiting for the starting shot to fire.

I smiled because it was impossible not to. He had his demons, but he'd never discussed them with me. Our friendship was light-hearted and fun. I'd never pushed for more and it was something I regretted. If he stumbled over Hope's infidelity, I wouldn't be the one he'd turn to. I might have been if it hadn't been Jack who had betrayed him.

I scrambled off the couch despite how it made me a little dizzy and raced toward the kitchen. "You're on." I beat him, but seated at the island counter, he looked too pleased with himself to not have let me win. I narrowed my eyes at him and he shrugged.

"I forgot how fast those little legs of yours are."

I nodded and put a hand on one hip. "I may be short, but my foot can still reach your ass."

He laughed. "Hey, I'll clean up."

"You'd better." I turned and started to search the contents of the fridge. "You're not allowed to get a big head just because you're a pro starter now."

He slapped the table. "Hold on, you're right, I am kind of a big deal now. So instead of one layer of pickles, put two. You know, thanks to you, I can't order a turkey sub now without them. You've ruined me."

I placed a jar of sliced pickles next to the luncheon meat and bread on the island between us. "There's a reason they've been around for thousands of years."

He opened the jar and plopped one into his mouth. "Are you officially done with school now?"

I hunted down plates and silverware. "I hope so."

He rolled up a piece of turkey and took a healthy bite of it. "Congratulations. You're officially an adult. Now get a damn job."

I laughed and paused from assembling the sandwiches. "I have several offers on the table. I just don't know what I want to do yet."

"Being a genius is hard, isn't it?" He didn't look the least bit serious. "Is there any company that *wouldn't* hire you?"

I pushed a finished sandwich across the island toward him. "Do you know that happiness is abstract and subjective regardless of the tools we attempt to measure it with? Despite circumstance or genetics, it often comes down to believing how a person says they are feeling. Medically, we try to measure it. Is the release of dopamine, brain derived neurotrophic proteins, or endorphins happiness? Maybe it's too much to expect one career to do all that. It might be time to start exploring mammalian mechanisms for releasing oxytocin."

He blinked a few times fast then said, "In English, Peanut."

"I'm looking for a job where not everyone is over forty. I want to make friends and date more."

He nodded and looked me over. "That shouldn't be hard. You're adorable."

I choked on a piece of bread. *Adorable.* I rolled my eyes skyward.

"But you shouldn't choose a job by how likely it is to get you laid. You're too smart for that."

"Says the football player who just did a commercial in boxers," I countered. I couldn't remember a time when he wasn't turning eager women away.

"The underwear gig was a seven-figure contract," he parried, then smiled again. "Besides, there's only one woman in my future." He checked his phone. "Did Hope say what time they'd be back?"

I shook my head. Technically, that was not a lie.

"I'm glad I had her come early. The snow was picking up and the roads were already slippery. The good thing about her being with Jack is I don't have to worry if she's okay." He finished his sandwich, grabbed a bottle of water and said, "I'll hit the shower then."

He left without remembering to clean up, but I didn't say anything. I sagged against the counter, feeling guilty and apprehensive. I tried to call Jack but got only his voicemail.

I had just finished rinsing the dishes when a towel clad Graham appeared in the doorway of the kitchen. His hair was still wet from the shower, and I could barely breathe as I took in the perfection of him.

His jovial mood from earlier was gone. He held up Hope's engagement ring, and said, "I found this in the bathroom. Hope never takes it off." He glared at me as if his mind was already running through all the possible explanations and not liking a single one of them. I was reasonably certain he hadn't yet factored Jack into the equation. He looked confused and upset, but not as angry as he soon would be.

This time my heart did break for him. I wished there were a way to protect him from this, but that wasn't an option.

I had two choices before me.

I could tell him the truth or I could lie.

CHAPTER 3

Graham

I never have been, and have never claimed to be a *nice guy*. I've always been a complete and total prick, a trait I'd always hoped that Lauren would never discover, but I was just about to blow my cover and completely lose my shit.

Hope *never* took her ring off, so I knew *something* was wrong. I had good instincts, and they had never steered me wrong, especially when it came to playing football. Unfortunately, my gut reaction was fucking screaming that whatever was happening with Hope, it wasn't good.

"Graham, I don't know what to say," Lauren said nervously.

"Tell me the truth," I demanded, my teeth gritted to keep me from having a goddamn meltdown.

Lauren Swift, one of the two friends I'd trusted for way over a decade, didn't lie to me, and I sure as hell didn't want her to start doing it now. She and Jack had been the only real friends I'd ever had. They were like the *family* I'd never had.

Okay, technically, I *did* have some blood relatives, but none of them had ever wanted to claim me. I was okay with that because

I didn't like any of my living relatives, either, so it worked out well for us not to communicate.

I learned a long time ago that a blood connection didn't mean much.

I watched as Lauren avoided eye contact and fidgeted with her glasses. Hell, that wasn't a good sign. The only time she messed with them was when she was nervous.

"Hope is gone. Jack took her to the airport," she blurted out. "She didn't say, but I think the engagement is definitely off."

The engagement is off? What. The. Fuck. There was no way Hope could be finished with me. The wedding invitations were in the mail. Everything was settled.

Hope *had* to marry me. She was part of my future plan. I was on track to finally be *somebody*. We'd had an agreement that worked for both of us. She couldn't back out now.

Marrying Hope was going to be one more strategic move to have the life I'd always wanted. Making her my wife would prove that I'd taken one more step up in the world.

"She just…left?" I knew Lauren wasn't telling me everything. "There has to be some reason why she split. We weren't fighting. Nothing was wrong."

Hope and I didn't *ever* argue. I had no reason to get mad at her.

She was from a very wealthy, respected family.

She was a supermodel.

And we made no unrealistic demands on each other.

She did her modeling thing.

I did my football thing.

And when we were available, we'd get together as a couple.

Who wouldn't want a marriage with somebody like Hope?

"She wasn't *angry*," Lauren confessed. "She was *upset*."

"For God's sake…why?" I loved Lauren like a sister, but I was starting to lose it.

Lauren finally stopped fidgeting and looked me in the eyes. "I can't lie to you. I can't."

Oh, holy shit. She was staring at me with *sympathy* in her expression, and I hated that. I didn't want pity. I never had. All I wanted was the truth. "If you're really my friend, tell me what happened. I know that you know. I can see it written all over your face."

I'd known Lauren since I was seven years old. Jack and I had met in elementary school, and had become fast friends, something I'd valued because I'd really had no friends. It had been a new school district for me when I'd met him. Luckily, I'd stayed in the same school district even though I'd changed foster homes more times than I could count after Jack and I had become friends, we'd been best buddies ever since.

I'd met Lauren one day at Jack's house. Ben, Jack's dad, had always been willing to go out of his way to come pick me up to play at their home, and Lauren had quickly become the second friend I could trust. Okay, maybe she was only all of four years old when we'd first met, but she'd already been attending a school for gifted kids.

I'd idolized her brilliant mind, and I'd adored the little girl who gave her affection so easily to a boy who had really never done anything to deserve it. In return, I'd made myself her protector when she was a kid. Strangely, I'd never really gotten away from that habit, even though I was now twenty-five and Lauren was twenty-two. We hadn't seen each other in person much in the last seven years since I'd left for the East Coast after I'd graduated high school, but I still considered Lauren one of my best friends.

"Tell me everything," I prompted, since Lauren still looked like she was considering the benefits and drawbacks of spilling her guts.

"She slept with somebody else, Graham. I'm so sorry."

Lauren's words hit me like a ton of bricks. "Not possible," I told her in a defensive tone. "She'd never do that."

Hope didn't exactly burn red-hot when it came to sex. Sure, the sex was good, but she'd never been all that enthusiastic about mating like bunnies. Most of the time, she *planned* out our nights together, and it *usually* ended with sex. But it wasn't down and dirty. I was okay with that since she was a woman I thought I needed to treat with respect.

"She *did* do it," Lauren corrected. "I'm telling you the truth. I saw it myself, or I wouldn't be telling you about it."

Wait! Lauren *saw* it?

The only way that could work is if it had happened...here.

My brain really didn't want to put together the facts. "Jack?" I asked hoarsely.

She nodded slowly. "Yes. I'm so sorry."

I looked away from her remorseful face. "I'll kill the bastard."

I tossed the expensive diamond on the counter and walked back to the bathroom, slamming the door behind me.

Rage built inside me, an over-the-top anger that I'd never completely been able to shake off. It had been there when I was a kid, and the only difference between my adolescence and now was that I had learned to control it.

Son of a bitch!!!

My fury was closely followed by the emotional pain of being betrayed by the one male friend I'd ever trusted to look after Hope when I wasn't around.

I dug into the pocket of the jeans I'd left on the floor until I found my cell phone. I hit the buttons to call Jack, but he didn't answer. It went to his voicemail.

"Goddammit!" I hurled my phone, enjoying the satisfying sound of the bathroom mirror shattering as I stood and watched the shards of glass explode all over the vanity and fall to the floor.

My chest was heaving and I felt like I couldn't breathe. Jack was my friend. He'd been my best buddy all through school, and for every single year after that. Why in the hell would he sleep with my fiancée?

And why would Hope run around with Jack? He wasn't even her type.

I lowered the lid of the toilet and sat my ass down, trying to make sense out of the surreal situation I was in.

I'd met Hope last year while I'd been playing for New England. I'd been a second-string quarterback with a chip on my shoulder. I'd barely been picked up in the draft after college because of a shoulder injury, and I had something to prove. All I'd needed was a chance...

I'd gotten the opportunity to prove myself when our starter went out with an injury. I'd played the best season of my life, which had opened doors everywhere. All of a sudden, I could pick my future team, and I'd gotten a ton of offers to become a starting quarterback in a bunch of different areas of the country. Coming back to Colorado to play for the Wildcats had been a logical choice for me since Lauren and Jack were both still living in Denver.

I'd wanted to be near somebody who gave a shit about me, and that meant moving back to Colorado to be with Lauren and Jack.

Honestly, it hadn't hurt that the Cats had made the best offer. They'd made me a millionaire overnight, with more guaranteed income to be delivered over the next few years of my contract.

All kinds of lucrative side deals had also come my way— which was why I'd been doing commercials in purple boxer shorts. Hell, if somebody wanted to pay me a fortune to talk up their colorful underwear, I was all over that.

It figured that just when my life was going exactly where I wanted it, somebody would throw me a fucking curve ball. But I'd never expected this.

Not from Jack.

Never from Jack.

But I'd deal with him. I'd make him sorry he'd ever touched Hope.

If I could find the motherfucker.

"Graham?" Lauren knocked hesitantly on the bathroom door. "Are you okay? I heard something crash."

I wasn't okay, but I bit back the urge to tell her to go the fuck away.

I'd always valued my relationship with my Peanut. So what in the hell was I supposed to do now? Her brother had made himself my enemy. I didn't want her to have to choose between her real brother and her honorary one.

Lauren and I had a unique relationship. She was one of the only people who didn't see me as a ruthless prick. I kind of liked it that not everybody on the planet hated my guts.

Jack knew what a dick I was, but he'd learned to blow off the jerk part of my personality—which wasn't an easy thing to do— and had chosen to see some kind of hero underneath my bullshit.

Problem was, I wasn't *anybody's* hero. I'd stepped over anybody who had gotten in the way of my success. I was a stubborn bastard, probably because I'd been a foster brat who had carried my belongings from one foster home to another in a plastic garbage bag. If *that* wasn't motivation to better my situation as an adult, I didn't know what would be.

I generally hadn't bothered to unpack when I was a kid. None of my temporary homes lasted for very long.

Back then, Jack and his sister had been the only stable things in a childhood of chaos.

I finally answered Lauren. "I'm good. The mirror broke."

"Did you break it?" she said suspiciously.

"Naw. It just spontaneously exploded."

I heard her snort. "The probability of that happening is pretty slim."

Hell, she was smart. Maybe that was one of the reasons I'd always worshipped her. "Shit happens," I said noncommittally.

"Okay." She sounded unconvinced. "I'll be in the kitchen if you want to talk."

I didn't want to talk. I wanted to smash her brother's ugly face in. I wanted to beat the crap out of him until he told me why in the hell he'd betray our friendship.

It had always been special to me.

It hurt to find out that Jack didn't rate our friendship quite so highly.

I let out a frustrated breath as I heard Lauren move away from the door.

Maybe I *should* talk to her, but I felt like she was the enemy, too. She was Jack's little sister. Could I still trust her?

I dropped my head into my hands.

Jesus! I was so fucked.

I didn't even know who was friend and who was foe anymore. It wasn't the first time I'd felt that way, so I'd learned to just write everybody I suspected of screwing me off, whether they were guilty or not.

Maybe it was better if I pretty much treated *everybody* like they were my enemy. It was a lot safer that way.

CHAPTER 4

Graham

My mom and dad were dead, and *nobody* wanted me. I set my trash bag down on the floor, and flopped on the bunk bed that my new foster parents had shown me just a few minutes before.

I tried to picture the faces of my biological parents, but I was starting to forget what they looked like, how their voices sounded, and how I'd felt while they were alive.

I was nine years old, so it had only been two years since my mom had died, but it seems like a really long time ago.

My dad had been a Navy SEAL, a tough guy who had always played with me when he was home between assignments—which wasn't very often. My mom used to tell me that my father was brave, and that he had an important job because he was fighting for our country. I had been pretty proud of him because he was a SEAL. Maybe I didn't see him a lot, but he was still my dad, and I'd idolized him.

Then one day, my mother came to my room and told me that my father had died. Not that I'd *completely* understood death back then, but I'd known that he was never coming home again to play with me. My mom had told me that he was in Heaven, but I'd seen his body go into the ground, so I didn't understand how he could be somewhere else when he was buried in a military cemetery.

I kind of understood the whole *Heaven* and *God* thing now, but I'd been pretty confused a couple of years ago.

After my dad was gone, my mom had never been the same. She cried all the time, and I'd had no idea how to comfort her. I'd tried, but it had been like she wasn't really hearing me.

Then, not long after my father died, my mother died, too.

I closed my eyes and tried harder to remember my parents, but it was no use. They were starting to fade away.

"Shit!" I exclaimed aloud, knowing I was saying a bad word, but I didn't care.

I'd learned plenty of cursing when I'd gone to live with my aunt, which had happened right after my grandparents had passed me over to her. My grandma and grandpa said they couldn't handle me anymore, so Dad's sister had taken me in.

I'd only been with my aunt a couple of months before she'd told me I couldn't stay with her, either.

I was something my relatives and foster families called hyperactive. I knew there was a longer name for whatever I had, but I couldn't remember the whole thing. But it didn't matter.

I was bad.

I was different.

I did things I shouldn't do because of the enormous amount of energy I felt sometimes.

Really, I didn't *want* to be bad, but sometimes I couldn't control what I did.

Mostly, I was angry. Why did I have to lose my mom and dad before I was grown up? Other kids had parents, so why didn't

I? Why didn't my family want me? Yeah, I broke stuff and I said things I shouldn't, but it wasn't like I did it on purpose.

I started going from place to place in foster care after I left my aunt's house, and sooner or later, I was always rejected.

I'd be sent away from this foster family, too, so I knew I couldn't love them. I didn't need to love them. I had two good friends now, and that was enough.

I'm glad I have Jack and Lauren.

Jack was my best friend, and Lauren was Jack's little sister. Neither of them thought I was *different* or *bad*.

I got off the bed, hefted my trash bag up, and put it into the closet.

I wanted to go find my friends, the only ones I knew I could trust.

It wasn't like I really talked to them about my problems, but at least when I was with them, I didn't feel like such a weirdo.

Because she was only six, I didn't talk to Lauren about much of anything. But if I was sad, she'd hug me. And she always seemed to know when I wasn't feeling good.

I'll never tell Lauren and Jack that people think I'm not worth the trouble I cause. Jack was my best friend, and Lauren looked at me like I was somebody special. I'm not, but I wanted her to keep thinking that I was. It felt good to be important to *somebody*.

It was a lot better than feeling all alone.

CHAPTER 5

Graham

"I need a drink," I grumbled to Lauren as I entered the kitchen.

I'd tried to get myself together. I'd gotten dressed, and tried to pull myself out of my full-blown rage over Jack's betrayal.

If I was truthful—which I generally wasn't—I'd admit that I really needed more explanation. Not that there was *any* excuse for what had happened, but I guess I needed some kind of insight as to why my fiancée and my best friend since childhood would throw our relationship away just for a fuck.

Strangely, I wasn't as sad about Hope as I was about Jack. My best friend and I were like brothers, and had been since we'd met in grade school. Jack had been one of the few people I trusted, and his betrayal had stunned me, not to mention it was making my gut ache with disappointment.

Lauren went to the fridge and pulled out a beer. She twisted the top off and plopped it down in front of me.

I looked at her and cocked an eyebrow. "I was hoping for something stronger."

Usually, I avoided alcohol. Me and adult beverages didn't mix together well. I had to stay in peak condition as an athlete. But I'd just lost my fiancée and my best friend, so fuck it.

She shrugged. "It has to be beer or wine. It's all we stocked."

I took the bottle and chugged half of it before I spoke. "Tell me what happened. I deserve to know what you saw."

"Graham, you don't need to know all of the dirty details—"

"Tell me," I interrupted with a demanding tone. "It's over. I might as well know everything. I'm still trying to understand."

I could tell that she was reluctant. She didn't share anything right away. I watched as she pulled out the Merlot, poured herself a glass, and downed half of it before she opened her mouth to speak. "There isn't a lot to tell. I came in and found them together. Hope was swallowing my brother's—penis."

The look on her face would have been comical if the outcome hadn't been so damn tragic. Her distaste of finding her brother in any kind of sexual situation was obvious.

"It's called a blow job," I informed her. "Is that what you're saying?"

She nodded hard, but didn't say a word. I actually had to bite back a smile because she didn't want to associate Jack with any kind of sex.

Hell, had Hope really been blowing Jack? That *really* pissed me off. Never once had she offered to swallow my dick. I had thought she just wasn't into it.

Apparently, she just hadn't been into...*me*.

"I found them together," Lauren explained. "We argued, and Jack left to take Hope to the airport."

"So she's already on her way to Boston?"

"I assume she is," Lauren mused. "I've been trying to call Jack, but he's not answering."

I slugged the rest of my beer before I said, "He isn't answering my calls either."

Once again, Lauren went into the fridge and slammed another open beer in front of me.

"I don't understand why he did it," I shared. "He doesn't even know Hope that well. She's beautiful, but getting off should never come before a friendship."

Normally, Lauren and I didn't talk about anything sexual. But I was way beyond being polite at this point. She wasn't a kid anymore.

"Jack and I didn't exactly have time to talk. He was mortified that I'd walked in on him and Hope, and he didn't really explain. But Graham, I have to believe that there's something there between the two of them. You know Jack isn't the type of guy who betrays his friends."

"I'm not sure I really knew him at all," I said huskily. "I guess I never really knew my fiancée either. And I'm still going to kill your brother, whether he cares about Hope or not."

Jack had betrayed my trust, and in my book, that was reason enough to hate the bastard now.

Lauren made another sandwich and sat that down in front of me. I inhaled it while I polished off my second beer.

"I don't know what to do," I finally told her. Life as I knew it was over, and I was going to have to adjust to the fact that I couldn't really trust anybody. Maybe I was better off being completely solo. It didn't hurt as damn much.

"Have another sandwich," she suggested as she set more food and another beer in front of me. "When you're done, I'll dish you up some chocolate peanut butter cup ice cream."

"You picked some up?" It was my favorite, and I was surprised that Lauren remembered. We hadn't seen much of each other over the last seven years. But I knew my memories of her hadn't faded. She'd always be like a little sister to me, even though she was all grown up now.

"Of course. You like it."

Lauren knew that one of my weaknesses was food. I had a hell of a time eating healthy because I loved food way too much. Candy. Chips. Popcorn. Ice cream. None of those things were safe around me.

Maybe because I'd never had any of that stuff as a kid.

"Thanks. But I don't think it will taste that great with beer."

"You could stop drinking," she suggested.

"Not happening. Not tonight."

She picked up her wineglass and sat down in a chair next to the counter. "I know you're hurt. I wish I knew what to say to make you feel better. But I don't really understand any of this myself. Jack has never done anything remotely like this before. As far as I know, he's always been faithful to any woman he's been with, and he's never been into stealing a woman who's already with another man. In fact, he thinks there's some kind of *guy code* against doing that. It doesn't make sense."

I had to agree with her. Jack had always been loyal to every woman in his life. But that didn't mean that I still wasn't going to kill her brother. "He's a dead man," I rasped.

"You aren't going to kill him. Stop saying that."

"You don't know me as well as you think you do," I informed her.

Lauren and I joked around.

We laughed.

We had a good time together.

But she didn't know the other side of me, the one who wanted to break every bone in Jack's body.

"We've known each other for a long time, Graham. I think you're hurt and you're angry. Honestly, I don't blame you. I'm mad, too. But I think you should at least hear Jack out. I have no idea what he has to say, but he said he was coming back. I'm sure he wanted to explain."

"He should have explained *before* he fucked my fiancée," I said angrily.

"Technically, they weren't having sex."

"So having his dick down her throat was better than screwing her?"

She shook her head. "I didn't say that. I think oral sex can be more intimate than intercourse."

I went and got myself another beer. If I was going to start having a sexual discussion with Lauren, I'd need it. "Thanks for that."

"Do you need help with any of the wedding plans?"

"You mean canceling them?"

"Yes."

"Hell, no. I think Hope can handle that since *she* decided to end it."

"I think that's a healthy attitude."

I looked at her in surprise. "Really? Is that what your psychology degree tells you?"

"Not really," she admitted. "But I think it's better if she does it."

I gave her a pointed stare. "That so? What else do you think? Is your brother going to end up married to my ex-fiancée, Dr. Freud?"

Even though she *did* have a degree in psychology, Lauren had never tried to actually analyze me. It was a good thing she hadn't. She might have discovered that I was a total head case.

For some reason, even after all the years that had passed, it was still important for Lauren to see me as her hero. Maybe because nobody else had ever seen me as an honorable guy.

"I'm not really a fan of Freud's psychological reality theories," Lauren answered. "And I have no idea what Jack's plans are concerning Hope. He didn't tell me."

The sadness in her voice made my chest ache just a little. "You're hurt, too," I observed.

Shit, I'd always been a sucker for Lauren's unhappiness.

Lauren and Jack were close, and I realized that there was every possibility that she felt as betrayed as I did. Well, maybe not *quite* as much, but Jack and Lauren usually didn't have that many secrets.

"A little," she confessed. "Okay, maybe a lot. I hate that he took something we loved and ruined it. Aspen has always been *our* trip: you, me and Jack. How could he do that? Being *here* was always special, and now it will never be that way again."

I hadn't thought about that earlier, but if Jack had wanted to do Hope, this really wasn't the place to nail her. We had way too many happy memories in these mountains. "Our friendship will never be the same."

"I know. And I hate him for that. I don't want to lose you as a friend, Graham. I don't have that many real friends who accept me for what I am. Most people think I'm a freak."

Fuck! I always hated it when Lauren talked that way about herself. She was gifted, and was capable of absorbing and applying more knowledge than most people would ever be capable of processing and understanding. She should be idolized just for her mental skills alone.

Lauren definitely *wasn't* a freak, but her intelligence level had always made her different to some people. Maybe that's why we'd bonded when we were younger. But her differences had never made her unlovable. Not to me. I didn't care how much knowledge she had. All that had ever mattered is that she treated me like somebody important to her, somebody worthy of being her friend and protector.

"I'm not going to blame you for the sins of your brother." I *wanted* to make her the enemy because she was Jack's sister, but I *couldn't*. We had way too much history together. My relationship had been different with Lauren. It hadn't been the same as what I'd had with Jack. I'd been Lauren's hero when she was younger, and she'd given me the same unconditional love that she'd give a brother.

"If you kill him, then we can't be friends anymore," she pointed out.

I shot her a small grin. In a way, I think she was almost angrier than I was. "Then you better keep his sorry ass away from me. No promises."

"I don't think he's coming back. He would have been here by now," she said solemnly.

"It might be better that way." If I saw Jack now, I'd *definitely* hurt him.

"So what do we do now?" she asked.

I went to the fridge and started loading my arms with beer. I grabbed the bottle of Merlot for Lauren. "We watch some TV and get drunk."

"I don't get drunk. Neither do you. I don't think I've ever seen you drunk."

"There's a first time for everything."

I hadn't been drunk since college. But tonight was going to be an exception.

Hope had just changed my entire life plan, but not everything was bad. I was, after all, the brand new starting quarterback for the Colorado Wildcats. I was a millionaire. And I was going to sell a hell of a lot of underwear over the next several years. My endorsements would earn me a fortune.

"We didn't get a chance to celebrate your new contract," she said in an apologetic voice.

I motioned for her to follow me into the living room as I took the alcohol, set it up on the coffee table, and then built up the fire. "The contract isn't final yet, so we can celebrate after I actually sign on the dotted line. It's late night movie time."

"We haven't done that in a long time." Lauren dropped back onto the couch I'd found her on when I'd arrived at the cabin.

She was right. We hadn't watched old movies late into the night for years. Not since I'd done sleepovers at Jack's house years ago. His dad had been cool with us all camping out in front of the television for hours at night.

I smiled as I remembered that, although Jack and I watched until we finally turned the TV off, Lauren had usually fallen asleep after the first movie or two. She'd been so damn cute when she was sleeping that I'd just covered her with a blanket and turned the television down so she didn't wake up during my marathon movie nights with Jack.

For whatever reason, Jack wasn't coming back to my expensive chalet, and I hadn't had a break since the playoffs. I'd been running around trying to secure my future. Now that I had some free time, I wanted and needed some downtime.

Just for tonight, I wanted to turn everything off in my brain and enjoy some time with Lauren. I'd really missed her, and I was still trying to come to terms with the fact that she was all grown up.

"Maybe I'm not going to end up married to Hope, but the rest of my life is good." The words left my mouth before I could think about them.

Strangely, I wasn't all that upset about the prospect of not having Hope as my wife. I'd liked the *idea* of the whole marriage thing, but I wasn't that broken up over losing *her*.

I was more upset over losing Jack as a friend.

"Then do you think you'll eventually be able to forgive Jack?" Lauren asked.

"Nope," I told her sternly. "Never."

"What about me?"

There was a vulnerable look on her face that I didn't like. My Peanut should never be insecure. "You didn't do anything, Lauren. There's nothing to forgive. Are you going to forgive your brother?"

"Eventually, I suppose. He's my blood. I love him. But I'm not sure I'll ever trust him as much as I did before."

For some reason, Lauren and Jack being at odds with each other bothered me. I flopped down on the couch next to her and opened another beer. I refilled her wineglass and handed it to her.

"Find us a channel." Unlike some guys, I always gave Lauren possession of the remote if she was still awake. She could find any channel a hell of a lot faster than I did.

Lauren made herself comfortable with her legs in my lap.

Somewhere between *Casablanca* and *Psycho*, I finished every single beer on the table.

CHAPTER 6

Lauren

Lying with my back against the arm of the couch and my legs draped across his thighs, I studied Graham's profile. He was hurting even though he was trying to play it off as though he wasn't devastated.

Me? I was testing my alcohol consumption limit that day, seeking the numbness people claimed they found in the bottom of a bottle. It wasn't that I didn't know the physiological effects of alcohol. People called it a depressant, but it was a much more complicated drug. Yes, it suppressed the release of glutamate, which resulted in a slowdown of the brain's pathways, making it harder to form coherent thoughts, but it also elevated dopamine levels which meant I felt pretty good despite what had happened.

What Jack had done wasn't my fault. I felt guilty about telling Graham the truth, even though given the same situation, I would have done it again. Graham deserved not to be sideswiped by this.

Graham's home life had toughened him. He didn't talk about it but Jack and I had gotten glimpses of it over the years. I knew that Graham wanted to keep that side from me and I let him because I selfishly wanted my version of him to be real. He was my protector, my cheerleader. There had been times when I'd wondered if he hid his other side for us or for him. Was he worried that if he was anything but the good friend, the "big brother," that we wouldn't still love him?

Jack had pretty much made that a moot point.

Even though Graham said it wouldn't change us, this was likely our last time like this. Jack would return that night or stay away to give Graham time to cool off—either way it would be ugly when they saw each other.

Aspen would never happen again.

Jack, Graham and I would never laugh over stupid shit we did as kids. Nothing would ever be the same.

I drank because my nerves were raw and I wanted this one last time with Graham. I drank for all the things I would never do again and all the things Graham and I had never done.

"I've had sex," I blurted out.

Graham shot me an amused look. "That's good to know." His cheeks were flushed and his eyes were heavy, but hours of movies and drinking did that to a person. By driving standards, he was inebriated, but he wasn't fall down drunk. At least, he hadn't fallen during his last trip to the bathroom. Apparently beer went through a person faster than wine.

Even though I told myself he was like a brother to me, my pride was a little dented that he did not see me in *any* other way. It felt important to prove to him that some men did. "You didn't have to teach me the term for fellatio. I'm familiar with it."

He looked at me then looked away. "I don't want to talk about this."

Strangely, I did. "Sorry. I don't know why I said that."

He shrugged and picked up the remote, flipping through the channels without stopping at any of them long enough to know what he was skipping over.

"Actually, I do know." I tipped my now empty wineglass sideways and watched the drops of Merlot gather into a small pool. It was fascinating in a way it wouldn't have been before I consumed the entire bottle on my own and been introduced to a new equation. The more I drank the easier it was to down the next glass. "Alcohol affects the prefrontal cortex which regulates impulse control."

"Bad news for Jack. I was hoping the beer would make me less likely to kill him," he said but kept his eyes on the television.

I put the glass down. "It may slow your reaction time sufficiently enough to allow him to dodge your swings," I said, hoping it didn't come to that.

He rubbed the shin of my leg. "Then all I have to do is stay drunk." Now that he said it, there was a noticeable slur to his words. Funny, I didn't feel like there was to mine. The disconnect in self-perception explained why people felt capable of driving when they clearly were not. *Holy shit, I may be drunk.*

I sat up, waving off the dizziness that followed the sudden move. His pain cut as deeply as my own. I wished there were something, anything I could do to ease it. "I'm so sorry, Graham."

He shook his head. We sat there quietly for several long minutes. "So, who was it?"

"Who was who?"

"The guy you slept with?" he asked as if it were a casual question about the weather.

"Tim Beller. My lab partner last year. Why do you say *guy* like you know it was only one? For all you know I might have slept with everyone I met at college. Men. Women. You don't know."

He chuckled and met my eyes again. "I *know.*"

That was a kick to my pride. "Because you think I couldn't find more than one person who'd sleep with me?" The expression in his eyes changed, at least I thought they did, his face was a little blurry.

"You're beautiful, Lauren, just in your own way."

I rolled back against the arm of the chair and covered my face with my arm. Not even beer goggles could change the way he saw me. "Ouch."

He tugged on my foot. "Stop."

"You stop." I pulled my foot away, running it over his cock by accident. It wasn't erect, but that wasn't a surprise. "I'm not insecure—I'm realistic. Men don't lust after women with a higher IQ than they have. And before you try to cheer me up about that, I'm okay with it. Sex wasn't that great anyway."

"Then you slept with a douche."

"Or a hundred of them. Maybe a thousand."

"Lauren, look at me."

I lowered my arm and did. "When you meet the right guy—and you will one day—tell him the truth. He won't care if it was a hundred or none. Don't let anyone make you feel bad about who you are."

Yes, there was a slur to his speech, but his words rang clear in my head. His smile was so beautiful I sat up so I could see it better. Flutters skidded through my stomach and filled me with a yearning I tried to suppress. This wasn't someone I needed to lie to. This was Graham. "One. Just one guy. I didn't want to graduate from another college still a virgin."

Graham let out an audible breath. "It'll get better."

"I hope so." I remembered my first time and suddenly it was funny. "At least he was quick."

Graham groaned. "TMI."

Okay, either it was the funniest story ever and had to be retold or I was drunk. Either way, I couldn't stop myself from sharing. "I was so disappointed I went home and masturbated just to make sure all my parts were still in working condition." I laughed as a joke came to me. "They were and I remembered a perk to sex with my hand—no morning after awkwardness, although there was a sense of jealousy from my other appendages."

He turned away again.

I moved to lay my leg back over his lap, grazing my foot over his cock for a second time and froze. *Whoa.* Unless I imagined it, he was sporting a huge boner. For me? I double checked by easing my calf over it.

He grabbed my leg to still it. "Don't, Lauren."

Don't what? Marvel that something I had done had turned him on? How could I not take a moment to bask in how it felt?

My breath caught in my throat. Sex would change our relationship but everything was already different. Even if he said it wasn't—this night felt like our goodbye.

He'd never forgive Jack. Never trust him again. How would that not take him from me as well? I couldn't close that door without tasting his kiss just once.

"Graham?"

He turned slowly toward me, looking tortured as he did. "Don't look at me like that. I'm holding on by a thread here. You matter to me, Lauren. I don't want to hurt you."

The desire in his eyes was what moved me onto my knees beside him. He'd never looked at me that way before and it was mesmerizing. I ran my hand over the strong muscles of his chest. His heart was beating wildly. For me. There was so much I wanted to say, but the words didn't come. Instead I leaned forward and kissed him.

He dug his hands into my hair and kissed me back roughly. There was no tenderness, no teasing. He took my mouth, claimed my tongue. This wasn't the vanilla foreplay I'd experienced, but I wasn't afraid. I wanted to be his even if it was only for one night.

He lifted me so I straddled his lap, then he tore away the front of my shirt. Cotton ripped beneath his strength. He unsnapped my bra and threw it on the floor. My breasts fit perfectly into his hands. I grasped his shoulders to steady myself as he kissed his way down my neck and to my breasts. He tongued one breast while he kneaded the other with his hand. I arched and moved my pelvis forward over his bulging cock.

His movements were angry, impatient, yet my body responded. He kissed his way back to my mouth. I met his passion with my own. As we kissed I unbuttoned his shirt and pushed it aside, then rubbed my bare breasts across his chest, loving how it drove him wild.

He fisted a hand in my hair and pulled my face back from his. His breathing was as ragged as mine. "Get away from me, Peanut. You could be anyone tonight. I wouldn't care."

His words had cut through me, but they didn't make me want to leave him. He was pushing me away but only because he wanted to protect me. I didn't need protecting, not from him. I wanted to experience him and to comfort him. It was an irresistible combination.

"I want this, Graham," I whispered. *I've always wanted you.* I kissed him before he had a chance to say more. I didn't want to talk—I wanted to feel.

He ground his mouth against mine in a kiss that was somewhere between a punishment and a pleasure. It blew every kiss I'd ever had out of the water. Maybe it was the wine. Maybe it was years of fantasizing about being with him, but I was all in.

He eased me back onto my feet and then stood. I tore at his clothing. In a glorious frenzied blur, he surrounded me with hard muscle. With him, I felt small and feminine. With him, there was no self-consciousness—only hunger to feel more of him, taste more of him.

Graham had never been anything but gentle with me, even when we disagreed on something. He wasn't gentle then. His hands were rough and demanding. His cock was huge and bold. I wanted it inside me, as deep as he could thrust it. No hesitation or consideration. I wanted him as crazy to have me as I was to have him.

I closed one hand around his cock and pumped up and down, loving how it felt—imagining how it would fill me. All the while, he kissed me relentlessly, deeply. He wanted everything and I wanted to give it all to him.

His fingers found my sex and while he fucked my mouth with his tongue, his fingers thrusted upward into me. I was wet and ready. He was hard and hungry. He picked me up as if I weighed nothing then stumbled backward before steadying himself against the couch. It was a physical reminder that we were FWI, fucking while impaired.

I thought that up even while the tip of his cock dipped into the folds of my sex. I've always been an over thinker. It's what I hated most about myself. There I was having wild sex for the first time in my life and my brain would not shut off.

I wondered if our ancestors chose to walk upright simply for this sexual position.

I warned myself not to confuse real intimacy with what I might feel right after an orgasm. Orgasms were a gift from the universe, but they also had a purpose. The hypothalamus releases extra oxytocin. There were studies that linked it to a biological element of trust building.

He grabbed my ass with both hands, thrusted upward, and something magical happened. I stopped thinking. It was all about the connection. He kissed my neck. I clung to his shoulders and linked my feet behind his back. For a while I moved up and down in hot abandon. This was what it was supposed to be like. I didn't want the moment to ever end. Each thrust took him deeper, drove me wilder.

A flush rose up my chest, spreading across my face. I was close, so close to coming. There I was, about to have my first non-solo orgasm and it was with Graham.

Graham. A man I'd loved most of my life.

A man I desperately didn't want to lose.

There was something deeply, wrenchingly sad about finally being intimate with him now that our time together was ending. I hated Jack for betraying him. I hated myself for making this night about me when it should have been about Graham.

I wanted to start the night over and do everything better.

What could I say to Graham that would make him not hate himself for fucking me? I didn't want him to feel guilty. I didn't want to add more to his pain.

He was pounding up into me and it felt good, so, so good, but I couldn't fully enjoy it. My brain was sabotaging what should have been the best orgasm of my life.

Once I'd imagined how Graham would feel the next morning, it was all I could think about. I'd put fulfilling a fantasy above what would have been best for my friend.

Was I any better than Jack?

An image of Graham holding up Hope's engagement ring entered my head and everything went to shit. I didn't want to think about her or what she'd done with Jack. I didn't want any of that to be part of this, but it was the reason for it.

Graham wasn't making love to *me*—he was proving he didn't need Hope.

I wasn't having sex with a man who loved me, I was saying goodbye to one who never would.

I wished I could've been a better friend for Graham.

Or at least a better fuck.

My orgasm faded away, the passion I'd felt now sadly elusive. All I wanted to do right then was hug Graham and tell him I was sorry for everything.

Graham sat back on the arm of the couch and growled. "Are you crying?"

With him still deep inside me, I hugged myself around him, hugged him tighter than I'd ever hugged anyone and burst into tears.

I learned another biological factoid that night—nothing kills an erection faster than sloppy sobbing. He wrapped his arms tightly around me and simply rocked me back and forth while swearing softly.

CHAPTER 7

Graham

What in the hell had I just done?

Okay. Yeah. I was drunk, but I wasn't *that* intoxicated. I should have put a stop to Lauren's explorations the moment I felt myself getting hard. But had I done that? *Hell, no.*

She was drunk, and I'd taken advantage of that fact the minute I'd gotten all hot and bothered while I was thinking about her making herself come. She hadn't exactly been coming on to me. It was a simple conversation about the woman in my arms fingering herself to ecstasy. But I'd been able to see it in my mind, and it was one of the hottest fantasies I'd ever had. I'd completely lost it.

I'd moved us to the couch with Lauren still in my lap, and I was hanging on to her like I couldn't fucking let her go. And to be honest, I was pretty sure I *couldn't* release her. Not like this. Not after I'd hurt her and made her cry.

Lauren is like a sister to me.

At least, that's what I'd always told myself. But I'd been feeling far from brotherly when she'd shared the fact that she'd lost her virginity to some prick at her college. I hadn't wanted to talk about her experience because it actually pissed me off. For some weird reason, I hated thinking about *anybody* touching Lauren. It made me want to kill the bastard who had initiated her to sex without pleasure.

For some reason, Lauren had never seen herself as beautiful. She'd accused me of not believing that anybody would want to nail her. In reality, I was surprised she'd stayed innocent as long as she had. She had to have guys crawling all over her. It wasn't like I'd never noticed her curvy body myself once she'd hit adulthood, but I'd instantly shut down any carnal thoughts about her. She was one of my best friends.

Now, I couldn't do *anything but* notice her. Lauren had a body made for sin. I was a big guy, and I loved the feel of her body against mine. She was full and lush, and she didn't shy away from passion. What had just happened had been completely raw and primitive.

Until I'd screwed up and hurt her in some way.

Her blonde hair was slightly curly, and I'd just discovered it was as soft as silk.

Her pussy had taken my cock like a tight, hot glove. Being inside her had been like coming home, and I'd never actually had a real place where I belonged. The sensation had been so damn heady that I hadn't been able to stop myself.

"You okay?" I rasped against her ear.

Jesus! I felt guilty as hell about hurting her. Had she been in physical pain? She was almost a virgin, and I was a pretty big guy.

"I'm fine. I'm sorry," she said in a hesitant voice.

"I hurt you. You don't need to be sorry."

"It didn't hurt," she said in a hushed voice.

As she lifted her head, I plucked the glasses off her face and cleaned them with my T-shirt, a habit I'd been doing for so long it was automatic. Lauren usually had a smudge or two on the lenses.

I glanced at her earnest blue eyes as I slid the glasses back onto her face. "Then why were you crying?"

"It's complicated."

Shit! I hated *anything* complicated unless it involved football, but I couldn't resist answering, "I've got nothing but time right now. Tell me."

"I wanted to have sex with you," she blurted out. "I feel like we'll never see each other again."

I was stroking a hand down her bare back, and I couldn't stop. Her skin was so damn soft. "We can't have sex, Lauren. What happened wasn't right."

She wasn't the type of woman I could just screw and forget about. We'd been through everything together, and we'd known each other forever. Losing her friendship would be like cutting off my throwing arm.

"It felt right," she said in a contemplative tone. "Until it didn't."

It had felt pretty damn good for me, too, but I wasn't going to admit that right now. "What happened?"

"I realized how selfish I was being. I wanted something for myself when you were the one who had his life destroyed. And now you'll probably feel guilty about having sex with me."

"We didn't technically have sex. We didn't finish." Much to my disappointment. But I couldn't come when she was practically sobbing.

Lauren's tears were definitely a boner killer. I never could stand to see her cry.

She rolled her eyes. "Does it matter?"

"It matters to me." I would have given my right nut to have finished inside her. "And I don't feel guilty. We're both single, and we both wanted it. That's not selfish. And just for the record, I have no intention of saying goodbye to you, Peanut."

She looked startled as she asked, "You don't? Really? After what happened with Jack, how can things ever be the same?"

I shrugged. "Maybe they won't be the same. Maybe things will be different. Jack won't be in the picture anymore because I'm going to kill him. But I'm not losing you over what happened with Jack and Hope. It's not your fault."

Something had happened tonight that had changed our relationship, and I knew we could never go back. Nothing was the same, but I sure as hell wasn't going to lose our friendship over it. I'd known her too long. We'd shared too much over the years.

She nodded slowly. "I was so afraid that tonight would be the last time we ever saw each other again. You cut people out of your life when you're hurting."

Both of my grandparents had passed away, but I still didn't talk to the aunt who had rejected me as a kid. So there was some truth to her statement.

Yeah, there was a whole other side of me that Lauren didn't know, but she knew me more than people ever would. I couldn't just throw that kind of relationship away.

"Not happening. I need you to come to my games and root for the Cats," I teased.

"I'll be there if you want me."

My chest ached as I watched her expression change from sadness to hope. "I'll always want you," I told her honestly.

Problem was, I needed her in a whole new horny guy kind of way now, and my dick wasn't going to let me forget how damn good she'd felt wrapped around my cock.

She sighed. "My brain sucks sometimes. Now I wish we could have finished. I didn't want it to end."

"Better than Timmy?" Hell, was I actually jealous of her only lover?

She shot me a smile that had my cock coming to life again.

I'd never understand why Lauren didn't see herself as a sexy, smart, caring woman. She was special, and it drove me crazy that she'd never found those characteristics in herself.

"It was almost orgasmic," she joked.

"Almost? You know you wanted to come," I grumbled.

"I want a lot of things that have never happened."

She sounded forlorn, and I couldn't resist asking, "What things?"

"I *did* want to come. It felt so much different than the orgasms I have when I play with myself."

"Don't go there," I warned. The last thing I needed to visualize was Lauren getting herself off again.

"I'm book smart," she continued. "But I haven't really *done* much. I've never really had…an adventure of any kind."

"Then do what you want to do," I suggested.

Lauren had never been able to just be a kid. She'd been attending special schools and college when she should have been playing with Barbie dolls.

She shook her head. "Those silly things would be a waste of time, and my logical brain can't comprehend doing something useless just to have the experience."

I grinned at her. "Then I've pretty much been throwing away some valuable time. You can't work or study all the time."

Lauren was so damn smart that she sabotaged herself. She needed to learn to stop thinking sometimes.

"Maybe I'll try," she said nonchalantly.

"You won't," I told her.

She shot me a stubborn look. "I will."

"I'll help you," I said, not thinking about my words before they came out of my mouth. "I know how to have fun, and how to do something just for the hell of it. But I'd need a list."

"You'll be busy with your new contract."

"Not right away. I'll have time before we start up the pre-season stuff. The season is over, and I promised myself a break. The only thing I really have to do is work on my throws. Since I injured my shoulder, my arm is a little bit off. I have to learn to compensate."

"That makes sense," she mused. "If you don't have full usage, or if some of the anatomy has changed since your injury, you have to calculate what needs to be adjusted so you're completely accurate again. But you had an amazing season."

"I got through, and I did well, but I could be better." I was determined to be the best damn quarterback the Cats had ever had. I wasn't the least bit shy about taking the rewards my work had earned, but I was always pushing for better.

"I could probably help," she suggested.

"How?"

"I do have a doctorate in condensed matter physics," she reminded me. "Really, throwing accurately is all about the laws of physics."

"Sometimes I forget how smart you are," I admitted. "I'll take any help I can get."

She yawned right before she answered, "That's always been something I've liked about you. You don't see me as a freak."

I gritted my teeth. "You're *not* a freak. There's nothing wrong with being gifted and focused. It makes you special. But you're also human. Everybody needs some downtime for their sanity. Even if you don't see the point of doing useless things. Consider it therapy."

I stood with Lauren still in my arms. She was exhausted, and she needed to get some sleep.

Her arms shot around my neck and she let out a surprised squeak as she settled more comfortably in my arms. "So we help each other?"

I hugged her naked form to my harder frame. Having fun wasn't the only thing I wanted to teach her, but I couldn't let myself go there. "We help each other," I confirmed in a voice filled with tension.

There was no way I could pretend that having her naked in my arms didn't affect me. My dick was as hard as a rock.

Desire thrummed through my body as I carried her into the bedroom she'd claimed when she'd arrived. I ripped back the covers and sat her on the pristine white sheet.

I tried to straighten up, but Lauren still had her arms around my neck.

"I really am sorry, Graham. I won't apologize for wanting to have sex with you, but I hate what happened with Jack and Hope."

Damned if I was going to apologize for those brief moments of ecstasy, either. I couldn't. It had felt too damn good, but I knew it couldn't happen again.

Lauren was the kind of woman who deserved a solid commitment from a guy she fucked.

And I was a man who couldn't commit.

Not to Lauren.

I cared about her too damn much.

Marrying Hope had been part of my life plan, and I'd been okay with that.

Lauren was a completely different situation.

I couldn't lose her friendship. She'd been one of the only stable people in my life, and she'd always been there for me no matter how poor and pathetic I'd been when I was younger. Lately, since I'd had such a phenomenal season and been offered the world, I had no idea who was friend or foe. I'd gotten a lot of attention, but only because I was suddenly in the limelight.

Leaning down, I kissed her softly on the forehead. "Forget about it," I suggested huskily. "I dodged a bullet with Hope. It's not all bad."

Strangely, my ex-fiancée had been the last thing on my mind for the last few hours.

"You deserve so much more," Lauren murmured.

I wanted to tell her I didn't deserve shit. It wasn't like I'd done a whole lot of admirable things in my life. But that was a side of my life I didn't discuss with anybody. "I won't be looking for a while."

I wasn't ready to go in search of another perfect woman who would get me closer to my goals. Focusing on my career seemed like a much better idea.

"We could be friends with benefits," Lauren said breathlessly. "It could work out. Neither one of us really want a relationship right now."

We were so close that I could feel the warmth of her breath on my face. I hesitated for a moment, my eyes glued to her hopeful expression. It would be so easy to fall into her gorgeous blue eyes, and bury myself inside her fucking perfect body. Hell, I knew I'd forget that Hope even existed if I was fucking Lauren.

I'm not going to take advantage of the fact that we're both drunk.

She'd feel differently after she slept off her buzz. I mentally noted that I hoped I'd sleep off this sudden obsession to fuck her, too. My sexual attraction to Lauren wasn't comfortable for me. I'd always been her hero, and she'd always been my little Peanut. Looking at her differently now that she was all grown up was awkward.

She was so familiar, yet suddenly so unknown.

Our eyes locked, and it took everything I had to pull her arms from around my neck and move away from her. "I can't," I answered with regret. "It won't work for me."

Once I'd had Lauren, I'd want more. I sensed it. There was no possible way we could be fuck buddies and remain friends when it was over.

Besides, I had some powerfully protective instincts when it came to Lauren, and I was far from safe for her. I never knew I'd end up fighting myself to keep her safe, but that's exactly what I was doing.

"Okay," she agreed in a soft voice. "I shouldn't have even suggested it, but what happened earlier made me want to complete the experience."

I knew exactly how she felt. My entire body was tense, and my cock hated me at the moment for depriving it from something it desperately wanted. "We can't always get what we want, Peanut," I said in a graveled tone as I walked to the door, exited, and closed it firmly behind me.

I understood *wanting*.

Nobody knew better than me how hard it was to stop desiring things I could never have.

CHAPTER 8

Graham

FOURTEEN YEARS AGO...

"I hate my life," eight-year-old Lauren said angrily as she came through the door of her home.

I looked at the tow-headed little girl, and wanted to smile at her statement, something that probably shouldn't be said by a grade school kid, but Lauren was in a school for the gifted, and most of her classmates had several years on her.

Lauren was the brightest of the bright, and she was setting all kinds of records for her lightning-fast progress through school.

Jack had needed to make a run to the store with his dad, and I was studying at the Swift kitchen table, waiting for them to come back with all the stuff they needed for dinner.

I'd had homework to do, and if I wanted to make the high school football team someday, my grades would have to be decent to make the cut.

Putting down my pencil and closing my book, I asked, "What happened?"

She put her backpack on the table, and I wondered, not for the first time, how she managed to carry all those heavy books. "Dennis's mother said I was a freak of nature," she said sadly. "She probably thought I didn't hear her, but I did."

"Who is Dennis?" I asked, confused.

"He goes to my school. He's only *slightly* gifted, so he's old," she huffed, tipping up her tiny chin in an effort to act like she wasn't upset.

"His mom brought you home?" I guessed. All of the students at Lauren's school who lived in the same area did a carpool schedule.

She nodded as she opened the refrigerator, obviously looking for a snack. "I was sitting in the back seat. But I heard her tell Dennis that I was a freak of nature in a quiet voice."

By old, Lauren probably meant that Dennis was several years older than her.

I was so proud of my Peanut, but I knew she wasn't having an easy time in school, and it wasn't going to get any better. At her current speed, she'd finish high school at least a year before Jack and I did. Maybe more.

Lauren got speculated about by a lot of people because of her brain power, but it made me mad when anybody insulted her. There was nothing wrong with her. "They're just jealous," I told her.

She sat down at the table with an apple in her hand. "I'm different," she said in a moody tone I'd gotten to know well.

"There's nothing wrong with being different," I said in her defense. I knew how she felt. "Who wants to be like everybody else?"

Truthfully, I knew what it was like to want to just blend in and not get anybody's attention. But Lauren had no reason to be ashamed of herself. She should be proud of herself. "Don't pay attention to them, Lauren. I think they just want to be like you."

She lifted a brow at me, and I really wanted to laugh. Sometimes she acted like an adult in a child's body. "Do you think so?" she asked timidly.

I nodded hard. "I do. You're brilliant, and everybody is just sad that they aren't as smart as you are." I picked up my pencil again and started to twirl it around. "I wish I was as smart as you, but I'm not jealous. I just wish I could do better in school. I'm not smart at all."

She finished chewing a bit of her apple before she answered, "You're not dumb, Graham," she said empathetically. "I can help you with your homework. You have attention deficit and hyperactivity disorder, but that doesn't mean you're ignorant or dumb."

"I can't even say the whole thing," I told her. "I just call it ADHD."

I would have preferred for Jack and Lauren not to know about my problems, but they'd discovered my ADHD because Jack's dad had to give me medication when I was hanging out here.

"Do you want to talk about it?" Lauren asked, making me think of her as an adult psychologist.

Peanut had never really been with kids her own age. Her dad had discovered she was gifted early, and she'd never had the chance to go to a regular school. But really, I didn't think she would have been happy with kids her own age, either.

I shook my head hard. "I don't want to talk about it."

Even though Lauren and Jack knew I had ADHD, I didn't talk about my problems with anybody.

She nodded. "Then I'll help you with your homework if you'll let me."

My chest ached as I saw her kind smile. It wasn't often that anybody offered to help me. But I was struggling with math class, and Lauren, once I got her to slow down, was good at helping me understand.

She was gifted in more than one area, but math was one of her talents.

"Okay," I agreed. I wasn't going to turn down the opportunity to do better in school. "Thanks."

She rose and threw her apple core away, and then washed her hands. After scooting a kitchen chair closer to mine, she climbed up on it. "Show me what's giving you difficulty right now?"

I grinned down at her as I put my pencil down to open up my book. It was always funny to see a little girl helping people who were way older than her. "Are you smarter than your teacher?" I asked as I snatched her glasses to clean them.

Lauren might be a genius, but she never cleaned her glasses.

She looked thoughtful for a moment before she answered, "Not yet."

I laughed before I showed Lauren the problems I'd had difficulty solving.

It had to suck when you knew you were almost as smart as your teacher at the age of eight. But I didn't see Lauren as different. I just saw her as my friend.

By the time I went home later that night, my homework was all done.

I owed Lauren big time, and I was going to repay her by buying her a teddy bear I'd seen in the store when I'd gone with my foster parents. I'd been saving my lunch money to get it. It didn't matter if I was a little hungry when I got home from school. Lauren had helped me a lot over the last year, and I wanted her to have a friend around even when I wasn't with her.

It might take me a few more weeks of saving, but I'd get it eventually.

I thought she'd love it because the teddy bear had glasses just like hers. Maybe she'd feel less alone if she had a smart stuffed animal that was just like her.

CHAPTER 9

Lauren

S leep came quickly to me—a gift of over indulging. The next morning, however, was not as kind. I woke with a headache I told myself I'd earned, and more than one regret about the night before.

Luckily, feeling awkward was a sensation I knew how to handle well. I'd felt some variation of it for most of my life. Just never with Graham.

I stumbled to the bathroom to relieve myself then shower. As I stood beneath the hot spray of water, I didn't want to wash away the memory of his touch. I wanted to bottle the sensation of being his, even if it was just for a few moments, and keep it with me. The brain's synapses didn't work that way. The details would naturally fade away over time unless they were repeated.

I soaped myself, closing my eyes while letting every sensation I could recall come back to me. And just as they had denied myself the final pleasure the night before, my thoughts sabotaged this reverie as well. He said there should be no guilt, but I *did* feel guilty. Graham was probably thinking he'd taken advantage of me, but the reverse was closer to the truth.

Jack was out there somewhere and I was so angry with him that if I didn't see him again it would be too soon. At least, that's how it felt. Would time change that as well?

Imagining not knowing where Graham was or how he was doing tangled my insides painfully. I turned off the shower and dressed in jeans and T-shirt while my mind ran through simulations and the probable outcomes.

I could attempt to pretend I didn't remember much about the night before. Graham might be relieved if I did. The lure of that option was I didn't have to face how many times I'd offered myself to him—even as he laid me on the bed. It might salvage some of my pride, but it would mean lying to Graham and I'd never done that. Also, where would it take us? There probably wasn't a better way to end my friendship with him than inserting that kind of lie into it.

I could apologize again. Honestly, I felt sorry enough about what Jack had done as well as how I'd used the situation to get what I'd always wanted that apologies would come easily—and with great frequency. I didn't want him to feel sorry for me, though. If I was hurt by last night, Graham would be, too. I couldn't bear the idea of hurting him more.

I could act as if being with him had left me unaffected. People fucked all the time and, by his definition, we didn't even get to the point where we needed to count it. I could be cool as a cucumber, sophisticated like some of the women I'd seen him date. The problem? Graham knew me too well. He'd know I was trying to be brave for him. It might not even be a lie I could sustain. And where would it lead? What's the next step? Fucking someone else to prove my indifference? I didn't want that. Not for me. Not for Graham.

As I blew my hair dry, I gave myself a stern look in the mirror. Graham said he didn't want to lose me. He was willing to separate what Jack had done from our friendship. He might not love me the way my heart ached for him to, but he did love me. I needed to honor that. Graham's life was full enough with people who wanted to take from him. There were many things I didn't know, but I was certain I didn't want to be one of those people.

What would being a loving friend to him look like after last night? It would require some painful honesty and then more love than lust. Since this was the first time I'd given into my craving for him, I suppose I had the restraint necessary to continue on that way—as long as we didn't drink together again.

Honesty then restraint. I found a notebook and pen beside the bed. He'd said if I wrote a list he'd help me fulfill it. That sounded healthy. Loving. And I'd promised to help him compensate for his injury. I already had ideas for how and having a new problem to solve was exciting.

Not as exciting as the idea of Graham showing up at my bedroom door because he decided finishing what we started was what he wanted, but it would have to suffice.

As soon as I opened the kitchen door I was assailed by the heavenly scent of my favorite breakfast—blueberry muffins. I had brought some mix myself, but it was now tucked into my luggage. The only way Graham would have been able to make muffins was if he'd also brought a box of mix with him. Even though he'd been engaged, even though he was there to celebrate his own success, he hadn't forgotten me. I hesitated at my door and blinked back tears.

Graham didn't give himself credit for the good in him. I wished he could see himself through my eyes.

Could designing the right list help him do that? *Yes, I believe it can.*

Could helping him restore stability to our friendship? *It just might.*

All I had to do was proceed openly, honestly, and remember that what we had was so much more than what our bodies wanted.

I took a fortifying breath and walked into the kitchen with the blank notepad in one hand and pen in the other. Dressed in a T-shirt that hugged his muscular chest and jeans that did nothing to conceal the power of his thighs, Graham looked up as I entered. He was leaning against the kitchen counter with his phone in one hand. Behind him was a rack of fresh muffins that were cooling on the stovetop. Our eyes met and held. I saw a myriad of emotions in his: concern, regret, and a flash of something I hadn't expected to—desire.

Holy shit. It rocked right through me and replaced the calm morning greeting with a more guttural, "I understand why it's better if we don't fuck."

He dropped his phone then swore. When he straightened, he looked both cautious and uncomfortable. Shit. I didn't want that to be how he felt around me.

I waved the notebook in the air. "I'm a woman and you're a man." I'm sure he's glad I'd clarified *that.* "It's natural for us to think about each other in a carnal fashion, but that doesn't mean we have to act on it or regret what we did while under the influence of an un-inhibitor. So, let's have a muffin and you can help me come up with my list."

He looked at me without saying a word.

I felt compelled to keep reassuring him, even though what I wanted to do was close the distance between us, wrap my arms around his neck and melt into him. I sat at the table and poised my pen above the notepad. "Ride a tandem bike," I said as I wrote it then waved the list at him again. "See, no sex on this list."

He rubbed his hand on the back of his neck then chuckled. "Who the hell puts riding a tandem bike on their bucket list?"

I raised my eyebrows. If this was going to work we'd have to find our footing again. "Well, Mr. Judgy, what would you add to my list?"

He took a moment to answer and I let myself imagine he was fighting back illicit fantasies of me. Hey, I was only human.

I could put my desires second to what I knew we should do, but that didn't mean the hunger I felt around him ceased to exist. He turned, put a muffin on a plate, and placed it in front of me with a glass of water. "I don't know how long I'll have to help you with that list before I have to go into preparation for the season."

He was laying out his options as well. I respected that. We could avoid each other and hope this goes away. I ran through all the ways that might go badly and decided my way had a higher probability of ending with us still friends.

As long as I stopped imagining how good it'd felt to be wrapped around him with his cock thrusting up into me. Surely, I could do that.

So, we started with painful honesty. "Graham, I know I made things awkward between us, but I want you in my life. So, let's do this. You help me. I'll help you. Last night doesn't have to define us. You didn't hurt me and I didn't mean to take it where it went. Your idea about the list was brilliant, and I don't throw that word around lightly. Yeah, it's going to be weird today, but you're worth it to me. I hope I am to you."

He poured himself a glass of water then joined me at the kitchen table. I couldn't decipher his expression, but I didn't expect to. Graham kept his feelings to himself. What I did have was faith in him. It went against my analytical side, but when it came to Graham it was just there.

We can do this, Graham.

He placed his phone on the table beside him. "Jack left me a message. He wants to see me today. We should keep your list to things you can do while visiting me in prison."

My gut twisted painfully. There I was thinking about myself again while he was still trudging through hell. "Don't let him take anything else away from you. Don't give him that satisfaction."

"Hope texted me as well."

"What did she say?"

"That she wants to talk. Really, what the fuck does she think there is to say?"

"Maybe sorry?"

His eyes blazed. "Do you think any man wants to hear that?"

"No. I guess not."

"The one I don't understand is Jack. What the fuck was he thinking?"

"He wasn't. You know how Jack is."

Graham turned his phone over. "Things were going well for me. I don't fucking need this."

"No, you don't."

"If I see Jack, I'm going to hit him. And if I hit him, I won't be able to stop."

His tone was scary cold. This was a side of Graham I hadn't seen before. It was brutally honest, though, and wasn't that what I'd said we'd need to move forward? "So, maybe you shouldn't see him—at least not yet."

"I'm not going to fucking hide from this."

I prayed I knew what the hell I was doing. "It's not hiding; it's letting him stew on what he did while you work it through on your own. I think he deserves a punch. Hell, he deserves the full beating you want to give him, but then what? Is it worth losing your career? Are you willing to let him take that from you as well?"

His hands fisted on the table. "No, I'm not."

Hoping I didn't sound like a sappy teenager, I said, "Then maybe the best revenge is doing well. Show them you don't need either of them to be happy."

I prayed he didn't announce he couldn't because he *does* need Hope to be happy. Could I be a good enough friend to help him work things out with her if that's what he wanted? I'd like to think so, but I didn't know. I held my breath and waited for his answer.

He nodded once. "I don't."

The tension in the kitchen was thick. I didn't know if I was doing this right. All I knew was that I cared about Graham and I was trying to be the friend he deserved.

He grabbed the notepad and wrote: parasailing.

"Oh, no. You know I hate heights."

His face relaxed. "Isn't this about pushing your boundaries?"

"Are you doing all of these with me?" I asked.

He seemed to think it over, then said, "Yes. I haven't signed my final contract yet, so the Cats can't say that I'm breaking contract by participating in anything dangerous. I'm technically a free agent at the moment."

I took the pad back and wrote: swimming with manatees.

He shuddered. "Hell no. Those things creep me out."

I sat back in my chair and folded my arms over my chest. "Big strong man afraid of a water cow? Poor baby. It stays on the list."

"Really?" A smile returned to his lips and he claimed the pad again. "So, that's how this goes, is it? If it's written it's non-negotiable?"

I licked my bottom lip, telling myself his mind didn't just go where mine did. "Within reason."

"That's bold of you. Not afraid of what I might add?" There was that spark in his eyes again, and I wanted to stand up, shed my clothing and beg him to add every decadent thing he could imagine to the list.

Instead, I leaned forward and tried to look less turned on than I was. "Bring it."

CHAPTER 10

Graham

I'd gone through several muffins and a cup of coffee before I finished my list. I'd hardly noticed when Lauren had gotten up to make the coffee and sat a cup in front of me.

"How long is this list?" Lauren asked nervously.

"Long enough," I answered vaguely.

We'd never be able to do everything I'd added to the list during the winter. I knew I had at least a few months until I needed to start squaring things away with the Cats and then get to training season.

I scrutinized the list, wondering what else I needed to add. Lauren would hate my entries, but she needed to learn to have a good time without thinking about anything else. She needed activities that would turn off her logical brain. She feared heights, but she could get over that. Her adrenaline would be pumping, taking over every thought except the thrill of the activity.

"You're scaring me," she said as she swiped the pad from my hand. "You've been at this for way too long."

"You can cross off the ones you've already done," I told her, knowing she'd never done a single one of those things.

"Are you insane?" she said, her eyes scanning my list.

"I guess I am because I've done every one of them. More than once."

"Tubing? I've never been tubing."

I grinned. "Isn't that the point? To do things you've never done. We have several more days here in Aspen. The chalet is already paid for. We can start with that and move up to snowmobiling."

She frowned. "I can't drive a snowmobile. I've never even tried. I have a perfectly good automobile."

Snowmobiling was something people did strictly for fun. And I liked speed. It was exhilarating to fly across the snow.

"You can ride with me. I'll make sure you're safe."

She'd be with me during every single activity so I could make damn sure she was okay.

She chewed her bottom lip for a moment before she said, "Okay. No problem."

No matter how brave Lauren claimed to be about bringing on some challenges, none of them would be easy for her. She wasn't used to doing things just for fun, or pushing her boundaries. Her mind was always working at problem solving, her reasoning ability so damn good that it didn't figure she needed to just cut loose.

"I'm not going skydiving," she said in a horrified tone.

"We can go tandem. I'm an instructor. I can take you with me."

"No!"

I shrugged. We could work our way into that. "You'd love it if you just try it. Maybe we could just do a zero gravity flight chamber?"

She was silent before she finally said, "I don't see the point, but I could probably do that."

Of course she didn't see *the point*. Having fun never made sense to her, but she needed to do it.

I motioned toward the pad in front of her and gave her the pen. "Write it down."

She added it to the list, then said, "Why is skiing on the list? We already ski."

"Because we're here in Aspen. That's something we could do later today. Maybe you could try a more challenging slope."

Lauren had been skiing for years, yet she'd never joined me and Jack on the more challenging runs. Her time was spent on the kiddie hills. She had the skill to at least bump herself up to a higher level. Not that I wanted to see her on anything dangerous, but there were runs that would be more suitable to her skills.

"I do just fine on my runs," she said hotly.

"With all of the five-year-old kids," I added. "You're better than that, Lauren. Challenge yourself just a little bit. You could handle any run on the mountain, but I'm not asking you to do the expert ones. Just step it up."

She was the most intelligent woman I'd ever known; she was brilliant. Scholastically, she was an achiever. But taking a risk on something she wasn't familiar or confident with seemed to scare the hell out of her.

Being gifted gave her a unique perspective of the world, but that didn't mean she didn't have emotions. I knew for a fact that she'd always felt like she was living outside of the world and analyzing it instead of living in the middle of the chaos. It was probably safer for her that way.

She looked up at me with apprehension, and I wanted to take the list back. My chest ached from seeing her worried expression.

What the hell did it matter if she wasn't exactly a daredevil? She didn't *need* to be. But I couldn't shake the niggling feeling that she needed to get over her fears of stepping outside her comfort zone to really be happy.

"Okay," she agreed, trying to hide her concern. "But I'm not doing number five, either."

I quirked a brow. "What's number five?"

"You wrote the list."

"I don't have your intellect and skills. I forgot the numbers. My recall isn't as advanced as yours."

"Disneyland."

"What's wrong with Disneyland? The rides are fairly tame."

"I'm not a kid."

I chuckled. "But you can act like one for the day."

She glanced at the list again. "And I'm definitely not scuba diving."

Yeah, I figured she'd object to that one. But I'd tackle that later. "Compromise?"

She gave me a skeptical look as she asked, "What kind of compromise?"

"You do Disneyworld with me instead of Disneyland, and I'll go swim with the big water cows since they're right there in Florida."

Her face lit up, and it made me suddenly regret that I'd pushed that off her list because it wasn't all that thrilling for me. It was obviously something she wanted to do.

"Deal," she said breathlessly. "But I'd need to save up for the trip."

"I'm taking care of all the expenses."

"Graham, I can't let you do that—"

"Yes, you can. That's non-negotiable. It's small money to me now. Let me do this, Lauren."

"We'll see."

I was covering the tab for everything. There was no argument, but since I knew she'd be stubborn, I'd just let her think I might consider her objection. But I wouldn't. After signing a lucrative deal with the Wildcats, I'd never be poor again. I'd majored in business in college, and although I didn't have anything close to Lauren's intelligence, I was smart enough to invest well.

"Are we agreed on the compromise?"

"Yes," she answered quickly as she changed the list to include our deal. "Why do you want me to eat at the best restaurant in Denver?"

I hesitated before I admitted, "That one is kind of for me, too. It's the one thing on the list *I've* never done. You know I love food, but I've always been too poor to try any of the good places. And I don't want to do it alone. You'd be doing me a favor if you agreed to that one."

She nodded immediately. "I'd love to go."

"Good. Anything else you don't like on the list?"

"Riding the Sky Coaster over Royal Gorge isn't going to happen. And I'm not excited with the idea of white water rafting."

"You will be," I assured her. "And those are things we probably can't do during the winter anyway. We'll save them for spring."

I'd add more stuff as I went along. One thing I wanted more than anything was to see Lauren laughing and happy. She was way too serious and focused, and I was going to teach her to just enjoy the moment. I doubted that she did anything that she didn't plan a year in advance, and none of *those* activities were exactly mindless and fun. Her idea of a trip for fun generally included a conference or some kind of think-tank.

"Will we still be friends in the spring?" she asked hesitantly.

My heart was racing as I asked, "Are you planning on kicking me to the curb? 'Cause that's the only way we won't still be in each other's lives."

"Of course not."

I was relieved. "Then consider us friends for life."

Hell, friendship wasn't all I wanted. I was getting to the point where I couldn't look at her without my dick getting hard. I had to put last night down to our drunkenness and leave it behind.

"What about Jack?"

My mood suddenly turned dark. "I know I can't kill him. But I'm also not planning to meet up with him right now. One slip-up with the law and I could lose my career. I can't go there. Hope and Jack aren't worth that to me. They both betrayed me."

Really, losing Hope had been like dodging a bullet. I couldn't be married to a woman I didn't trust. I was lucky to find out about her before we tied the knot. Jack was a different story. We'd been friends since childhood, and his betrayal hurt like a bitch. And that hurt was manifesting in anger. That was always the way I handled being let down. I got pissed as hell and cut that person out of my life. It wasn't going to go any differently this time.

"I'll call both of them and tell them to give you some time," Lauren said.

"It won't help," I said huskily. "I'll never trust either one of them again."

"I know. But it's too soon to have a discussion about what they did."

I knew Lauren was right, so I nodded. "I don't want to hear from either one of them right now."

"I'll take care of it," she said in a stoic tone.

"We need to get dressed for the slopes," I reminded her. I needed to be active. If I sat around thinking about how much I wanted to pin Lauren to the kitchen counter and fuck her until she was screaming my name, I'd totally lose it.

How had I never realized how much I wanted her before this trip? Okay, I *had* been engaged, but I'd never struggled with this kind of lust before—ever!

Granted, I hadn't seen Lauren that often in person for the last several years, but I'd tried to get back to Colorado at least once a year, usually at the holidays. I'd seen her and hung out with her several times as an adult, but I'd *never* seen her as anything *except* a good friend.

Maybe I'd blocked it because she *was* my friend, but all of those emotions had broken free. I think it would have been better if my lust-filled thoughts about Lauren had stayed hidden from my conscious mind. I wanted to spend time with her, but I knew it would come with a price. My balls would be blue forever, or at least they would until one of us decided on another committed relationship.

The thought of Lauren dumping me because she'd found another guy didn't sit well with me. Nor did I care for the idea of tying myself to another woman like Hope.

"I'll be ready shortly," Lauren said as she headed toward her room.

I caught her around her upper arm to keep her from leaving the kitchen for a moment. "I'm really sorry about last night, Peanut. I know that I hurt you, and I'm not convinced that it wasn't physical. I hate myself for that."

She backed up so she could look up at me. "It wasn't physical. I swear. I wanted what happened. I just didn't want you to regret it or feel guilty about it."

I *didn't* regret it, and I *didn't* feel guilty. I *did* hate the fact that she cried. "I don't feel guilty for wanting you. Hell, if I thought we could just be fuck buddies, we'd never leave this cabin today, but I can't do it, Peanut. I can't."

"Why?" she asked breathlessly.

It was a question she hadn't asked last night, and I'd been grateful. I shifted and grasped one of her hands. When it landed on my cock, I almost groaned. "Because of this. I can't see you without wanting you, Lauren."

"But you aren't drunk anymore," she said, sounding confused as her palm stroked over my jeans.

"No, I'm not. It seems that alcohol wasn't responsible for the way I wanted you. I guess I lied when I said you could be any woman last night. I only wanted you."

Maybe I was being a little too honest, but I wanted Lauren to know that I wasn't rejecting the offer of being friends with benefits because I didn't want her. In fact, it was just the opposite. I wanted her too damn much.

I lifted her hand off my crotch and let it fall to her side. "We're friends. We can't complicate this," I told her.

She nodded. "I know. You don't do complicated."

"I *can't* do complicated. This isn't a choice," I said in a raspy voice.

I was mesmerized as I looked into her beautiful blue eyes, her reaction so open and raw.

Mine!

Every damn cell in my body wanted to claim her, and knowing I couldn't was fucking agony.

To keep myself busy, I plucked off her glasses and cleaned them with my T-shirt before placing them back on her face again.

I couldn't seem to forget the way her wet heat had surrounded my cock, and the sultry little noises she made when I was fucking her. I'd felt so damn lost inside her, and it had been a fucking incredible state to be in.

Now, I wanted more.

Don't touch her. If you do, you'll be screwed.

"Go get ready. We're missing time on the mountain." I slapped her ass to set her in gear. If she didn't get going, I was going to pin her against the nearest solid object and show her how damn good sexual pleasure could really be.

Last night had been sloppy for me. But I knew how to pleasure a female until she was completely sated. I might fuck and run, but I made damn sure any woman in my bed was satisfied before I left.

"Just for the record, I don't regret it, either. I only regret not finishing what we started," she confessed in a wistful voice.

It took my body a long time to settle down after she'd exited the kitchen. I hadn't satisfied her, and that bugged the shit out of me.

Did I really care if I hadn't come? Actually, I didn't. It bothered me a hell of a lot more that I left Lauren wanting and crying.

I wanted a damn do-over, but I knew that I wasn't going to have that chance ever again.

CHAPTER 11

Lauren

I started hyperventilating halfway to my room. Did that just happen? Had Graham just confessed he wanted me and then shown me an impressive amount of proof? I closed the door of my bedroom and leaned forward, closed my eyes and braced my hands on my knees.

Okay, first it was necessary to determine if I was dreaming. To do this I used a method I'd come up with as a child. I imagined a hatch door in my head and opened it. My subconscious could take me to some scary places but I'd never let it beat me. The method was effective with nightmares so it was reasonable to theorize it would be with fantasy fulfilling dreams as well. I didn't want to buy into the idea of Graham wanting me only to wake and realize I was still on the couch waiting for him to arrive after Jack and Hope left.

I opened my eyes. Still here.

Oh, my God. So, this was real.

I called Jack but he didn't answer. He obviously didn't want to hear my opinion. Telling him off wasn't the purpose of my call, though, so I kept to what was. I told him Graham needed time to work through what had happened before he'd talk to either of them. I was debating what else to add when the voicemail beeped and asked me if I was satisfied with my message. I said yes because, really, what else was there to say?

I straightened then, and on autopilot began to hunt through my suitcase for my ski pants. I couldn't stop thinking about what he'd said. *Last night wasn't about any woman—he wanted me.*

I hugged my pants to my chest and sat on the edge of my bed. *I might have been offered my one and only chance with him and ruined it. I made things complicated when they could have been gloriously simple.*

How simple would the next day have been even if we'd gone all the way?

I took several calming breaths. Very few things in life or nature were one-time occurrences. Patterns were everywhere.

And they often repeated.

Over-thinking a situation until I couldn't enjoy it was a prime example.

I mentally ran through Graham's additions to my list. There wasn't a single thing on there that I normally would have chosen to do. It wasn't that I was afraid, per se. I just knew myself. Snow tubing sounded fun in theory, but casualties happened each year—some fatal. The circular nature of the tube provided a rider with only a minimal amount of control. Ice. Speed. Trajectory. Path obstructions. There were too many unknown variables for me to ever enjoy it.

Unknown variables—just like sex with Graham held.

The night before I had held myself back and it had cost me my chance to know an intimate side of him. If I said no to the list I would cheat myself of knowing another piece of him.

Was mitigating risk worth the cost of what it kept me from experiencing? The concept of risk itself was subjective and relied on more than external observable factors. People viewed the same event differently based on personality, experience, or cultural norms—and those variables were not constants—making growth and change possible. Graham applied that philosophy to his football career. He'd designed a plan for me to grow from.

Snow tubing.

Sky diving.

Disney.

At least, that was what I wanted to believe the list was about. He might be trying to regain control of an impossible situation. Or his goal might be to prove to himself that we're too different for each other.

A memory came back to me from years before. I was on the porch bench swing of my parents' home—crying. Jack walked by, but Graham stopped and asked me if I was okay. I'd tried to say I was, but had ended up gushing to him that no one at the college I was attending talked to me. He sat next to me on the swing and gave me a playful punch to the arm. "Fuck them, you've got me." I smiled at the memory.

I no longer had to ask why he'd written the list. In my heart I knew. He knew I needed this—we needed this. Suddenly I was less opposed to the idea of skiing one of the more challenging hills. Broken bones heal; I never would if I lost Graham.

Life was full of repeating patterns, and if doing everything on that list gave me another chance with Graham, I was all in. I stood and stepped into my ski pants. I gathered the rest of my gear and headed out of my room to find Graham.

He was dressed and waiting for me near the door. His expression was dark until he saw me and a teasing smile lit his face. "I thought I might have to come in after you."

I almost said, "I would have liked that." Instead, I rolled my eyes skyward. He said he couldn't do complicated and that was understandable considering everything that was going on with Jack and Hope. "You aren't going to be unbearably smug the *whole* day, are you?"

He shrugged as if it were a distinct possibility.

I added, "Because then I may have to leave your ass in my dust."

"Oh, really?" he chuckled, as he held my jacket out for me.

I turned, slid my arms in and glanced at him over my shoulder. "Really," I said cheekily. Desire flashed in his eyes and it set my heart thudding wildly. Maybe we couldn't go back to exactly how we were before last night, but maybe, just maybe, if I took it slowly and didn't over-think it we could have something even better.

His smile turned tender and he turned to open the door for me. When I stepped forward and next to him, he said, "All it takes, Lauren, is believing you can and you will."

It might have sounded like recycled locker room speech, but his expression was tender. Referencing us and not the challenges, I said, "I'm not afraid anymore."

We exchanged a long look.

He closed the door behind me. "Don't look at me that way, Peanut. What Jack and Hope did was fucked up, but I can handle it. If I hurt you, it would gut me. I'd never be the same. I look at you and I want to carry you right to my bed and finish what we started. But I need you to be the strong one. Don't let me become someone I'll hate."

In my mind we were back on the swing at my parents' house and this time he needed me. I could over-think it and make it all about me or I could be the kind of friend he'd always been to me. Wherever this went, the idea of hurting him gutted me as well. So, I gave him what he was asking for. I punched him playfully in the arm and said, "I don't know about you, but I came here to ski. Can we forget all the other shit and hit the slopes?"

His smile returned. "Please."

We talked about the weather and the run options on the way to the lifts. He looked torn about which one to choose. I dragged him toward the one with a black diamond, the toughest course. I told myself I wasn't scared, but I could barely breathe as I took a seat next to him and our feet left the ground.

"I've done this hill before. It's not so bad."

There was no time to confirm his impression of the hills with statistics. No time to check the conditions or the challenges of the course. I would soon be racing forward with no idea of what lay ahead. Enjoying it would require believing in myself as well as Graham.

We reached the top of the run and slid off the ski lift. The view was breathtaking, unlike anything I'd seen from below. *Okay, let's do this.*

Graham was at my side. "Take it slow, Peanut. You don't have to become a daredevil all in one day. In fact, I'd prefer that you wouldn't."

I felt the first rush of adrenaline but this time embraced it. "I'm fine, Graham. I know I can do it. Do you know why?"

He looked at me in bemusement. "No."

I pushed off instead of answering. I'd tell him one day, but not that day. The pitch brought speed I'd never experienced. I dug in, used what I'd learned from years of instruction to go even faster.

A side glance confirmed he was skiing with me but at a distance, there to pick me up if I fell—just as he'd been doing most of my life. How could I not love him?

I returned my attention to the course and let myself really fly for the first time in my life.

CHAPTER 12

Graham

ELEVEN YEARS AGO...

I felt elated as I arrived at Jack's house.

I was only a freshman in high school, but I'd made the football team. In fact, I was chosen to be the quarterback.

As long as I don't get in trouble.

For me, that was a pretty difficult stipulation, but I was determined to keep my nose clean.

Most of the time, I wanted to do well in school. I had a talent for math, a skill I could thank Lauren and all her tutoring through the years for, but more often than not, I didn't do my homework because I was on the field tossing a football.

Jack had made the team, too, but I didn't know if he knew about it yet. He hadn't hung around to get the roster. Lauren was at home alone, and he'd mentioned that he had to go take care of some problem.

"Graham?"

I stopped as I saw Lauren sitting in her swing as I cut across the backyard.

As usual, just seeing the adoration on her sweet little face made me feel ten-feet-tall.

I sat on the swing next to her. "Whatcha doing, Peanut?"

"I'm sad," she said directly, her gaze diverted to the ground.

For Lauren, cutting to emotion without analysis was unusual.

"Why?" *Dammit!* I hated seeing Lauren upset. I could tell that she'd been crying, and her glasses were smeared. I plucked them off her face and cleaned them with my T-shirt.

"Milly died," she said with a quiver in her voice.

I put her glasses back on her face, my heart aching as I realized why Jack had needed to go home.

"What happened?" I knew her little poodle was old. Actually, Milly had been older than Lauren was, and I was pretty sure she'd probably had more years on her than Jack. The bitch had been a rescue dog, and I don't think anybody had ever figured out her exact age.

But Lauren had adored Milly, and I hated to see her lose an old friend.

Her eyes filled with tears, and she squeezed the large teddy bear on her lap, a gift I'd given her over three years ago. Max, the stuffed animal, had been well worth the money I'd had to save to give it to her for her birthday. He was somewhat dilapidated, but by the looks of the bear, she used it well and often when she was upset. She looked up at me, obviously in distress. "I don't know. I came home, and she was dead."

I balked at the idea of Lauren coming home to find the dog she adored dead in the house. But I wanted to be strong for her. This wasn't about me.

"She was old, Peanut. It was probably her time."

"But I wasn't ready yet."

I thought about all of the losses I'd had in my life. I'd never been prepared for *any* of them, nor had I totally understood why they happened. "I don't think you ever would have been ready," I observed.

She tilted her head like she was considering my words. "Do you think so? I'm going to miss her terribly."

When I looked at Lauren, I saw an adult trapped in a sweet little girl. That shit couldn't be easy. She was smarter than the large percentage of adults, yet she wasn't mature enough to handle all of that brain power.

One minute she reminded me of a college professor, and then at next glance, I could only see a little girl who was hurting.

I stood up and knelt beside her, swiping at the tears on her face with my shirt. "You gave her a good life, Peanut. She knew that you loved her. And you rescued her from a crappy life at a shelter."

A few of my previous foster homes had animals, but I'd never gotten close to them. I didn't know what it was like to love a pet. Hell, I didn't know how to love people, much less a dog.

She gave me a worried look. "But she died all alone. That shouldn't have happened."

I flinched and tried to hide the fact that her comment hit a nerve. "Sometimes we can't control what happens."

"I know. But I don't have to like death."

As far as I knew, *nobody* liked anybody or anything they loved dying on them. I know I sure as hell didn't.

I shook my head. "Nope. You don't. Take your time and miss Milly if you want. Think about all the good memories you have of her. Eventually, it won't hurt so much."

"Did you ever have anybody die?" she asked curiously.

I nodded, but my throat closed up because of the knot that was lodged smack in the middle of my vocal cords.

She continued, "So you hurt, too?"

I found my voice. "Not so much anymore," I told her. "But when my parents died, it was pretty bad."

Honestly, it had been so long that I couldn't quite remember their faces, but I knew I'd been hurt and confused.

"I'm sorry they died," she said earnestly.

I cracked a small smile. "Thanks."

Lauren almost knocked me over as she threw her little body into my arms. "I love you, Graham. Please don't ever leave me."

I put my arms around her and hugged her tight, squashing Max between us. She was afraid of losing anybody else she cared about. Genius or not, she was still emotionally sensitive. Maybe more so than the average kid because she couldn't quite justify being unhappy in her head.

Death sucked. I knew the fear of experiencing it again after my father died. And my worst nightmare had come true. I didn't want that for the girl I adored. "I won't leave you. I promise," I vowed.

She wiped her wet face on my T-shirt, but I didn't give a damn. Lauren was the only person on Earth who told me that she loved me, and I cherished every damn word.

"I swear it will be okay," I said hoarsely. "Should we go get some blueberry muffins?" They were Lauren's favorite, and I'd go buy some if there wasn't a mix in the house.

She drew back and looked at me with a dubious expression. "You realize that I'm smart enough to know that sweets won't solve any of my problems?"

I ruffled her hair. "But it won't hurt."

She appeared to be analyzing my words before she replied, "I suppose not."

I rose to my feet and handed Max to her. "Let's go, smarty-pants."

She smiled up at me and took my hand. "I feel a *little* bit better."

Some of the pressure on my chest lifted as I walked her into the house. I wanted to protect her from anything dark or ugly in her life, and sometimes I felt so damn helpless. What in the hell did a fourteen-year-old guy say to an eleven-year-old girl to cheer her up?

I knew very little about happiness. All I knew was survival.

It was probably all I'd ever understood.

I love you, too, Peanut.

Maybe if I could tell Lauren just once that I loved her like the sister I'd never had, it would make her feel better. She said it all the time, but I'd never once voiced my own emotions.

I'd thought about it, but saying the words was something I never did.

Maybe it was better that way.

CHAPTER 13

Graham

*I*never felt as free as I did when I was on the slopes racing at a breakneck pace down a challenging run on the mountain.

But today was different.

I was fucking terrified.

I stayed with Lauren as she took control of her run, expertly maneuvering her way down the black diamond slope.

She'd shocked the hell out of me when she'd chosen one of the hardest courses. I'd been proud of her for just stepping up to the longer runs. There was no way in hell I could have predicted what had just happened.

I was terrified that she'd get injured. Yeah, she had the skill to handle this run, but she didn't have the experience.

Now, I didn't know if I was proud or horrified. If she got hurt, I'd never fucking forgive myself for wanting her to step up to a bigger challenge.

I wish I had kept my mouth shut.

And, dammit, she'd never told me *why* she was okay with pushing off from one of the most advanced slopes she could conquer.

Of course, I knew she could do it. I wouldn't have challenged her with a harder run if I didn't know for sure that she could ski at an expert level. I'd watched her over the years, wondering how she didn't get bored on the kiddie slopes. She was an amazing skier. With her kind of skill, she probably could kick my ass if she really wanted to compete.

But experience was everything, and to go straight to one of the hardest courses wasn't wise. I'd wanted her to work her way up.

I began to relax as I followed her close enough to keep an eye on her, but not enough to make her nervous or distracted. She was good. Really good. She was blazing her own trail, and all I had to do was ride slightly behind.

When we were about halfway down, I willed myself to relax. Lauren was tearing up the mountainside, and she wasn't going to fall. She was looking pretty damn relaxed and confident as she took on every new challenge the course could throw at her.

I'd done this course hundreds of times with Jack.

But being with Lauren made it all seem new and different.

There's a curve ahead. Be careful, Peanut.

We were fast approaching one of the trickiest sections, and it involved avoiding the trees and taking some tight, fast turns.

Lauren maneuvered spectacularly.

I...didn't.

I was so concerned about her making the turns that I missed one myself, and it had me tumbling down the mountain like a damn novice.

"Shit!" I took a face full of snow as I finally came to a stop.

"Graham! Oh, God. Talk to me. Are you okay?" Lauren had circled around, shed her skis, and climbed back up to check on me.

She sounded breathless with worry, and I ate *that* up like I'd never had somebody who cared about me before. Probably because I hadn't. Generally, if I fell on my head, nobody gave a damn. Jack would make sure I was okay…eventually. But he was usually laughing at my dumb ass after he knew I'd survive.

I was tempted to keep silent when I felt her hands running over my hair and my forehead. She'd shucked off her gloves and her fingers were gingerly touching my face, looking for injuries. I really *did* want to bask in her response to thinking I was hurt because it was such a novelty. But I couldn't do that to her. "I'm okay."

I sat up and reached for the hat that had fallen off my head. "I was stupid."

"You're *not* stupid," she said emphatically. "All it takes is one minor judgment error to end up on your ass with this course."

I pulled on my hat and looked at her as she crouched down beside me. Her expression was concerned, but her cheeks were bright with excitement. "Yeah. I kind of found that out," I said drily as I stood up and retrieved my skis. I'd lost both of them when I'd taken my tumble.

Lauren's mind worked in ways I couldn't possibly understand. No doubt she could calculate every turn, and do what she needed to do to fly through all of the obstacles. While she called herself a freak, I'd always idolized her skills. Having a brain like hers was special. She was gifted, and she didn't waste that talent.

"Are you sure you're okay?" she asked.

I grinned at her as we both got back into our skis. "Other than the fact that I have to bow to your superior skills, I'm fine."

"You took a fall. My skills aren't superior," she denied.

God, I loved the fact that Lauren could joke around, yet be so sensitive. She was defending my stupidity because she didn't want to hurt my ego. Hell, my ego wasn't suffering. I knew I had good skills. I'd just lost them temporarily while I watched her fearlessly flying ahead of me.

"You're a distraction," I claimed jokingly.

She put her hands on her hips. "Is that so?"

"Yep. I never would have eaten snow if I hadn't been watching your beautiful ass in front of me. I lost my concentration. It's entirely your fault."

Her smile was worth every ache I had from wiping out on the side of the mountain.

"Then I'll let you lead this time," she offered.

I shook my head. "Oh, hell no. It seems that I really like torturing myself."

"Are you really okay?" she asked breathlessly. "You took a pretty hard fall."

"I've always had a hard head." *Jesus!* It was nice to have somebody who cared about whether or not I was okay. Why had I never seen just how damn lucky I was to have a friend like Lauren? Honestly, she'd always been my inspiration to succeed because I wanted to make her proud. The fact that she'd always had faith in me had been motivation in the back of my mind, even when I was across the country physically.

"I'll go slow," she told me.

"I can keep up."

She frowned, but she turned around and looked out for other skiers before she set herself in motion again.

Lauren *did* go slow, but I didn't give a damn. It gave me that much longer to watch her from behind. And her beautiful ass was definitely worth watching.

When we got to the bottom, I took us both out of our skis and picked Lauren up and twirled her around. "You were incredible up there, Peanut."

She looked down at me with a happy smile. "Put me down or you'll end up with back strain."

I snorted as I let her slide down my body and find her feet again. "You're a lightweight."

"You're just strong," she argued.

"You're so fucking beautiful." The words came out of my mouth without a second thought.

Lauren's blue eyes were mesmerizing, and I couldn't look away from her happy, smiling expression. I wanted to see her like that every single day. I didn't understand my reaction to her, and I wasn't going to analyze it. The way I felt...it just *was*. I knew I needed to stifle my physical desire for Lauren, but I just couldn't do it.

I couldn't go back to the friendship we'd had before I'd touched her.

I couldn't erase the sensation of the incendiary heat I'd felt when her pussy was wrapped around my cock like she wanted to keep me there.

Yet, I couldn't be the guy for her, either.

It put me in one hell of an uncomfortable position.

She shook her head slowly, her eyes still locked with mine. "I've never been beautiful, Graham. I've always been a geek."

I put a hand on her cheek. "Bullshit. You've just never *seen* yourself the way I do."

Unable to stop myself, I lowered my head and kissed her. She responded to me immediately, wrapping her arms around my neck as we got lost in each other. We were totally oblivious to any other skiers around. As long as I was touching her, nothing else really mattered.

I devoured her mouth like I was terrified it was suddenly going to go away. I was greedy, and Lauren responded with an equal amount of fire.

My chest was heaving by the time I finally let her go. "If there weren't other people around, I'd be fucking you against one of these trees," I said in a rough voice.

"I'd let you," she answered breathlessly.

My dick was already diamond hard, and her affirmation that she felt the same way that I did nearly killed me. "I don't know how to handle this, Lauren. I don't think I can *not* want you anymore. That need won't go away no matter how hard I try to push it into the back of my mind. It's always there." And it was fucking eating me alive.

I felt like we'd opened a door that would never close. Had I felt this way for several years—since she'd grown up—and I'd buried it, or had I just finally looked at her with a new set of eyes that could see *her*?

She wasn't just my friend anymore, but she wasn't technically my lover.

At some point, Lauren *had* grown up, and I'd missed it. She wasn't like a sister to me now. In fact, she was rapidly becoming a damn obsession that I couldn't control.

"I want you, too," she confessed in a soft voice.

"Don't say that," I snapped.

She shrugged. "It's true. And we don't lie to each other."

Her words hit me like a sucker punch. Maybe she'd always been honest, but there was a side of me that she didn't know—a messed up part of me that I never wanted to show her. "I've lied to you," I admitted brusquely. "Don't trust me, Lauren. Don't *ever* put your faith in me. You'll be disappointed if you do."

"Graham, I don't understand—"

I nodded my head toward the ski lift. "Are we going back up?"

"Yes. I suppose. If you're feeling okay. But can you explain—"

"I can't." I looked away from her and stepped back into my skis.

I never wanted Lauren to know just how fucked up I really was. That meant that I could never take this relationship further, whether I wanted to or not.

She stepped back into her skis and followed behind me as I made my way to the lift.

We caught the chair that would take us back up the mountain before I said, "Let's just forget about everything else today, okay? Can we just enjoy the day?"

I didn't want to spoil her accomplishment. This day was for Lauren. And I had plenty of other days that were going to revolve around her, days I hoped would be just like today.

Fuck what I wanted. Lauren had helped me become what I was today. If not for her unwavering faith and help with my schoolwork, I never would have been in the NFL. It was time for me to pay her back for everything she'd done to help me get to my current life.

She was silent for a moment before she answered, "Yes, we can. I won't ask any more questions you don't want to answer."

"It isn't that I don't *want* to," I admitted. "I can't. I don't *understand* what's happening. I was engaged to Hope. We were supposed to get married. And I don't even feel angry about her fucking around on me right now, even though I'm pissed at Jack. I don't miss her. I don't even think about her."

"Maybe you never loved her," Lauren suggested.

"I didn't. I never did. I thought she was the perfect woman because she was a supermodel and well-connected. She was all part of my life plan. I have no fucking idea how to love *anyone*."

It was a truth that I hadn't meant to blurt out that way, but maybe it was time to tell Lauren some of my not-so-nice traits. Maybe it would put some well-needed distance between us.

"So you knew you didn't love her?"

"Jesus, Lauren. I don't even know what love *feels* like. Not really. Other than you and Jack, I've never felt like anybody gave a damn about me."

"You're right," she said quietly. "Let's just enjoy the day."

I didn't blame her for being confused or not knowing exactly what to say. She was a woman who had so much love to give, and she gave of herself every single damn day. How could she possibly comprehend a guy who had no problem screwing everybody else to get exactly what he wanted?

I ignored her last comment as I said, "Hope didn't love me, either. In some ways, it made our relationship perfect because

I don't know how to give anybody anything. I was engaged to her because I thought she'd benefit me with her connections and family. She agreed to marry me because I think she liked the idea of being with a pro football player. Hell, maybe we were good for each other because neither one of us had to put much emotional effort into our relationship. Maybe she didn't know what love was, either."

"Graham, I—"

"Don't, Lauren. Don't say anything. Even though we've always been friends, there are a lot of things about me that you don't know." Maybe I'd said too much, but I wasn't going to go back now.

I'd wanted her to keep on caring about me, even when I probably didn't deserve it. I was silent, on edge as I waited to see if she was going to react to my confession about me and Hope.

"I never wanted to push for any information you didn't want to share," she said as we both exited the lift.

"I appreciate that." In some ways, I wanted Lauren to know everything, even my darker side. But I was afraid I'd scare her off.

She nodded. "You pick the run."

When I went to a much tamer course, she laughed. "Now who is being cautious?" she asked with humor in her voice.

"My heart won't take another black diamond run, even though I know you can handle it," I said, trying to exit my dark mood so we could enjoy the slopes.

"Lead the way," she challenged.

I pushed myself off, letting Lauren follow closely behind me.

CHAPTER 14

Graham

I t had been *almost* a perfect day.

But I'd spoiled it somewhat by opening my stupid mouth about my faults. There had been tension between me and Lauren since I'd blurted out the fact that I hadn't loved Hope.

Maybe she'd thought it was cold, and maybe it was, but the relationship *had* fit my life.

Being with Hope had seemed like a brilliant idea at the time, and it had worked for both of us.

Now, I was starting to realize that it might not have been the brightest idea I'd ever had.

Lauren and I had come back to the cabin lighthearted and laughing like the old days, but I knew it wasn't going to last. Lauren wasn't going to let me get away with not explaining my earlier words. She'd just delayed it for a while.

I gave her credit. We'd eaten a take-out pizza and were settled on the couch before she opened that door again.

"So you didn't love Hope, and she didn't love you," she mused as she sipped a glass of Merlot. "If you were both okay with that kind of relationship, that doesn't really make it bad. But you deserve so much more, Graham."

I took a slug of my beer before I answered. "It's completely fucked up. And we obviously weren't happy. Hope had her mouth wrapped around another guy's dick."

"It's not your fault that Hope cheated. And everybody makes mistakes, Graham."

"I've made a shit-ton of them, Peanut."

"Tell me," she encouraged.

"Other than the times I spent with you and Jack, I've always been a prick. You know I was always moving from one foster home to another."

"You never said why. Was it because of your attention deficit hyperactivity disorder?"

"I was a hard kid to handle, and I didn't have much impulse control. I'd do something and then regret it later. I fought constantly. I was always angry. There were some homes that really weren't good for me, but after a while, I didn't even try to make my foster parents like me anymore. Most of them had kids of their own, and I couldn't compete with them."

"You shouldn't have had to compete. You just needed somebody to care about you."

I shrugged. "None of them did. So I didn't give a damn about them, either."

"You could have," Lauren argued. "I think you needed someone to care about you."

"I just wanted to survive. I'm not sure you can understand that, but all I wanted was to feel safe. I got into some pretty bad situations in the beginning. By the time I hit my teens, I was just pissed off. All the time. You, Jack, and football were the only things that kept me grounded."

"You were afraid," she corrected. "I could always see that, but I didn't know how to help you."

I shrugged. "You didn't need to help me. I had to help myself."

It was strange how Lauren had seen my fear when everybody else had seen me as just a bad kid. "Football was my only out. I needed to be *somebody*, and I promised myself that it would happen no matter what. I wanted to make you and Jack proud."

"You have a lot to be proud of. But I've always admired you. You didn't have to be a millionaire for me to care about you."

My gut ached from the words I wanted to hear so much—that somebody cared regardless of my profession or wealth. She cared about me. But I wondered if she still would if she knew everything.

"I have a lot to regret, too," I told her. "I was an asshole to anybody who might have shown me some kindness. Then when I went to play in college, I wasn't exactly a team player. I cared about *me*. I didn't care about my team or my teammates. It didn't matter whether we won or lost. *My* stats and performance were my only concern. Did I have enough completions and passing yards for the NFL to look at me? To hell with the team."

"Graham, you were struggling to survive. Considering your background, it's understandable. It's admirable that you can even do a self-evaluation and recognize that you don't like some of the things you did. But you can't keep blaming yourself. You've never been a jerk to me or to Jack."

"You two were the exception," I rasped.

Lauren slid across the couch and put her hand on my face. "There's nothing you're ever going to tell me that's going to make me hate you. Whether you realize it or not...I do know you. I knew that you were scared when we were kids. Yes, you let it out in anger, but who in the hell was listening to you? Who really cared? I'd get angry, too. And since you had to fight your way out of a really shitty life with football, I don't care if you were selfish. You *deserved* to be selfish. Nobody had ever taken care of you. And if you didn't know what love was, it wasn't your fault. Nobody ever taught you how to love anybody."

"Maybe I didn't want to know," I argued.

"I call bullshit."

I looked into her eyes, and I knew I was fucked. Her trust in me was way more than I deserved. But I was getting addicted to it. I was getting addicted to *her.* Maybe I always had been.

"So there's nothing I can tell you that will make you run away screaming?"

She rolled her eyes in that adorable way that made me want to get her naked and show her who was boss.

Of course, just about *everything* she did now made me want to fuck her.

"Not a thing," she said as she dropped her hands and made herself comfortable next to me. "Honestly, it's nothing I didn't already know. I was younger, but I knew every time you got in trouble in school for fighting. And I knew you'd have to be completely focused to become a pro starter. You aren't a dick. You were just protecting yourself emotionally. You were driven."

"Nope. I'm an asshole. Most of my teammates hated me. And I don't blame them. Every game was about *me* instead of being about our *team.*"

"Clean slate," she said. "You're starting with a brand-new team."

She was right. It was a whole new group of guys. I'd known some of them from college or by reputation, but I was starting over in a way. "So what you're saying is that I can become a nice guy."

"You already are. You always have been. What I'm saying is that you can let more people know who you really are."

Honestly, I wasn't sure I could do that. "I don't trust easily."

"There are valid reasons for that. So you take your time."

Maybe it was a bit clichéd, but for some reason, Lauren made me want to be a better guy. "I'll try."

"Good. Because I'll care whether you win or lose because the Wildcats are my team. So you better win."

"I want to win our division this time," I confessed. "I want the Super Bowl."

"Then you'll have to be a team player," she observed. "Those teams succeed because all areas of the team are the best."

"I know," I answered. "I'm just not sure how to trust other team members." But I was aware that something had to change if I wanted to go all the way.

I looked at Lauren and frowned. "*Shit!* Don't cry." I hated seeing tears in her beautiful eyes.

"I can't help it. I hate what happened to you. It wasn't fair."

"Life often isn't fair," I told her. "But I've got a new shot at something great now."

She swiped a tear from her cheek. "You deserve it, Graham. And you earned it."

I *had* earned it with sweat, blood and plenty of injuries.

"I'm going to be the best I can be next season, Lauren." No way was I willing to let my favorite Cats fan down.

"I'll help any way that I can," she vowed.

I was taking her up on coming with me when I was practicing my throws. She was a genius. I'd be crazy not to let her try to help me figure things out to be better. Peanut was way too good at finding ways to help me understand things I couldn't figure out myself.

Now that I'd dumped out how I felt about myself, I was ready to leave it all behind. Maybe Lauren was right. Maybe some of my behavior had been justified. But I still didn't like my darker side. It took me to places I didn't want to go. But I was doing all I could to get that side of me under control.

"I think I need ice cream," I declared, trying to lighten the mood.

What the hell. If I was going to blow my healthy eating routine while we were in Aspen, I might as well go all the way. It had been too long since I'd had ice cream.

"Your favorite is in the freezer."

"With whipped cream?"

Damn! I could think of so many uses for whipped cream, and all of them entailed licking it off Lauren's gorgeous body.

"Do I ever forget?"

Nope. She never did. Lauren did sweet little things that I'd probably taken for granted. "No. You never forget."

She started to rise to go to the kitchen, but I stopped her. "Thanks for today," I said huskily.

Lauren smiled at me as she said, "It probably wasn't all that thrilling for you. You've done those runs so many times."

"I don't mean that. Thanks for believing in me even after I told you what a dick I can be."

"You believe in me. Why wouldn't I feel the same way?"

I stood and pulled her to her feet. "Because it's unusual for anybody to support me."

"I've always been there for you, Graham, and I've always known you'd be successful."

Yeah, I'd just never opened my eyes to really *see her* as a woman before yesterday. If I had, I would have broken down and told her every crappy thing I'd ever done. I would have known she'd still support me even if I'd made some mistakes.

Lauren was forgiving; I was not.

Now that I did see her, I was starting to realize that I fucking needed her.

Mine!

A possessive instinct slammed me in the gut so hard I nearly flinched. I didn't know how I was going to keep myself from touching her.

The more I was around Lauren, the more desperately I needed her to belong to me. I didn't understand why I had to have her. But the primitive emotions were all too real, and something I'd never experienced before.

Before Hope, I'd fucked plenty of women. Maybe too many. And I hadn't ever *needed* any of them. I hadn't needed Hope, either.

Yeah, my contract had made me wealthy, but I wasn't exactly a great partner. Hell, I'd realized that fact since the moment Lauren had told me about Hope and Jack. I hadn't been enough for Hope, so I knew I'd never be the kind of guy Lauren would want. I'd never be able to satisfy her long-term because I had no clue how to love somebody the way she deserved to be loved.

I hadn't been lying when I'd told her I didn't know how to love. I just...didn't. That was part of the reason I'd proposed to Hope. I wasn't really into needing romantic love. I think Hope and I were both convinced it didn't exist. We understood each other, or we *had* before she'd needed...more.

"Need ice cream," I growled playfully as I slapped her on the ass.

"Grouch," she countered.

I wasn't unhappy. I just needed something to cool me down. Food was also a great distraction for me. But I had a feeling that whipped cream would fuel more fantasies than I needed to consider right now.

When she went to open the refrigerator door, I stopped her by putting a hand and some of my weight on the door. "Hold the whipped cream," I requested gruffly.

She looked up at me in surprise, possibly reading the raw desire on my face before she agreed, "Probably not good for *either of us.*"

Shooting me a knowing smile, she moved my hand away and opened the freezer.

She only took out the ice cream.

CHAPTER 15

Lauren

I told myself we'd made the right choice. I breathed in the cool air from the freezer, hoping it might strengthen my resolve. If only he would stop looking at me as if I was his favorite dessert. If only I could forget he *wanted* me.

I closed the freezer and focused on scooping the ice cream into two bowls. If I'd needed to, I couldn't have said how many times we'd snuck off like naughty children to indulge in sweets together. It wasn't so much that anyone would have denied us the treats, but it always felt like a guilty pleasure.

Just like wanting Graham did.

There wasn't a part of Graham I didn't love, hadn't spent most of my life loving. What had started as a crush had grown into a yearning-filled friendship and was changing again. I didn't know if I could stop it or if I even wanted to.

I put a spoon in his bowl and turned. He was standing closer than I thought and I accidently hit him in the chest with the bowl.

He grabbed my hand to steady it and fire shot through me. His eyes were burning with the same need I was fighting. I licked my bottom lip and swayed toward him. "Graham—"

His breathing became ragged. "I—We—Fuck me."

Whether he said it as an expletive or an order, I didn't know, but I welcomed either. He put the bowl on the counter and pulled me to him. I wound my arms around his neck as he devoured my mouth. It was the kiss from the mountainside and more because there was no reason we had to stop.

There was no patience or tenderness in our caresses. He roughly slid his hands beneath my sweater, undid my bra and cupped my breasts. I arched against his touch. *Heaven.*

Graham was a feast for my hungry hands: the bulging muscles of his shoulders, wide chest, tight six-pack. Yes, I had touched him before, but not sober. This was an entirely different level of hot. My body shuddered from the intensity of need overtaking me.

My hands went to his belt. I wanted to finish what we'd started the day before and I wanted it right then.

He growled into my ear. "Easy, Peanut. I want you so fucking much, but I'll make it good for you this time. So good."

I should have told him the first time was my fault, but he was kissing me again and the last thing I wanted to do was talk or cry. He pulled my shirt up, breaking off the kiss just long enough to whip it over my head. I dropped my bra to the floor and yanked at his shirt, but he was too tall for me to repeat his move.

He chuckled against my lips and shed his shirt. His chest was warm against my excited nipples. I writhed against him, loving how he responded with a guttural sound of pleasure.

This was the Graham of my fantasies. I ran my hands over every inch he'd bared until it was no longer enough. I needed more.

As if he came to the same conclusion, he undid my jeans and with a thumb looped on either side, lowered them with my underwear. I stepped out of both, then used my feet to rid myself of my socks. Naked didn't feel vulnerable, not with Graham—it felt like a promise.

He held me back from him. "You're so fucking beautiful."

"So are you." I didn't care if that sounded stupid. He *was* beautiful. Inside and out. Someday, somehow, I would prove it to him. He deserved a much better life than the one that had been given to him.

I looked away as my mind began to race. We might not be together long enough for me to prove anything to him at all. He already thought sex between us was a bad idea.

What if by not respecting his decision I made our friendship impossible?

Oh, no, I cannot get emotional and start to cry again. This was *not* our last time together. It *didn't* have to be goodbye.

Graham had already reassured me on those fears.

He took my face between his hands and raised my eyes back to his. "Hey."

There was no time to compose myself. I met his gaze, blinked and cursed myself for ruining my second chance with him as well. If I couldn't hold myself together, maybe I wasn't what he needed. I hated that I wasn't stronger.

He ran a thumb over my mouth gently. "I can see the wheels turning in your head. Do you want to stop?"

"God, no," I breathed. "I want this so much. I'm sorry."

The understanding look he gave me was a familiar expression. He'd always celebrated my best and somehow understood my worst. "What are you sorry about?"

"I can't turn my thoughts off. They start racing around and I get all tangled up. You didn't do anything wrong last time. It was me. It's always me."

He pulled me to his chest and tucked me beneath his chin, simply holding me for a long time. Against my hair he murmured, "There is nothing wrong with you. Not one damn thing."

I nodded for his benefit rather than because I believed him.

"Look at me." He ran one hand roughly through my hair while his other slid down my stomach to my sex. He dipped a finger into me and groaned. "You're so wet. Tell me what you want."

I raised my eyes back to his and gasped as his confident fingers found my clit and stroked it with a rhythm that sent heat rushing through me. "I want you."

His hand tightened in my hair and he arched my head back. "Not good enough," he growled and thrusted a thick finger upward into my tight sex. "Say it. I want to hear that sweet mouth of yours crying out your filthiest desires. You want me to fuck you, don't you?"

I nodded, holding on to his shoulders to steady myself. He bent me further back and took one of my nipples between his teeth and gave it a deliciously painful nip. He pumped his finger in and out, circling my clit with his thumb each time. His tongue replaced his teeth, circling and flicking my excited nub.

Then he paused and raised his head. "What do you want?"

Barely able to breathe, I said, "I want you to fuck me."

His hand began its talented caress again. His mouth loved my other breast and I shuddered with pleasure. "Don't stop," I demanded.

"You like that? What else do you like?"

"Anything," I said breathlessly. In that moment I meant it. Everything he did felt good. I trusted him completely. "What do you want?"

"This time isn't about me." He lifted me and sat me on the counter. I spread my legs for him and was rewarded with a slow, pleased smile. "You're so fucking perfect. All I want is to see you come."

I smiled. His gaze was a caress of its own. I brought my hand to my clit and began to rub it. His nostrils flared and he breathed in audibly. I'd never been sexually bold, but knowing that I could turn Graham on gave me confidence. With his cock bulging in his jeans, he watched me as I increased the speed of my hand across my clit. My eyelids grew heavy and my core began to spasm. It was a small wave of warm release.

I stopped, gripped the counter on either side of me and was about to open my eyes when I felt his breath on my sex. He parted me with his fingers and began to adore my clit with his huge, hot tongue. The pleasure I'd brought myself was nothing compared to the fire his touch sent through me.

He slid one finger inside me, then another and then began to pump them in and out—faster and faster. I whimpered as I started toward a second and much more powerful climax.

I shifted closer to the edge, wanting his tongue to go deeper. He'd created a need his fingers could not fulfill.

I was out of my mind by the time I heard him unzip his jeans. There was an excruciatingly long pause while he stepped out of them and rolled on a condom. Then his hands gripped my hips and he teased me by dipping just the tip of his cock into me.

I wrapped my legs around his waist, pulling him closer. His hands bit into my ass as he lifted me off the counter and held me effortlessly just above his rock-hard cock. I couldn't take it anymore. I started begging. "Fuck me, Graham. I want to feel you inside me. Now."

"Good, baby. That's so good." He claimed my mouth then thrusted upward into me. He was so big and for a second I worried that taking him all in might hurt, but it didn't. He moved slowly at first, then more powerfully. Deeper and deeper. Harder and faster.

He turned so my back rested against the coolness of the fridge and pounded into me. I dug my nails into his shoulders and gave myself over to my first out-of-body-mindlessly-wonderful orgasm.

I cried out as I came. He didn't break stride. He was lost to our passion as well. There was a primal fierceness to how he kissed my neck and held me as he took his own pleasure. I held on, clenching around each powerful thrust. I wouldn't have thought it possible, but my body began to hum again. I had to know if it could get even better. I dug my hands into his hair and growled, "Hard. Fuck me harder."

"Fuck, yeah." Whatever control he'd had disappeared then. He drove into me with an abandon that had me calling out his name and soaring out of control again.

With a grunt, he buried himself inside me one last time and came.

It was so good I almost started to cry, but dragged his mouth back to mine instead. I kissed him with all the love in my heart. He kissed me back tenderly, then slowly lowered me to my feet. He cleaned himself off, tossed the condom in the trash, then lifted me so I was settled around his hips again.

I wasn't one of those petite women that most men could pick up, but Graham wasn't most men. He made me feel small and beautiful. "I told you there was nothing wrong with you, Peanut."

I hugged him because I knew gushing gratitude would make him feel awkward. "That was amazing."

He carried me out of the kitchen with his hands cupping my ass casually. "I could use a hot shower."

Smiling adoringly up at him, I asked, "With or without me?"

He shifted me and I felt the tip of his cock teasing the slit of my sex. "With. We'll wash each other down, then I want your lips wrapped around my cock before I turn around and fuck you from behind." He slid the tip of himself between my folds positioning himself against my clit. "What do you say?"

I shifted my hips back and forth, rubbing my clit along his hardening shaft. "Yes. Yes. Shit, yes."

We exchanged a look that was part easy friendship and part lustful partners. "Peanut, I need you to know—"

"Not now." I claimed his mouth and robbed him of the chance to say whatever he was about to. I didn't want to start thinking again—not yet.

He gave my ass a slap. "Have I created a monster?"

I ran my hands over his chest and said, "If your definition of a monster is someone who desperately wants that shower you promised, then yes."

"Desperately, huh?" He wiggled his eyebrows at me.

I smacked his chest. "Don't be an ass."

His hands tightened on me and he thrusted his bare cock balls-deep into my wet pussy. I gasped. He growled. "The shower can wait. I can't."

I would have countered with something witty, but instead my answer was to clench around his shaft and pull him in deeper. We didn't make it out of the living room until much, much later.

CHAPTER 16

Lauren

*I*n a blissful state between sleep and waking, I smiled and rolled onto my side in my bed. I'd never known sex could be like what I'd experienced with Graham, and loved that my discovery had been literally at his hands. *Hands. Tongue. Cock.* I wondered why more studies weren't done on how to attain quality orgasms. Now that I'd had one, I didn't want to go back to what I was able to produce on my own.

One might argue that both released the same chemicals into the body, but the difference defied conventional descriptions. I tried to imagine what my professors would have said had I chosen that topic for my dissertation. Supporting data required more than anecdotal evidence.

Or perhaps seeing my perma-smile would have been sufficient. Really, who could argue with that?

I threw my arm out, seeking Graham. I'd fallen asleep in his arms and had thought I'd wake to the same. Reluctantly I opened my eyes to the bright late morning sun. He wasn't in the bed anymore.

I cocked my head and listened for the shower. Would either of us be able to walk later if I joined him in there? It was a risk I would have taken had I heard water running.

Still glowing from our marathon of lovemaking, I sat up and stretched. I caught a glimpse of myself in the bureau mirror. My hair was wildly tussled, my face pink and happy. I looked exactly as sated as I felt.

Knowing Graham, he was probably out for a run. Although he indulged in sweets occasionally, there wasn't an ounce of fat on him because he worked out daily.

Deciding he was a better person than I was, I trudged to the bathroom to shower. Beneath the hot spray, I planned the start of the day. If he hadn't already made something, I'd make breakfast for us. After that, we'd talk. I prayed that by then I'd have the words to convince him that he was so much better of a person than he gave himself credit for. Somehow I'd find a way to make him feel as right with himself as he made me feel with myself.

On impulse, I applied makeup—not because Graham hadn't seen me a thousand times without it, but because I felt beautiful and sexy and wanted to reflect that.

I shook my head at my conservative underclothing. None of it represented how I felt. Did I dare go without? I'd never. I didn't have a dress with me. I did, however, have an oversized sweater that could double as a mid-thigh dress if I were brave enough to wear it as one.

Bra or no bra?

I decided the likelihood of us leaving the chalet that day was slim so I slid only the sweater on and walked out of my bedroom. There was no sign of Graham in the house so I started a pot of coffee. A moment later, I was blissfully sipping at a cup of some while hunting for my phone.

After locating it, I curled up on the living room couch, put on some soft music and checked my messages.

Jack wanted to know how Graham was doing. I made a face at the phone. *Really, Jack?* I was tempted to tell him that Graham was surprisingly just fine—better than fine and that we didn't need either him or Hope in our lives.

I sent Graham a quick text asking him what time he'd be back so I would know when to start breakfast. He didn't answer. Possibly because he couldn't hear his phone's notifications while he was running. There was also a chance he'd left his phone somewhere in the chalet.

One cup of coffee became two. I snacked on a leftover muffin while waiting for him to either answer me or return.

Eventually I wandered to the front room of the chalet and looked out at the driveway. Graham's car was gone. My stomach tightened nervously, but I told myself I was being silly. Graham wouldn't leave me—not after what we'd shared. Even if he wasn't in love with me, he cared about me. This wasn't a one-night stand scenario where he would run off after having gotten what he wanted.

He hadn't even been the one who'd initiated the sex.

Telling myself I was in danger of once again focusing on the worst-case scenario instead of letting myself have this day of wonder, I made my way to his bedroom. I didn't immediately open the door. I stood there, holding the doorknob, telling myself that last night had been possible only because I didn't let my fears ruin it.

With a defiant flip of my hair, I swung the door wide open. His bed was unmade and empty. I rushed to the closet then to the bathroom. His luggage was gone.

Gone.

In a dazed state, I made my way back to my phone and checked for a message from him. Nothing. Just the message from Jack asking how Graham was.

I laughed without humor. *I thought I knew him, but I guess I didn't.*

I didn't know how he was, where he was, or why he had left.

I sank back onto the couch, fighting back nausea as tears welled in my eyes. I wanted to text him, but I'd already sent him a message. I didn't want to write anything while my emotions were so raw and confused.

I was a science driven person who didn't put a lot of stock in things that couldn't be measured or quantified—except when it came to Graham. I believed in him as I believed in almost nothing else.

Why did you leave, Graham? I didn't understand.

And I didn't know what I was supposed to do now.

CHAPTER 17

Graham

SEVEN YEARS AGO...

"*I*'m going to miss you so much, Graham," a tearful, fifteen-year-old Lauren said sadly during a quiet moment alone at the high school graduation party that her dad was having for both me and Jack.

If Ben hadn't stepped in to include me with Jack, making this a joint graduation party, I'd probably be alone. My current foster parents—I'd lost track of what number foster family they were—wanted me gone now that I was graduating, and I couldn't wait to make that dream come true for them. I was off to the East Coast to attend college. And I couldn't wait to get there.

I'd been awarded a full scholarship to college for playing football there, and I was getting closer and closer to my goals.

Unfortunately, I was having a harder time achieving those goals because my body and mind didn't seem to be cooperating lately. But I'd get through that. I wasn't going to blow the opportunity I had right now.

My only regret was saying goodbye to the best friends I'd ever had. But Lauren was already done with high school, and was in college putting her incredible brain to work, even though it didn't seem like much of a challenge for her.

And Jack was attending college here in Colorado.

"I'll miss you, too, Peanut," I said huskily as we sat on a very familiar porch swing together.

God, how I'd miss her. She was the little sister I'd never had, but also like a friend who always had my back.

"I got you something," she said quietly as she passed me a neatly wrapped, small package. "I don't have much money, but I had to put a lot of time into finding it. It's kind of silly, but I couldn't think of anything else."

I grinned at her and started tearing off the wrapping paper. "You didn't have to do this, Peanut. You've helped me plenty with getting decent grades to graduate."

There was no way I could repay Lauren for all the time she'd spent helping me with my classes. She'd been the reason I'd actually graduated.

"I wanted you to have something from me," she answered. "It's nothing, really."

I opened the lid on the small box, and stared at the tiny shamrock inside the box.

I counted the leaves.

One. Two. Three... Four?

I put a finger to the delicate leaves. "You found a four-leafed clover?"

For fun, we'd searched for the elusive symbol of luck many times as kids, but we'd never found one.

"I had to find different locations to search, but I finally did it," she said shyly.

I could picture Lauren methodically searching for it. "It must have taken days." I was in awe of her tenacity. It took patience to comb through greenery to find what was beneath my fingertip. More discipline than I'd ever had.

She nodded solemnly. "It took a long time, but maybe it will help you with your football."

Lauren wasn't the whimsical type. I got a lump in my throat and my stomach ached from imagining how much she'd had to fight her analytic instincts to look for something like this.

I put the lid back on the box carefully. "Thanks, Peanut," I said hoarsely. "I'll always appreciate this."

There was no doubt I'd keep it with me to remind me of how much *somebody* believed in me.

She shrugged. "I know it will die, and you'll eventually throw it away, but I wanted you to know that I'll be here rooting for you."

I punched her in the arm playfully. "I'm not losing it. This is the best present I've ever gotten."

Maybe I didn't believe in luck because I'd had to fight for everything I'd gotten. Sometimes literally. But her gift would always mean a lot to me just because she'd had to comb through fields to finally find it.

And she'd done it for me, even though her logical mind didn't believe much in luck, either.

"Will you call me?" she asked.

"You know I will," I answered immediately. Jack's dad had bought us each a cell phone last Christmas.

"I know you'll be busy," she said rationally. "You can just text if you want."

I grinned at her. "I might need to hear your voice. I might need a friend."

College was going to be a whole new world, and I was going to have to face it without Jack and Lauren. The thought terrified me, but I wanted to make the whole Swift family proud.

Maybe I'd never needed anybody but them, but now I was going to be totally alone in a place where everybody wanted the position of star quarterback. I was determined to get and keep that job, no matter what I had to do to get it.

"Don't forget I'm here if you need me," she reminded me for the hundredth time.

I never got tired of hearing her say it.

We both saw more people arriving, so we stood. She hesitated for a moment before she threw herself in my arms the way she always did when she was troubled.

"I love you, Graham. Be careful on the East Coast."

My heart thumped as I put my arms around her. I wanted to tell her that I loved her, too. That I'd always loved her like a sister. But the words just wouldn't come out of my mouth.

"I'll miss you, too, Peanut," I said, forcing the words through the enormous lump that was still sitting in my throat.

I gave her a quick peck on top of her head as I released her.

Letting go of the only person who had ever said that they loved me, at least the only person I could remember, was much harder than I thought it would be.

CHAPTER 18

Graham

THE PRESENT...

*I*t had been an entire week since I'd slept with Lauren.

And I was barely fucking surviving.

I'd had to hold myself back from answering her text. In fact, I'd come so close to begging her for forgiveness that I finally slammed my phone against the wall, breaking it so I wouldn't use the damn thing to do something dangerous—like calling her just to see if she was okay.

I couldn't see her. I couldn't talk to her. I couldn't explain what I'd done.

I'd gotten a new phone, but I couldn't shake the emptiness that had been eating at me since the moment I'd stepped outside the cabin in Aspen to head for Denver.

"I'm a chicken shit son-of-a-bitch," I cursed as I aimed and let go of the football, hitting my target just a little off-center.

I should have stayed and told Lauren in person that I couldn't fuck her again, that I wanted to go back to being friends, but I hadn't. Probably because I'd been afraid that I wouldn't be able to say the words I needed to say.

Fucking Lauren was like a drug. She was addicting, and I knew if I saw her eyes open the morning I'd left, I wouldn't have been able to walk away. Every instinct had been screaming at me to stay, but my rational mind knew I couldn't be with her again.

I had to think about her well-being, something I hadn't thought about once the whole time I'd been screwing her. But I was thinking pretty damn hard about it now.

Tyler "Ty" Miller, my new wide receiver, had needed to adjust quickly to catch the pass, but he'd pulled the ball in effortlessly.

It was probably just as well that Ty had called me to see if I wanted to get some practice in well before we started officially on the practice field. I needed to work off steam. I'd been so fucking restless that I'd actually been glad he called, even though I'd promised myself a break before I got back on the field again.

Tossing balls beat getting off with my hand every damn day. Yeah, I probably could have found a woman who would fuck me, but I was pretty sure Lauren had ruined me, at least for now.

I lifted another ball from the ground as I prepared to toss another long pass.

I tried not to think about what Lauren was doing.

And I failed fucking miserably.

She was safe. I knew that. I'd checked on her myself. There was no way I could keep from stalking her dad's place to see if she got home okay. Her car had been in front of the house before nightfall the same day I'd left Aspen.

Lauren had left a voicemail earlier this morning. I hadn't answered. I hadn't replied to her in any way. It was the only way I could keep myself in check.

And even *that* wasn't working out well for me.

How in the hell could I explain why I'd gone? I spent one fucking perfect night with her, and then walked out the door before she even woke up.

What kind of asshole did that shit?

Just. Me.

And I hated myself for it.

I'd woken up a little after sunrise, and the realization of what I'd allowed myself to do really sank in.

I'd screwed the woman who'd always been there for me, cared about me.

Lauren. My Peanut. What in the hell had I been thinking?

Honestly, I probably hadn't been thinking *anything*. My dick had been totally in control.

Ty motioned to me that he was ready, and I forced myself to concentrate as I tossed the football.

It was still a little off, but I didn't have to worry about Ty. He was the type of guy who was going to get the football into his hands regardless of how I was throwing.

Then again, Ty Miller was a first-round draft pick who'd scored a pretty decent contract for a guy who was just out of college. He *should* be good. The Cats had paid a lot of money to get him on their team.

My receiver trotted toward the sidelines, so I followed him.

"Jesus Christ, it's cold," Ty said with a grin.

"Get used to it," I stated flatly. "You're not in Florida anymore."

The field was clear of snow, but the temperatures were pretty frigid. I had no doubt Tyler was feeling it. He'd grown up in Florida, and he'd played college ball there, too.

I watched as he threw back a bottle of water. He seemed like a decent guy, but I wasn't exactly chatty. I pretty much minded my own business in a team setting unless the players were fucking up. It was safer that way. My best friend had just lost my trust, and I wasn't willing to stick my neck out again.

Tyler didn't know me, and I didn't know him.

Just the way I liked it.

"You married?" he asked me innocently.

"I was engaged. We broke up." I grabbed my water bottle and quenched my thirst.

"You cheat on her?"

God, the bastard was curious. Too curious.

I dropped the water bottle back onto the bench. "Nope. She screwed my best friend."

Maybe I was counting on honesty shutting him up. I figured if I blurted out the truth, he'd stop asking questions.

I was wrong.

He scowled as he answered, "That's fucked up, man."

I shrugged. "She made her choice."

"You're okay with that?"

I lost my patience. "Hell, no, I'm *not* okay with it." I was still hurting over what Jack had done. "I lost my best friend."

"What about her?" he asked as he set his empty water bottle on the bench. "You sound more put out about your buddy than your fiancée."

"Why in the hell would I be upset over a woman who wanted to fuck another guy?"

Ty shrugged. "If you were going to marry her, it had to hurt."

"It didn't," I denied, knowing I was telling him the truth. I'd thought a lot about Hope. She'd probably done me a favor. My pride was more injured than my emotions.

He hesitated before he said carefully, "I've heard that you're an asshole to work with. My buddy who plays left tackle for New England warned me about you. I'm not trying to be rude, but I just wanted to get that out there. I'm hoping we can have a better relationship than you had with your receivers on your last team."

I'd been a dick to my last team. I let them know every damn time they'd made a mistake. I knew it, but I guess I didn't like him saying it out loud. "I had to take my chance when our QB went out with an injury. Maybe I was a jerk, but I just wanted all of them to work as hard as I did. It's too damn competitive not to give it everything you've got on the field."

I sized Ty Miller up, trying to decide which one of us would win in a fight. I did that a lot with other members of the team. He was a little bit shorter than me, and probably leaner, but he had speed and agility on his side. I wasn't fooled by his friendly mannerisms. He might look like an all-American surfer dude with his blond hair and blue eyes, but if he'd been a first-round draft pick, the guy was tough.

I'd watched his college career. He was nearly flawless.

"I get it," he replied as he took a seat on the cold bench. "I don't want to play football forever, but I need it right now."

I sat my ass down on the other side of the bench. "It's all I have," I said defensively.

"So I guess we understand each other," Ty answered. "I'll catch the balls if you put them into my range."

His statement was kind of like a promise. "I'll put them in the right place," I agreed.

He nodded. "So now that we have that out of the way, what else is on your mind?"

"Not a damn thing," I lied.

"Bullshit," he said.

"You don't know anything about me," I said angrily.

"Now seems like a good time to get to know you. My career is going to be partially dependent on how well you throw."

"If I get the balls there, why in the hell do you care about anything else?"

"I'm curious," he said calmly. "You're a guy with a reputation. I want to know if you deserve it."

"Everything is true. I was a dick in New England, and I haven't changed much."

"Changing is your choice," he mentioned casually. "You can either be part of a team, or you can continue to be an asshole. I just want to know which one I'm getting before practice starts."

His candidness threw me off-balance, but I respected a guy who spoke the truth.

I thought about what Lauren had said about this being a new start for me, but I wasn't sure how to make things different with the Wildcats.

"I'm not a team player," I admitted grudgingly. "I've learned not to count on anybody except myself. It's safer."

"You want to get to the playoffs?" he asked.

"I want more than that. I want a damn Super Bowl ring and the bonus that goes along with it." My contract was going to include a seven figure bonus for winning the Super Bowl.

"No team gets there when they're disconnected," Ty observed. "I'm not saying you have to kiss anybody's ass. But you need to think about the big picture. Super Bowl teams are organized. The guys get to know each other well enough to anticipate what another player is going to do. Plus, they have to outsmart the other team."

"Mental toughness is just as important as communication," I pointed out.

"Agreed. But we're all going to have to get along to some extent. If you want the Super Bowl, everything has to gel."

I frowned. "Then I'll make it gel."

"You can't control the behavior of everybody else on the Cats. But you can start by being an example."

Damned if he didn't sound like Lauren. "What in the hell was your major in college?"

He hesitated for a moment before he answered, "Neuroscience. Once my football career is over, I'd like to be able to go back to school without worrying about money. I'm continuing my studies here, but I want a doctorate so I can do research. I get off on how the brain works."

"Jesus. Just what I need is another Dr. Freud," I grumbled.

"What?"

I shook my head. "Nothing. You just remind me of a friend."

"Is that good or bad? Tell me it's not the dude who just screwed your fiancée."

"It's a female friend. She's gifted. Twenty-two years old and she has a doctorate in physics, *and* a degree in psychology."

"Is she single?" he asked enthusiastically. "I have a thing for smart women. Hey, it's not the woman who broke all the age records for college studies, is it? I've heard about her. Sounds like the same person. She lives here in Colorado. I'd love to meet her."

My head turned sharply to give him a dirty look. "Don't even think about it," I warned.

It didn't matter that I'd walked out on Lauren. She wasn't fucking one of my teammates. It would destroy me.

Ty put a hand up as he said, "Hey, I didn't mean anything by that. I do like smart women, but I don't tread on a friend's territory. I take it she's more than a friend?"

I didn't know how to answer his question, so I was silent for a minute before I said, "We've known each other since we were kids. Her brother slept with my fiancée."

"Shit, man. That's complicated."

"You have no idea," I responded.

Ty stood. "Let's go get some lunch and talk about it. I'm starving."

I was grateful for the reprieve, but I didn't usually hang out with other guys on my team. And I wasn't sure I wanted to start now.

Ty was too damn introspective, and I wasn't the type of person to analyze myself when I didn't have to. I was too afraid of what I'd discover.

"It's just lunch, dude," he said as he folded his arms in front of him. "It's not like I'm asking for a lifelong friendship."

Ty was right. "No talk about Lauren," I insisted as I stood up. "She's off-limits."

"Fine," he said with humor in his voice. "Then I'll pick your brain about other stuff."

"No brain picking," I said irritably. "Can't we just fucking eat?"

He grinned. "I'm talented. I can do both at the same time."

Smart-ass!

We both grabbed our stuff and picked up our athletic bags. "Then you can tell me about *your* life," I rumbled. "I don't want to talk about mine."

I turned around and started walking, letting him fall into step beside me.

We were almost to the parking lot before I stopped.

Ty halted beside me. "You know that guy coming toward us?" he asked, his tone wary.

I knew exactly who it was. I'd stopped because I didn't really want to talk to *him*, but his determined stride didn't falter, so he kept getting closer and closer.

It was Jack.

"Fuck! I don't want to talk to that bastard," I rasped.

"Then don't," Ty suggested calmly. "Is he cool?"

I knew he was asking if Jack was going to start any trouble.

"He's not looking for a fight," I answered. "He's the one who slept with my fiancée."

Jack obviously wanted to talk about what happened. He'd called me several times. More than likely, he wanted to explain— unless he'd found out that I'd screwed Lauren.

I found that highly unlikely.

"That's him?" Ty asked, his voice rougher than I'd heard it since we'd met.

"Unfortunately," I confirmed.

Jack stopped right in front of me. Shit, I didn't want to hit him, but I knew I wasn't going to be able to stop myself.

Just the sight of him had me in a rage that had nothing to do with him messing with Hope and everything to do with his betrayal.

Jack had been all I had, the only male friend I'd ever trusted for as long as I could remember, and the asshole had just thrown that friendship away for a blow job.

"I got this," Ty said, his tone dangerous.

Turns out, I didn't need to beat the shit out of Jack. Ty pushed me aside, drew his arm back, and then hit Jack with so much power that he laid him out on the ground with one punch.

"We're done here," Ty said calmly, like he hadn't just punched a guy hard enough for his brains to scramble. "I'm starving. Let's go."

I looked at Jack, his face bleeding, but looking like he was about to recover. He was moving. He was breathing. I guess that was all I really needed to know.

Ty was already making his way to his truck when I finally started to walk again.

Son-of-a-bitch!

"Why in the hell did you do that?" I asked Ty as I caught up with him.

He shrugged. "You were hesitating. You were obviously conflicted. I wasn't." He hesitated before he added, "I want you healthy for the season, and I don't want you landing in jail. Our backup quarterback sucks."

I wasn't used to anybody helping me out, so I wasn't sure what to say.

"Thanks," I answered simply.

He acknowledged my gratitude with a nod, and we didn't talk about it again for the rest of the day.

CHAPTER 19

Lauren

I stood on a grassy area next to a small airfield in Northern California and closed my eyes, turning my face toward the warmth of the sun. It had been 29 days, 696 hours, 41,760 minutes, or 2,505,600 seconds since I'd woken up and realized I'd lost Graham. No calls. No texts. He'd cut me from his life—exactly the way I'd known he would.

Leaving the chalet had been hard for me because I'd wanted to believe he would return, when he didn't, I'd headed back to my dad's. I'd spent the next few days wandering around in confused shock. Every text I sent him, every voicemail I left, would surely change his mind.

Anger followed desperation. I left him hateful messages and told my father I never wanted to see Graham or Jack again. Dad said I'd feel differently in time. He didn't ask me what had happened. On some level, he knew there was nothing he could say. Probably because Jack told him about Hope—not the details or imagery I was subjected to—but enough that Dad looked like he felt sorry for all of us. Graham had never let himself get super close to my father, but Dad cared about him. I didn't say anything about what had happened between me and Graham. Even though I was angry with Graham, I hated the idea of him losing another person.

My phone rang. I considered letting it ring through but from the tone I knew it was Kelley. I'd seen her once when I'd first arrived in California, but she was only part of the reason I was in that state. I dug my phone out of the inside pocket of my light jacket. "Hey, I'm waiting to be called so I may have to abruptly hang up."

"Are you sure you want to do this?"

"I ended up enjoying scuba diving."

"I'd feel a lot safer if you started with a tandem jump."

No way. Being strapped to an instructor, relying on that person to make me less afraid was the opposite of what I was systematically proving to myself. "Don't worry, I'm fully certified to jump, having passed the courses and clocked several hours in the simulator."

"Yes. Yes. *On paper* you're ready, but I'm sure it's an entirely different experience when you're 12,000 feet and falling."

"I'll tell you when I know."

Kelley sighed. "I just want to make sure you're doing this for the right reason."

"And that would be?"

"Because you want to experience free falling and a rush of adrenaline."

I've already done that—emotionally and it didn't turn out well, but I kept that thought to myself. The more I said, the more she worried. "Why else would I be here?"

Kelley took a moment before answering. "Because you think doing everything on the list Graham gave you will bring him back to you."

"I realize it won't."

"Or worse—you're hoping something off that list gets you seriously hurt—and he'll return out of guilt or fear."

"I would never do that and this is not about Graham."

"I can't tell if you're lying to me or yourself. Tell me again why you're about to jump out of a plane because my friend Lauren would never do that."

I watched a plane take off with a group of jumpers and hated how much it hurt not to have Graham there with me. He should have been right there, making me laugh so I wouldn't over-think. But he wasn't. "Graham wrote the list because he knew I needed this. There are a multitude of solutions to any given problem. Sure, it would have been nice to complete the list with him, but he won't even take my calls so that option is not available at this time."

"You're hurting. Admit it. It's okay to be."

My hand clenched on the phone. "I am angry and hurt and confused and sad. None of those feelings, however, make the list less valuable of a tool. I have a few weeks left before I go to the Washington think-tank. I need to clear my head before I do." My instructor waved for me to join him with a group of three others. "It's time. I'll call you later."

"Be careful, Lauren."

"Don't worry. The probability of me dying from a car crash on my way home is higher than that of my parachute not opening. You're statistically more likely to fall down the stairs at your office building."

Kelley chuckled. "I know. Good talk. Call me later."

I hung up, replaced my phone in the zippered inner pocket of my jacket and headed over to my jump group.

"How do you feel?" my instructor asked in encouragement. He was in his late twenties, physically fit with the lean body of a runner, and obviously attractive to the other women in the group. They'd been flirting and hanging on his every word all through the course. Even though he looked like he could model on the side, I felt nothing when I looked at him. *He's not Graham.*

"I'm ready."

As a group we walked to a rigging tent where we put on our harnesses and parachute. Then off to the plane. Last minute advice: keep your head back, knees bent, jump. Stay together. Remember hand signals and the cue to open the chute. Bring arms to chest as the parachute opens.

I ducked beneath the tail of the plane and smelled burnt rubber. I almost asked for the flight and maintenance log, but I stopped myself. My instructor motioned for me to enter the plane first. I closed my hand around a metal handle and forced my feet up the ladder, rung by rung.

I was in. I sat on one of the benches. The two women looked nervous now. The man sat beside me on the bench. "This is my second first time," he said with a wide, toothy smile. He was older than any of us, maybe in his late forties. If I had to guess, he'd spent most of his life in an office. He wasn't overweight, but he was pale and soft looking. "I didn't jump the first time. The woman next to me started hyperventilating and I choked. This time I'm choosing a better flight partner."

I was no one's partner, but I didn't want to say that and be the reason he failed to jump a second time. "There are very few documented deaths from sky diving. Although, considering your age and gender, I'm sure you had a physical. Still, your beta receptors will respond to the adrenaline release by increasing your heart rate. A panic attack can mimic many of the symptoms of heart failure." I noticed the man growing paler with each word I said. "You'll be fine."

He nodded.

My instructor sat at my other side and smiled. "You look as cool as a cucumber. Are you sure you haven't done this before?"

I met his eyes. "I'm terrified, but I'm not letting it stop me."

He nodded. "That's what this is all about. People usually come here after having a life changing event or while gearing up for one. Which are you?"

The door closed before I had a chance to answer. The plane bounced down the runway. Squashed onto one of two benches I reminded myself to breathe deeply. I checked my goggles and tried to clear my head.

I'd once found the idea of being close to one hundred feet *below* sea level inconceivable, but I went there and it was undeniably a life changing experience. This would be, too. And hopefully, I would be stronger because of both.

I needed to be stronger.

I refused to give in to the pain of losing Graham. He'd hurt me, but it was my choice if that broke me or not.

We shot up into the sky. I looked at the now green man to my right, then the excited instructor to my left. "You love this, don't you?" I asked.

My instructor smiled. "It never gets old. Every jump is just as good as my first. It's an addictive rush if you can get past the fear."

I thought about Graham and how it had felt to be with him. "I fucked my best friend and now he won't talk to me. I can't imagine my life without him, but I don't want to be afraid. That's why I'm here."

"My wife left me for her plastic surgeon," Mr. Office Man said.

The brunette woman across from me contributed, "I'm turning thirty."

"I found a lump," the blonde woman next to her said and we all fell quiet.

I hadn't realized they'd all be able to hear me. Had we bared our souls because we weren't sure we'd survive? I looked at the instructor again and wondered if every flight involved this level of confession.

He gave me a long steady look. "Your friend's an asshole."

"He's not. He's just scared. A lot of people have disappointed him."

"You one of them?"

"No."

"Forget him."

"I don't want to." *I love him.*

The instructor stood and nodded toward the door. He rattled off instructions again and we followed him to the door. Office Man tapped my shoulder. The door opened and he had to yell near my ear to be heard. "I would marry my ex all over again even knowing how it would turn out." He stepped past me, received a signal and jumped out of the plane. The two women went before me.

I made the mistake of looking down from the plane and tensed. Time slowed. Suddenly there was no way I could imagine doing anything but returning to the bench. I stood there for what seemed like forever, but was likely only an additional second or two before the instructor said loudly into my ear, "I can't push you out. Jump or sit back down."

I've never been a spontaneous person. I measured the risk. I studied the stats. And until sleeping with Graham I would have chosen to sit. There was no rational reason for me to risk bodily injury. No one would care if I didn't jump. No one would even need to know.

But I would know.

Life was full of unknowns and difficult choices. My co-jumpers were prime examples of people at such crossroads. None of them were letting life beat them.

I adjusted my goggles, bent my knees and jumped. Somewhere between regaining my ability to breathe, following the instructor's directions, and clenching my anus so I wouldn't shit myself—I decided I was done waiting for Graham to come to me.

I needed to return to Denver before heading to Washington for a week. If Graham *really* wanted our friendship to be over, he would have to say it—to my face.

Twenty-four hours later, I knocked on the door of his apartment telling myself that everything would work out. No matter what had happened between us, he was still the angry boy who had yearned for a home and never found one and I was still his awkward friend who wanted him to find that home even if it wasn't with me. This didn't have to be the end of us.

Through the door he demanded to know who was there.

I knocked again—louder.

It's me, Graham. Let me in.

CHAPTER 20

Lauren

"This had better be important." The door flew open revealing a wet Graham with a towel draped around his hips and another in his hand.

He froze.

I froze.

Every conversation I'd had with Jack since he'd seen Graham flew through my mind. Jack warned me that he was still angry. Of course, he'd been most vocal after one of Graham's teammates had broken his nose.

Jack hadn't liked it when I'd told him he'd deserved it, but I didn't care. My brother could try to justify what he'd done all he wanted, even tell me it wasn't any of my business, but he'd selfishly changed all of our lives.

"Lauren." Graham didn't need to say more than my name. His tone said enough. I was an *unwelcome* surprise on his door-step. "Shit."

I stood there looking for the man I loved in the face of this stranger. Graham had to still be inside his body, but he wasn't showing. "Are you going to invite me in?"

He glanced over his shoulder then said, "Give me a minute," and closed the door in my face. If I hadn't known him most of my life, if he didn't have an entire section of my heart dedicated to him, I would have walked away. My pride told me I should. I hadn't gone to see him to appease my pride, though.

Kelley had advised me to make sure I was there for the right reason. Answers. Possibly closure. I swore I was. Waiting gave me too much time to hope I knew what I was doing. Just like a month without Graham had shown me some of the best and the worst I could be.

I didn't want to be angry anymore. I didn't want to wake up each morning asking myself where we would be if I had done things differently. I wanted to take back every nasty message I'd left Graham—or for him to say that he'd wisely deleted them—unheard.

Unrealistic and selfish, but impossible to deny, was the hope I held in my heart that when I saw him I would say something so perfect that I'd find myself once again in his arms, his bed, his heart.

What felt like an eternity later, he opened the door again dressed in a T-shirt and jogging pants. "Come in."

I stepped inside and took a quick look around. It was definitely a successful man's apartment, dark furniture, dark carpeting, modern. Was there a woman in the other room? I didn't know how I would handle it if one walked out of his bedroom. I folded my arms across my chest. "Is this a bad time?"

Graham pocketed his hands and shook his head. "I was going to call you."

"Were you?"

He ran a hand through his hair. "Leaving the way I did was a dick move. I know. I'm sorry."

He didn't sound sorry. He was angry. Impatient. And he looked tenser than I'd ever seen him before. Where was the

Graham I loved? The one who had always brought a smile to my face? "That's it?"

"What do you want me to say?"

"I want you to tell me why you left while I was still sleeping. Why you haven't so much as answered one of my texts since then." Time became elastic, stretching each painful second I waited for his response until I couldn't hold my silence. "Say something."

"I don't know what you want me to say. I'm sorry."

"That you're not cutting me out of your life," I said in a strangled voice.

"I'm not." His hands fisted at his sides. "I've got some stuff I need to figure out then I'll call you. I promise. But you should go."

Bile rose in my throat. "No. Not until you talk to me. We can fix this."

He turned away from me. "Don't do this to yourself. I'm not worth it."

"Yes, you are. I don't hate you. I could forgive you anything, Graham, if you just tell me why." I meant every word. Our history of laughter and kindness was a solid base—at least in my heart. "Everything happened so fast. You had just lost Hope—"

He whipped back around, his eyes flashed with anger. "I don't give a shit about Hope."

"It's understandable to be confused."

"I'm not confused. And don't try to analyze me. One year of psychology doesn't make you a fucking shrink."

"I do have a psych degree—never mind. You're obviously angry. Is it with me? Talk to me." He met my gaze but said nothing. There was a wall up between us that had never been there. I was desperate to break past it and talk to my best friend. I took out my phone and opened my photos. "I went scuba diving in the Bahamas."

His eyebrows furrowed and he leaned closer to see the photo. "No shit. I'm proud of you."

With my heart beating wildly in my chest, I swiped to another photo. "This is me skydiving in California." His expression was tight and pained, much like how my chest felt. "I did almost everything on the list, but I left some to do with you. I can't let you remain a pussy when it comes to swimming with manatees."

He almost smiled at that, but then his expression darkened again. "I know I hurt you, Peanut."

I stepped closer and flipped to photos of me white water rafting and then on a Skycoaster. "You didn't. You *challenged* me and I grew from it. You're not bad for me, Graham. Look." I tried to hand him my phone.

He stepped back. "Go home, Lauren."

I advanced. "Not until I know you're okay. We're okay. Are we still friends? Do you hate me? What can I do to make this better?"

His face went white. "I don't want you here. What do I have to do for you to hear me?"

"You don't mean that."

"I do."

"Oh." I did what I swore I wouldn't do: I started to tear up.

He grabbed my arms and pulled me to him for an angry, painful kiss I didn't understand. I pushed away and he released me. My hand went to my tender lips and I shook my head while I backed away.

"Lauren," he said in a tortured tone.

I backed my way across the room, knowing that I had to leave. He'd given me no choice. I wasn't afraid of him because he was Graham, but I wasn't communicating with the man I loved. *He* was obviously locked away in the body of the man I didn't understand. The Graham I knew didn't want to come out and talk to me. But at least I tried. "It's okay," I said because I didn't know what else to say.

Things *weren't* okay, but I'd have to live with his decision somehow.

"No," he said as he advanced to the door with me. "It's not."

CHAPTER 21

Graham

SIX YEARS AGO...

I never knew how lonely being in a hospital by myself could be. But then, I'd never *been* in a hospital before, alone or with anybody else.

For the first time in my life, I was doubting whether or not I could *ever* reach my life goals.

It wasn't going to happen like this.

I was going to lose everything that was important to me.

I was restless, but I knew I wasn't going to be discharged, so I grabbed my wallet off the nightstand and flipped through it until I found my four-leafed clover from Lauren.

I clenched it in my hand, wishing I could talk to her. Maybe she could help me figure all this out, but I was too ashamed of myself to tell her or Jack.

Peanut looked up to me. What in the hell would she think about me now?

I grabbed my cell phone and looked at her most recent text:

Lauren: *Are you okay? I haven't heard from you for a few weeks.*

Turned out, she was pretty damn good at helping me with my college courses, too, and we'd been communicating by phone or text since I'd left Colorado over a year ago. With video and audio, she still tutored me, helping me keep my grades up.

Fuck! I wanted to talk to her. I wanted to talk to Jack. I wanted somebody to tell me that everything would be okay, even though my entire life was falling down on top of my head.

I finally sent her a text.

Graham: *I'm okay. Just busy. I'll call you as soon as I can.*

I was such a fucking liar, and I hated people who didn't tell the truth. But I was now becoming one of those liars I hated.

I was becoming a lot of things I hated, and I didn't want to go there.

I had dreams.

I had fucking goals.

I wanted control of my life, but I wasn't getting it right now.

Clutching the four-leafed clover harder, I closed my eyes. I tried to picture Lauren's face, and the vision came immediately. I could see her bright blonde hair and inquisitive features in my mind, and it drowned out some of the other noise I was hearing.

What would she tell me right now if she knew the truth?

She'd probably kick my ass into gear and tell me that nothing could stop me from succeeding except...myself.

And she would be right. I was in my own way right now, but I felt helpless to change my situation. What in the hell *could* I do when I couldn't help myself or gain control of my own body?

I looked down at my phone as it buzzed her reply.

Lauren: *I'm so glad you're okay. I'm here if you need me. Talk to you when you have time available.*

I needed her as a friend, but I sure as hell wasn't calling her or Jack. I didn't want them to know what a mess I was at the moment.

Setting my phone aside, I let Lauren's comforting image stay in the back of my mind as I opened my eyes. It seemed to help.

"Graham?" a deep voice queried from the side of the bed.

I looked up to see my doctor hanging out beside me. He was middle-aged, and non-threatening in his approach. But I was worried anyway.

The doctor had the ability to make or break my career.

"We need to talk," he said, his expression almost unreadable.

I didn't let go of my four-leafed clover as he began to explain what had happened to me, and why I might never play football ever again.

CHAPTER 22

Graham

THE PRESENT...

*L*auren was opening the door, and I knew she'd probably run like her ass was on fire.

It wasn't like I didn't know I was being a prick, but my need to get her out of my condo was my biggest fucking goal. Or it was...until I heard her breath hitch as she swung the door open, making a whimpering noise that sounded very much like she was in pain.

"Fuck!" I growled, and then slapped my hand on the door above her head, making it slam closed with her still inside my condo. "I can't do this. I *cannot* do this," I said as I leaned my weight on the door, cutting off her escape. My breath was audibly ragged as I kept her trapped with me.

"Just let me go," Lauren demanded with a tiny sob. "I already made an ass out of myself. I'd like to salvage a little bit of my pride."

I put my hands on her shoulders and turned her around.

The tears flowing down her cheeks lashed at my heart.

She'd been so brave, trying to complete every challenge I'd given her even though she had nothing to really prove. She was fucking perfect. And I was being the biggest coward in the world.

Finally, I answered through gritted teeth, "I can't let you leave like this. You're upset. You shouldn't drive when you can't completely focus on what you're doing."

"I'm fine," she said angrily. "I just realized that I care about a guy who doesn't give a damn about me. My mistake. I wanted some kind of closure since we had the best sex of my life, but it doesn't matter anymore."

I'd always loved her tenacity, but I knew it would get her in trouble eventually. I just hadn't imagined it would involve me. "You don't understand. I *do* care."

She looked at me dubiously. "No offense, but your behavior says differently."

I had to force myself not to touch her, not to wipe away every single tear on her face.

"I'm not a man worth putting your emotions into, Lauren. I never will be."

She pushed at my chest, and I let her slip past me. "Fine," she said in a clipped voice. "Then just let me leave. I don't plan on bothering you again."

I turned and leaned against the door. "I don't want to leave things like this. I never meant to hurt you."

"You don't always get everything you want," she replied bitterly.

"You don't have to tell me that," I rasped, trying to hold my anger in check. "I learned that lesson a long time ago."

She crossed her arms over her chest. "Since we're never going to see each other again, why don't you just tell me why you left. Tell me why you couldn't even bring yourself to talk to me again. Was it that bad for you? Were you disappointed?"

Shit! That pissed me off. I hated it when she said anything derogatory about herself or even insinuated that she wasn't good enough. "You know damn well it wasn't bad. It was the best sex I've ever had, too." I'd had a lot of sex to compare that night to, and not a single one of those experiences even compared to the night I'd spent with Lauren.

"So do you always run away when you have a great orgasm?" she asked sarcastically.

"I *had* to go," I told her. "I never should have touched you. You were one of my best friends. One of my *only* friends."

"It's your choice to end that relationship," she snapped. "You made it perfectly clear that you regret what happened."

"I don't regret it," I answered hotly.

"But you don't want it to happen again," she countered.

"It *can't* happen again," I said.

"Why?" she pressed.

My hands were starting to shake from suppressed frustration, so I dropped my arms to my sides and clenched my fists, trying to get myself under control before I lost it.

I wanted to touch Lauren so badly that it physically hurt.

"Tell me," she prodded.

"I can't," I said gruffly.

"You *won't*," she corrected. "You can *do* anything you want. You could always tell me anything. What happened to that? What happened to us?"

"I've *never* told you everything," I said roughly.

"I know," she answered simply. "But that was your choice, too. Jack and I would have listened if you had wanted to talk. We were *always* there for you."

I'd already lost Jack, and I was going to lose Lauren, too. My heart was so damn heavy that I didn't give a shit about my secrets anymore. It didn't matter what anybody thought about me because I was about to lose the best friend I'd ever had, all to keep my damn secrets.

Lauren probably hated me right now, and I didn't blame her. Maybe it was just better to tell her, and then she'd understand.

It was a hell of a lot kinder for her to know I wasn't rejecting her. I needed to stop being so damn selfish, trying to protect myself, and let her see who I *really* was. She needed to understand why a woman like her could never be with a guy like me. If she already thought the worst, what did it matter anymore?

Both of the people I cared about the most weren't going to be in my life in the future. I had absolutely nothing to lose.

I pushed off the door and wandered into the living room, more confused than I'd ever been in my life. I knew Lauren had followed as I sat down in a chair, feeling completely defeated. "I left because I knew I wasn't good for you," I told her honestly.

She sat in a chair across from me. "I think that's my decision to make," she said quietly.

"Why do you have to be so damn stubborn?"

"Why do you have to be such a jerk?" she said in an ornery tone I'd never heard come out of her mouth before. "Who are you to tell me what I should do? I'm all grown up, Graham. I make my own decisions."

"Then you should be running out that door right now," he warned. "Because every time I see you I'm always going to want to get you naked. I can't take that back. I can't make what happened go away."

"I don't want it to go away," she answered stubbornly. "I don't regret what happened because for one damn night, I felt like I was beautiful. I felt special, and not in a weird and different way. I felt desired. Why would I want that experience erased like it never happened?"

Goddammit! I didn't want it to disappear, either. And I *should* want that, but I didn't. "I'm a selfish bastard," I growled.

"Right now, I'm not going to argue with you about that," she said drily.

I finally looked up at her, and I could see her eyes glistening with unshed tears. She was upset, and she had every right to be. It sucked that I had fucked her and left her. "I didn't have a choice, Lauren."

"You *had* a choice," she argued. "At least be accountable for the fact that you hurt me."

"I could have hurt you more if I hadn't left," I said, casting my eyes down again so I couldn't see her face. It was killing me to see her damaged expression.

She got up. "I disagree. I couldn't have been more confused than I was at the cabin. I waited for you, Graham. I thought you would come back. It never even occurred to me that you'd left me there alone without even a note, a text or phone call because I've always had faith in you. I sat there like an idiot waiting for your explanation, and it never came."

I didn't move. I had to let her go, even though every cell in my body wanted her to stay.

"Goodbye, Graham," she said in a quiet, resigned voice.

I looked up just in time to see her walking away.

Jesus Christ! I couldn't let her go without an explanation. Not like this. I couldn't let all those years be nothing. Lauren and Jack had saved my life when we were young, and they'd been my motivation after that. "Wait," I bellowed, just as Lauren was reaching for the doorknob.

I got to my feet and crossed the distance between us. "I did it because I really *didn't* feel like I was good enough for you. And I knew that when you woke up, I'd fuck you again. I can't be with you without wanting that anymore."

She froze, but she didn't turn around. "Why is that so bad? I know we were entering into a relationship we'd never had before, but I wanted it to happen."

I had to will myself to speak. "I can't be with anybody, Lauren. It isn't you, it's me. I know that someday, I could drag you down in my issues, and you don't need that. You deserve everything, and I can't give it to you."

She still didn't turn around. "Everybody has issues, Graham."

I ran an irritated hand through my hair. "Not like mine. Most people don't have to wonder if they are going to lose their fucking mind. I do."

"What are you trying to say?" she asked cautiously.

I saw her shoulders tense, but she still kept her back to me.

"I'm trying to tell you that I'm not right in the head. I'm not fucking normal. I've always had problems, but it wasn't until college that I found out why. I was diagnosed with bipolar disorder, Lauren. I was drinking pretty heavy to try to make it go away, but it didn't help. It screwed me up even worse. I ended up in the hospital at the university after I'd gotten so confused that my roommates had to take me in. I almost lost my scholarship over it. After they got my medications right, I was able to play football again, but my chances of being picked up pro weren't very good since I'd spent two years on a fucking roller coaster before they found the right med combination for me. I played well in my last year, so I did get a pro gig, but just barely."

Lauren finally turned around as she asked, "Why didn't you call me if you were in the hospital?"

"And tell you what exactly?" I asked curtly. "Should I have told you that I'd lost my mind so badly that I needed to be hospitalized for my safety and everybody else's?"

"Yes."

"I couldn't. I had to make sure I wasn't going to end up like my mother."

"What was wrong with your mother?"

"She was bipolar, too," I told her flatly. "She didn't care about anything after my father was killed in the line of duty. She didn't take her meds, and she got to the point where she didn't even know I existed anymore. And then, she committed suicide. I came home from school one day and she was dead. She'd left me alone, even though she knew I didn't have anybody else."

Forcing myself to stay numb, I turned away from Lauren and returned to the living room, pretty sure that after my confession, she wasn't going to follow me.

If nothing else, the truth would force Lauren away, just like I'd wanted.

CHAPTER 23

Graham

"*Y*ou're not crazy, Graham," Lauren said gently as she sat back down in the chair she'd vacated just moments before, which surprised the hell out of me. "Bipolar disorder is a disease. Something that isn't working right in your brain, and it's probably hereditary. It's no different than having any other medical disorder."

I let out a bark of bitter laughter. "You don't have to tell me the clinical definition. Believe me, I already know."

"I wish you would have told me," she said wistfully. "Jack and I could have helped. I would have found a way to get to the East Coast to be with you if I'd known about this when it was happening. I'm sorry about your mom. And I'm sorry about your dad. You never seemed to want to talk about your parents."

Now that I'd blurted out my biggest secret, I wanted to pour out the whole story. "He was a Navy SEAL. He died in action. Once he was gone, my mother was so distraught that she stopped taking her medications. Eventually, she lost touch with reality and her only kid. I came home one day from school and she was dead. She'd shot herself in the head with one of Dad's side arms."

"Oh, my God," Lauren said with a gasp. "You found her? That must have destroyed you."

I looked up and met her eyes cautiously as I nodded. "For years, I wondered if it was my fault. I felt like if I had helped her more, it might not have happened. If she loved me more, she would have stayed with me. Eventually, I started to forget both of them. Maybe I wanted to forget. By the time I met Jack in school, I'd already been through all of the relatives I had, and I'd already had multiple foster families. Nobody wanted an angry, crazy kid."

"You *are not* crazy," Lauren repeated. "Were you having symptoms as a child? Bipolar disorder isn't usually diagnosed until the effected person is an adult."

I didn't see pity in Lauren's soothing gaze. All I saw was... understanding.

I finally answered, "You know I was diagnosed with ADHD as a kid, but my doctor thinks it was probably the early manifestation of bipolar disorder. Getting misdiagnosed happens a lot."

"What happened at the college?" she asked, her eyes fixed on my face.

I shrugged. "Just like I told you. I had manic episodes closely followed by bipolar depression. It happened several times, but I fought it. I wanted to be somebody, and losing my damn mind wasn't part of my plan. But I eventually found out that my will couldn't fight my disorder. I *had* to ask for help. I didn't have any choice. I was lucky to be at a university that had tons of studies going on with bipolar disorder, and good doctors. It took a couple of years, but they finally got me stable."

"You haven't lost touch with reality since you were in the hospital?"

I shook my head. "No. But the possibility is always there, and it scares the shit out of me. I don't want to drag anybody down with me, especially not you or Jack."

"It could happen," Lauren admitted. "But it hasn't. You were treated young, and there are studies that show early treatment could help you stay stable." She took a deep breath before she continued, "Nobody can say what the future holds, Graham."

My jaw was tight, my body tense as I answered, "That's why I don't want to be with anybody. I *can't* be with anybody. I don't know what the hell will happen."

"Nobody can predict the future. Bad things happen sometimes, and we don't have control over those episodes. What about Hope?" she asked.

"She's as fucked up as I am in many ways, so we understood each other," I explained. "I had to tell her, but she didn't care. Outward images meant more than private ones to her, and she wanted to be married to an NFL player. If I had an episode, she wasn't going to get hurt. She was what I needed."

"No. She's what you thought you deserved," Lauren said tearfully.

I opened my mouth to deny her observation, but I closed it again. She was right. I'd settled with Hope because she'd been safe for me.

No real emotions.

No real pain.

But it didn't change the fact that I couldn't be with somebody who cared about me. I'd never know if and when I was going to lose my shit, and the things that could happen during a meltdown could destroy lives.

"It hasn't happened, Graham," Lauren said like she was reading my mind.

"That doesn't mean it won't," I answered tightly.

"It's a very real fear," Lauren acknowledged. "But you can't let that possibility change your life. Medications can be changed if it happens."

"This whole damn thing has changed my life," I growled. "One day I'm in college on a football scholarship with a good chance of going pro, and the next day I'm in the fucking hospital trying to remember what in the hell I'd done the previous night at a party."

"You shouldn't have had to go through that alone," Lauren said with a hint of admonishment.

"It was better that way. I didn't want anybody I cared about to see me like that."

Lauren saw me as a hero. The last thing I wanted her to see was me rattling on like an idiot in a hospital bed.

Honestly, I was pretty surprised she was still sitting in my apartment like I hadn't just told her that I was fucked up.

"Better for you, maybe," she mused. "But I would have preferred to know so Jack and I could have been there to help you get through something that had to have been terrifying."

"I'm good now," I said, wanting to stop talking about my condition. "Now that the doctors have me on the right meds, and I've stayed in counseling, I'm playing the best ball of my life. I try to avoid all the triggers. I eat right. I exercise. I try to stay away from anything mind-altering. I succeeded until that night in the cabin when I decided to drink more beer than I should have. Not that I'm all that sure that I wouldn't have done the same thing sober."

"Why didn't you answer my call after our time at the cabin?" she asked, sounding vulnerable.

"I thought it would be best if we just ended it. I knew if I talked to you again, I was never going to want to give you up." I hesitated before adding, "I was being a coward."

"I know about your mental illness now," she pointed out. "And I'm not running away."

"Then I have to assume you're losing your mind, too."

"I'm not afraid of you, Graham," she said, rising to her feet.

My chest ached, knowing she was going to walk away. But I couldn't say I blamed her. "You got your closure?" I asked sharply.

She moved until she was standing in front of me, and then lowered down to sit on her haunches. Taking my hand, she muttered, "What happens between you and me is your decision. I have to go out of state for my new opportunity at a think-tank, but I have my cell phone. You can text me if you still want my help with the accuracy of your throwing arm. Or if you just need to talk."

I felt like somebody had opened up my chest and was ripping my heart out with a pair of very sharp claws. "Why? Tell me why you even want to see me again after what I did to you."

Her eyebrows scrunched together. "Because I understand that you were motivated by fear. I get that you don't want to hurt me, but if you want to stay friends, you have to be honest with me from now on. I'm done with fairy tales. I don't need my friends to be perfect. I just need them to let me know who they really are."

"Even now, when you know that I could go off the deep end?" I asked gruffly, my throat suddenly going dry.

She snorted. "I could go off the deep end, too. And I don't have bipolar disorder."

"I don't know if I can just be your friend, Lauren."

"I think that's all either one of us can handle right now," she said with a sigh. "I have to trust you're not going to bolt, and that's going to take time. You need to focus on being well and playing football."

My heart was racing as I asked, "Did you really do all those things on the list?"

She smiled weakly. "I have the pictures to prove it."

"But not the sea cows?"

"Not that one. It was one of the things I saved because I'd hoped I could do that with you. You did promise me a trip to Disney."

I owed her a hell of a lot more than a trip to Florida. "Thanks for understanding," I said huskily. "I'm sorry. About everything."

Lauren slowly rose to her feet. "Thank you for trusting me."

I stood up. "I always trusted you," I told her. "I guess I just don't trust myself."

There was probably never going to be a day when I didn't wake up normal and was pretty damn grateful that I'd gone another day without going over the edge.

When we were face-to-face, I took off her glasses, cleaned the lenses with my T-shirt, and slipped them back on again. "Be careful on your trip."

She nodded at me, and then turned to leave.

I sprinted to the door, catching her just the way I had when she'd wanted to leave before.

"Lauren, I—"

She turned and quickly put her fingers to my lips. "Don't say anything else. Just think about my offer. If I don't hear from you, I'll assume you decided to end our friendship, but at least I'll have my closure. I'm grateful to you for that."

"You've changed," I observed. I wasn't quite sure what had happened to her since I'd left her sleeping at the cabin, but she was different, more confident. The self-assured demeanor suited her.

"Maybe it was just time for me to grow up," she said as she turned around and opened the door.

She left my condo quietly, not saying another word as she walked through the door.

I closed it behind her, feeling like an enormous weight had been lifted off my shoulders.

She knew, and it hadn't changed the way she felt about me. I could see the same look in her eyes that she'd always had when we were together.

For some reason, I was *still* her hero.

Lauren cared, and I'd hurt her pretty badly. I couldn't expect her to just take me back as a friend. I'd need to prove myself to her.

But she was willing to give me another shot.

The ball was in my court, and I knew I was going to take advantage of that for all it was worth. I wasn't the type of guy who wasted a good opportunity, but this time, I'd be playing ball for something a hell of a lot more important to me than football.

And I wasn't planning on losing.

CHAPTER 24

Lauren

The next day I was in my bedroom at my childhood desk looking over my hiring packet from the Jeffersonian. Jack knocked on my door even though it was open. "May I come in?"

I closed the binder before answering. "Sure." I hadn't seen Jack in person since Aspen. He was still on my shit list, but he was also my only sibling. The thought of losing him as well as Graham was unsettling.

He sat on the edge of my bed and rested his elbows on his knees. "Hope and I broke up."

I was tempted to cheer, but I didn't. Dad had told me several times that he had never seen Jack behave the way he had recently. "Love makes men stupid sometimes," he'd said.

I could have told him it wasn't an exclusively male affliction. No matter how many times Graham pushed me away, no matter what my rational brain told me, my heart refused to give up on him. So, really, could I judge Jack for following his heart? "Sorry to hear that."

"Actually, she broke it off with me."

If he was looking for pity from me I didn't have any for him. Not yet. I put a hand on my hip and simply stared at him.

His shoulders slumped forward. "She was already dating someone new."

"Shocker."

"I thought she was *the one*. I'm such a fucking idiot."

I moved to sit beside him. "Yeah, you are."

He shook his head with a sad smile. "Dad said you saw Graham. How was he?"

"I thought you no longer gave a shit about him."

"You know I didn't mean that. I was angry."

"You had no right to be. You deserved that punch."

"I know. I feel like someone gutted me. Nothing matters right now. Not my new job. Nothing. What is fucking wrong with me? Why would I do this?"

I sighed and remembered something Kelley had once said regarding couple counseling. "Most people don't set out to hurt anyone. Betrayals start as small lapses in judgment. Like a married person who goes to bars every night without their spouse. Purely based on statistical probability, eventually they will meet someone who makes them take a second look, then laugh—or yearn. I don't think you set out to break Hope and Graham up. Knowing you, at first you were just trying to be nice to her. The two of you clicked. That led to—well, we know where that led."

"It felt real, you know? When I was with her nothing else mattered. My brain knew it was wrong, but my di—my heart had other plans."

I totally understood that feeling. "I'm glad you're sorry. Not glad you're sad or that Hope left you, but I didn't feel like I knew you when you were with her."

"I didn't know myself."

We sat in silence for a long time. I didn't know what else to say and it seemed that Jack felt the same way. Eventually, he asked, "Is Graham okay?"

It was a simple question that if answered honestly would require a complicated response. Graham had shared a side of himself with me that I didn't think he'd ever even shared with Jack. It wouldn't have felt right to divulge what I had learned. One day, if Graham wanted him to know, he would tell him in his own time and on his terms.

How was Graham? He'd sought treatment early and was maintaining a lifestyle to support it. If he continued on that path, there was no reason to believe he couldn't succeed both in football and in his personal relationships. Good communication with someone who understood the challenges he'd face and who could support him if he faltered. Medications sometimes required adjustments, but if he remained proactive he would be more than okay.

Me? I still felt like everything I cared about was sand slipping away between my fingers. How could I be so widely accepted as intelligent and feel so lost when it came to knowing what to do next? Gutted. Yes, Jack had described exactly how I felt. "He's doing better than I am. I miss him."

"Me, too. I didn't believe Graham really loved her. I knew she didn't love him. She couldn't and look at me the way she did. I feel even worse knowing I messed up your friendship with Graham, too. If I could go back and undo it, I would."

I looked across the room at my collage of the three of us over the years. Never, ever had I imagined it would end. "It wasn't all you. I screwed up, too."

"You slept with Graham?"

He didn't sound shocked so I didn't deny it. "I thought it was our chance to finally be together. I was just as stupid as you were. I rushed him and it fell apart. We're not friends now. I don't know what we are."

Jack put his arm around my shoulders. "You've always had a thing for him."

"Yeah."

"I'm sorry, Lauren. I know how much it sucks to love someone who doesn't feel the same way."

I sighed.

"Do you remember when he brought his prom date here so Dad could take photos of them? And you spilled your chocolate milk on her dress?"

"By accident," I defended even as the memory brought nostalgic warm feelings back.

"Sure. That story might have worked with Dad and Graham, but I saw you flash your braces at her before you tripped. You wanted to bite her."

"I have never and would never bite anyone." I remembered hating that the perfect body and features of his date that night had made me wonder if we were the same species. I wondered how I'd feel if I were faced with that scenario again. Being with Graham had taught me as much about myself as it had him. I no longer thought I was ugly. In my own way, I was beautiful. And brave. And resilient.

Jack chuckled then sobered. "You're human. Just like me. Just like Graham. Do you remember when you were thirteen and had a crush on some geek at school?"

That felt like another lifetime, but I vaguely remembered it. "Yes, Steven Bins. He asked me out on a date then he stood me up."

Jack smiled. "Oh, he showed up, but Graham and I agreed you were too young to date. We were tossing a ball around the front yard. Graham and I asked him a few questions, just to make sure we were all on the same page as far as how he would behave with you, and he pissed himself when Graham described exactly what would happen if he touched you."

"Oh, my God, he didn't."

"It was fucking hilarious."

"Why didn't you say anything? You let me believe I was stood up." I shook my head. "No wonder Steve never looked me in the eye again. I thought he'd changed his mind about liking me."

"No, he pissed himself like a scared five-year-old and is probably still in therapy about it."

"That's not funny."

Jack cocked his head to one side and measured an inch in the air. "Not even this much?"

I shook my head.

Jack shrugged. "I'm just saying that none of us are perfect. Maybe that's why we all get along so well."

I smiled reluctantly and pinched the air. "I'm this much less fucked up than you are."

Jack shook his head and showed a smaller section of nothing. "This much if at all."

Just like that Jack and I were back. I took a moment to soak it in. My brother could be the bane of my life. Over the years he'd often been the reason I would go into my room and slam the door. Later, though, we always made up because there was a better side to him—this side. I knew he loved me, and I knew he loved Graham.

Jack stood. "Dad's cooking dinner. You coming down?"

I looked over at the binder on my desk. I still had time before my job started, but thinking about the extensive probationary process was a welcome escape I wasn't ready to put aside. "I don't know."

Jack picked up one of my pillows and wacked me on the arm with it. "You're not staying in your room. Come on."

I grabbed the pillow from him and threw it at him. "Don't tell me what to do."

He wacked me with the pillow again. "Get up." When I rose to my feet, he said, "You're going to be okay."

"I know." I hugged the pillow to my chest. "It'll take time, though."

"Everything that's worth it does."

I tossed the pillow back on the bed. "Stop. Wait. Grab a calendar. Did you just say something that might be considered mature? I need to document this anomaly."

"Says the woman who still sleeps with a teddy bear." He held up a stuffed animal from my bed and waved it in my face.

"It's better than your VHS porn collection." I grabbed the bear from him and threw a pillow at him. He threw it back.

Dad popped his head in the door of my bedroom. "Still trying to kill each other. Looks like things are back to normal. Who's hungry?"

CHAPTER 25

Lauren

The sound of my phone beeping woke me from a fitful sleep. I rolled over and checked the time. *Eleven thirty.* I picked up my phone.

Graham: *You awake?*

I sat straight up in bed, my heart racing as I texted him back.

Lauren: *Yes.*

My phone rang. "I have a surprise for you," Graham said.

I used to like surprises, but I wasn't sure I could handle any more. "What is it?"

He chuckled. "If I told you, it wouldn't be much of a surprise, would it?"

I laid back on my bed, holding the phone to my chest. He sounded different from the last time we had spoken. He didn't sound defensive or unsure. His voice was a warm purr that made me want to say yes to whatever he had planned.

When I'd left him I'd suggested that we should start as friends. Had he confused that with my initial offer of friends with benefits? I couldn't go there. My feelings were still too raw to be able to fully trust him yet—never mind what I had once imagined sharing with him.

I wanted to see him again more than I wanted to breathe, but trusting him with more than friendship hadn't worked out. I didn't want to go back to being friends. I didn't want to be left again—with only questions and tears.

No, no surprises.

"Lauren? Are you still there?"

I lifted the phone back to my ear. "Yes."

"I want to make things right with you."

I had no idea what that meant. As friends? As lovers? Oh, God, I wanted to ask him but I didn't know which I wanted to hear. We needed to find our footing again and that would mean going slowly. But what if friendship was all he'd decided he wanted? Could I be there, pretending to be happy, as he dated someone else? I took a deep breath and decided that sometimes more information was required before leaping. "What does that mean?"

"It means you need to pack for a four-day vacation somewhere warm. I'm picking you up tomorrow morning."

"No," I said out of panic.

"When does your think-tank start?"

"Two weeks."

"Then come on a trip with me, Peanut. I borrowed a friend's plane. I know I hurt you. Let me do this for you." He sounded so sure of himself that I was filled with doubts. I wanted to believe it could be this easy. Who wouldn't? Too much had happened, though.

"Graham, we don't have to go anywhere. If you want to see me I'm right here at my dad's. We could go for a bike ride or a walk."

He was quiet for a moment. "What do you need from me, Peanut? How do I make this better?"

Finally, the Graham I knew. "I need to trust you, Graham. I heard you yesterday. I understand why you did what you did, but it hurt. I thought we were unshakeable. I put everything out there for you and you walked away from it. I don't know if you're hoping we can go back—or forward—" My throat closed and tears sprung to my eyes.

He cleared his throat. "What do you want?"

In a thick voice I said, "I don't know if it's that easy. . ."

"I thought no one and nothing could ever hurt me again, but knowing that I hurt you is killing me. I want you in my life, Peanut. You deserve a lot better than I gave you, and I understand that you need time, but things will be different this time."

"I don't know." I wanted to believe him. I wanted to jump. But the difference between that moment and skydiving was that I had already experienced a nasty crash with Graham. My fears weren't based on abstract statistics—the memory of waking up alone and slowly coming to the realization that he'd left me was still painfully clear.

"I do. Don't give up on me. Come with me tomorrow. We'll take it as slow as you want."

"Separate rooms."

"Done."

"No sex." I felt like an idiot for saying it, but I was attempting to maintain a degree of control.

"Okay." He agreed easily and I kicked myself for wishing he'd made it sound like more of a struggle.

A hundred questions were still swirling through me. I wanted to be happy about going somewhere with him, but there were enough unknowns that my stomach was doing nervous flips.

"Peanut?"

"Yes?"

"Don't over-think this. There's a point when I'm throwing a ball that I have to let it go and trust that it will land in the right place."

I could have countered with how correctly calculating trajectory would remove the need to hope, but he wasn't looking for throwing tips. I gave him the best answer I could. "I'll try."

"Can you be packed tomorrow around noon?"

"Yes."

"I'll see you tomorrow then. Good night, Peanut."

"Good night, Graham."

I laid awake for a long time after we hung up, staring at the ceiling, telling myself that he would be there the next day. I hated that I doubted him at all, but I told myself to value my feelings as much as I valued his.

Science tried to explain and quantify human emotions, but I didn't know an equation that could reflect the complexity and fragility of trust or predict the outcome when it came to relationships. On this matter, I needed to believe in things I couldn't measure.

Not a strength of mine.

Noon the next day took an eternity to arrive, but when it finally did I came downstairs to find Graham talking to my father. It looked like a serious conversation, but not one that upset either of them. When Graham saw me he came over and took my luggage from my hand.

We stood there looking at each other for several long minutes. At first I thought he was going to kiss me. His face came down close to mine and I froze. Part of me wanted to throw my arms around him and lose myself in that kiss, but another part thought turning tail and running was the safest course.

I was no longer a woman who let my fears dominate, though, so I stayed.

"Ready?" he asked, his breath warming my lips.

I nodded.

"Graham," my father said in the tone he used to use to remind me about my curfew. "Take care of my baby."

I almost protested but the sincerity of his tone stopped me.

"I will," Graham said and shook my father's hand.

I hugged my father and promised him I'd call when we landed. He didn't look worried which meant Graham had likely told him where we were going. There was something reassuring about my father still trusting Graham.

Graham opened the passenger door of his car for me. I slid in and adjusted my seat belt. He was beside me a moment later, studying my expression. "You look nervous."

I held his gaze and said, "I am."

"I hate that I put that look in your eyes."

The torment in his pulled at my heart. "I hate that you went through everything you did alone. I wish I had known. I could have been there for you."

He took my hand in his, laid it on his thigh, then revved his car. "You were, Peanut. You and Jack were what kept me sane. Even without knowing the details, you always knew when I needed a hug."

We shot off into traffic.

The tension in the car was thick and I felt that if I didn't find a way to lesson it I would change the mood by vomiting. "Jack came by last night."

Graham's thigh tensed beneath my hand. "And?"

"We talked. He regrets what he did."

"He should."

"Like me, he probably said things to you in the heat of the moment that he didn't mean. He cares about you."

Graham changed gears with more force than necessary. "Yeah, well, we might have different definitions of what that means."

I looked out the window then back at Graham's profile. "Don't give up on him yet, either. Talk to him. Not now if you're not ready, but keep that option open. We all make mistakes."

Graham's expression tightened. "Yes, we do."

It wasn't the tone I thought my surprise trip would take and I worried that I was bringing it there. "Hey, when were you going to tell me that Steven Bins didn't stand me up?"

"Who?"

"The guy you scared until he peed himself. Jack told me what the two of you did."

"Oh, yeah." Graham smiled. "You were too young to date."

"Wasn't that for me to decide?"

"You were fourteen and innocent. We did you a favor."

I smiled. "Well, then I returned the favor when I spilled that drink on your prom date. I didn't like her."

"Ah ha, I wondered if that was an accident."

We laughed together and it felt good. "Were there any other guys you scared off?"

His grin was telling. "Maybe one or two."

"No wonder I was a virgin for so long."

His nostrils flared and his chest rose and fell, but he didn't say anything. I glanced down and noticed his bulge growing beside my hand and cursed myself for bringing up sex. Even though I ached for him, I didn't want to go there yet.

I needed to change the subject fast. "Guess who I saw in the supermarket the other day? Do you remember Mr. Peckerman? My Latin teacher who you said had to be using an alias because no one would actually have that last name? I met his wife and kids. He introduced her as Mrs. Peckerman. . .and since they have kids I waited but oddly enough he didn't introduce them the way I hoped." I paused for emphasis, then joked, "As a peck of pickled peppers."

Graham laughed. "My mind is so much filthier than yours."

"Why?" I asked, then got it. "Oh, my God, he has three little peckers now."

We swapped funny stories for the rest of the ride to the airport. When we arrived we were met by a pilot who took our baggage and led us into the private plane.

"Fancy," I said, admiring the interior.

"Private," Graham said, wiggling his eyebrows outrageously. My eyes widened. "Not that we'll need privacy. I just thought you might not want an audience when I kick your ass at cards." He smiled and I relaxed.

We took seats facing each other with a small table between us. I was a tangled combination of grateful and frustrated. My mind knew it was too soon. My body remembered and craved every inch of his. Distracted as I was, I had no doubt he'd win— regardless of the game he chose.

Fearless—that's how I wanted to live, but I didn't know what that meant as far as Graham. I didn't want to lose him again, but I didn't want my fear of losing him to be the reason I gave us a second chance.

Was it unrealistic to hope that Graham's surprise took us where I wanted us to land? Could I let go and trust it to?

CHAPTER 26

Lauren

Several hours later we landed at a small airport in Crystal River, Florida. Graham hadn't yet told me where we were going, but the location was enough of a hint that I guessed. The area was known for manatees.

As soon as we stepped out of the plane I hugged Graham. I couldn't help myself. Continuing on with my list was his way of keeping a promise I'd convinced myself to let go of.

He held me tight then kissed my forehead. "This is what you get for calling me a pussy. It's a pride thing."

"Sure it is," I said against his strong chest. Then, because we were about to go somewhere neither of us was ready for, I stepped back. "Let's see what song you're singing when your butt is in the water with them."

He smiled broadly. "I researched the perfect tour. I'll be fine."

I walked with him to the car that was waiting for us and loved how easy it was once again becoming between us. This was how Aspen would have felt had it not started the way it had. "By research you mean you asked one guy and this was the place he knew."

Graham tried to look offended, then simply smiled back. "I resemble that comment."

"Yes, you do."

We slid into the back of the car together and he took my hand. It felt as natural as breathing. "They say this is the absolute best place to swim with them."

"They?"

"Are you doubting my sources? My doorman says his aunt's neighbor's dentist did the tour and it was amazing."

The data collector in me shuddered but I refused to give in to it. "It sounds fantastic."

Graham sat back and squared his shoulders as if I'd offended him, but there was a playful light in his eyes. "I can give you the name of the tour company and you can research it. . ." He gave me soulful don't-do-that-to-me eyes. "If you want to kill all the fun in this."

I threw my free hand up and conceded with a laugh. "If it's good enough for your doorman's aunt's neighbor's dentist, it's good enough for me." I turned to look out the window. It was my first trip to Florida. The lush foliage and palm trees reminded me of California, but we weren't in a commercialized tourist area like Orlando. I was itching to check the population, demographics and history on my phone but I didn't. Instead I took the average density of homes, estimated the number of people who might live in each according to size and wildly guessed two thousand, depending on how accurate my memory of the size of the town was from the time I'd seen a story about it on the news. Had they mentioned the population? Was I correct? Did it matter? I smiled as I realized it didn't. I was so used to people expecting me to always be correct that I had begun to hold myself to that impossible standard.

"What are you thinking?" Graham asked with a slight squeeze of my hand.

I turned back to him. With anyone else I would have kept my thoughts to myself, but this was the Graham I'd grown up with, the one who accepted me the way I was. "I was estimating the number of people in Crystal River based solely on what I can see. I realized my guess might be completely off but that it doesn't matter. Sometimes it's fun to not know. I get it now. This is an adventure."

"Exactly," he studied my expression and looked like he wanted to say more, but didn't.

We pulled up to a small hotel on the water. The driver stopped before pulling up to the office and turned in his seat. "Is this the right place?"

Less than pleased, Graham looked around and said the name again.

I scanned for signs. "That's where we are."

The driver pulled up to the check in office. "I'll wait."

Graham shook his head. "There has to be somewhere nicer than this. Let's go."

I touched his arm, hating that he looked disappointed. "It looks fine, Graham. And it's right on the water. I don't need anything fancy. Let's try it. How bad could it be?"

A few minutes later we were standing just inside the doorway of my room. I wanted to love it—after all I was in adventure mode. The room was warm and smelled like something might be decaying in a corner of it. The blinds on one window were hanging slightly askew and beneath our feet was a large, dark stain.

"All that's missing is an outline of a body," Graham joked.

I was relieved that he was having a similar response to the room. "How did you find this place?"

A slight flush rose on Graham's cheeks and I began to question the recentness of that dentist's last trip to Crystal River. "I bet this was a nice place—fifty years ago."

Graham looked irritated, but not with me. "Fuck. I really wanted this to be nice for you."

I pulled him back out into the hallway. "I'm fine, Graham. Do I look disappointed?"

He met my gaze. "No, but I should have booked a room at the four-star Hilton a few towns away. My doorman said he'd heard you could see manatee right from this place's boardwalk."

I touched his face gently and joked, "I bet you see a lot of things here."

I felt his smile before it spread across his face. "You deserve better than this."

I glanced over my shoulder. "I sure as shit do," I answered, but I was smiling, too. "You think the driver is still waiting for us?"

Graham took my hand in his and started to lead me back toward the front office. "He didn't look like he wanted us to get out of the car here so I'm sure he is."

We turned in our keys at the front office to a young man who was not surprised that we did. I explained about the smell and the stain, but he looked bored with the topic before I even finished.

Graham leaned in. "We're going on The Greatest Manatee Tour tomorrow. Have you heard of it?"

The young man's attention perked up. "With Captain Sid?"

Graham frowned. "I think so. It meets a few buildings down from here."

The man laughed like he was in on a private joke he wasn't prepared to share. Then he sobered slightly and said, "Don't do everything he says. We have strict laws about not disturbing the manatees. People get in trouble for it. Look, don't touch and you'll be fine."

"Okay, thanks," Graham said and guided me away. Once in the car again, he asked the driver for the best local hotel. After seeing the area's potential, I didn't argue with that.

After checking in to an upscale chain hotel, we had dinner and listened to a live band in the downstairs bar. Neither of us drank. We laughed. Conversation was light and easy. There were things we still needed to work out, but we also needed this reprieve.

And it felt good—so good.

Until he walked me to my door and I clung to the door handle like a lifeline. My body hummed for his and he appeared equally affected by me. It would have been so easy to ask him in. "Good night, Graham," I said as I opened the door behind me.

He leaned closer. "Lauren—"

I heard the hunger in his voice and it seared through me. I countered it with a memory of me yelling obscenities to his voicemail. I never wanted to be that person again. "Good night," I said quickly and shut the door in his face.

Right in his face.

Yep, real mature.

I leaned back against the closed door and imagined him still there, waiting for me to open it. In reality he'd probably walked away, but I stayed there for a long time, fighting the desire to open the door and check.

There or not, I needed to stay the course I'd chosen. We'd tried fast and free and it didn't work for us. Graham wasn't proclaiming a love for me. He wanted me back in his life. Part of me rejoiced at the knowledge that I was indeed important to him, but I forced myself to face that he wasn't defining our relationship. Friends? Lovers? Did he even know what he wanted?

I wasn't sure I did anymore. Being with him was wonderful and painful at the same time. Was this our new normal? Pretending we could go back to how things were before? I didn't know how long I could sustain that.

CHAPTER 27

Lauren

Dressed in bathing suits beneath our clothing, we headed out early the next morning. Captain Sid met us at his office and explained that we would be snorkeling off the side of his houseboat near where he had exclusive knowledge of where many manatees gathered this season. Each time he bragged, he flashed us a sparsely-toothed smile. I told myself that his personal hygiene habits did not necessarily predict his ability to safely guide us along the river.

Graham and I exchanged a look just before we boarded his houseboat. He was adorably uncertain and my doubts fell away. Unlike the first hotel room, I would love this tour—regardless of how it went because Graham was with me and doing this solely for me.

The water around the boat was covered with a plant I didn't recognize but that reminded me of ocean seaweed. The idea of swimming in it wasn't appealing, but I would do it. "Is the plant covering the surface native?" I asked. I remembered once hearing that Florida, like many places in the United States, was constantly battling invasive species.

Captain Sid looked from me to the plants. "It's harmless." He picked up a piece and stuffed it in his mouth. "Don't know if it's invasive, but it won't kill you."

Graham and I exchanged another look and I burst out laughing. "Good to know."

Graham put his arm around me. When Captain Sid walked away to navigate the boat away from the dock, Graham said, "Go ahead. Say it. I should have read up on him as well."

I tucked myself into his side. "What kind of adventure would it have been then? This is perfect. I have no idea if we're going to swim with or be fed to the manatees by this guy. It's kind of exciting."

He hugged me closer. "Manatees don't bite."

"They're mammals. There are documented cases of them attacking people."

He tensed beside me. "What the fuck?"

"But it's rare."

He grumbled. "That would be my luck to be injured this way before the season starts. I can just imagine trying to explain that one. Taken out by a fucking sea cow. If you're going to feed me to something can it at least be something cool like a shark or a gator?"

"There must be gators in here, too."

"You're serious."

I waved a hand at our captain. "I'm sure Sid would never take us anywhere dangerous."

Graham chuckled, then laughed louder. "We're so fucked."

The tour surprised both of us by being both informative and fun. We saw a good portion of river coastline and heard all about Sid's life there. What he lacked in teeth he made up for with his storytelling abilities and number of local family.

We snorkeled several times. I tried to keep my focus each time off how Graham's body looked incredible in and out of the water. Most of the time we watched manatee from a distance but during one swim a cow approached us with her baby. The mother stayed a distance away, but the baby was curious and swam under us several times. It was so close I could have reached out and touched it, but I remembered what the man at the shady hotel had said and didn't.

The mother seemed to approve of our restraint because she allowed her baby to stay and interact with us for a significant amount of time. I was impressed by how well Graham handled being around them—at least until one large manatee swam up in front of him and looked as if he wanted to dance with Graham.

I couldn't blame Graham for motioning that it was time to return to the boat. Captain Sid was shocked when we told him what had happened. He said some people waited their whole lives for a manatee to engage with them that way and that Graham had missed a real opportunity.

Neither of us asked him what that meant.

We ended the tour by swimming in a cold, but crystal clear spring that was truly beautiful. Sid aside, we were alone and dove repeatedly to explore. It was perfection.

Too soon Sid announced it was time to return to the boat. I swam up to Graham. "Tell your doorman's aunt's neighbor's dentist that he sure knows how to pick a tour. This was perfect."

Graham pulled me closer and my body slid along the length of his. "I'm glad you liked it."

Oh, I liked it and the feel of him against me, but I pushed off slightly. The only way this would work was if we were physically careful. It was a bit like juggling dynamite. One false move and we'd be right back where we were in Aspen.

That possibility was as exciting as it was frightening. It reminded me that neither of us was who we'd been before Aspen and all the pretending in the world couldn't change that. Eventually we'd have to face it.

But not that day.

Graham had promised me manatees, Disney, and a tandem bike ride. I needed to finish the list with him even though I wouldn't have been able to explain to Kelley why. Rationally it didn't make sense, but being with Graham wasn't a decision I was making based on logic and facts.

With a few inches of cold water between us, I looked into his eyes and saw a similar confusion. Even before he spoke, my heart began to pound wildly.

"We're going back tonight," he growled.

"Back?"

"To Denver."

My heart sunk. No Disney. "Okay."

"Don't look at me that way."

"I'm fine. If you want to go back tonight, we'll go back tonight," I said, irritation rising within me. "It's better than you just disappearing the first time I look away."

"You don't understand."

I started to swim away. "Now that is something we agree on."

He grabbed my arm to stop me, but wet as I was I slid out of his grasp easily. "Could you try to appreciate that I'm trying to do the right thing, Lauren? I could just haul you off to my bed and do what both of us can't stop thinking about."

I pulled myself up the ladder of the houseboat, snapping at him over my shoulder, "No you couldn't because I told you we're not going there—not again—not until we figure out what we're doing."

He was standing behind me, around me, on the ladder. "What we're doing is driving each other insane. I thought—I hoped—"

Captain Sid wisely retreated to the other side of the houseboat.

"We can't, Graham. We can't go back." There, I'd said it. I picked up a towel, wrapped it around myself and sat down on one of the benches.

Graham, all two hundred twenty-five pounds of him, hauled himself onto the boat, began to towel himself off as well and sat across from me.

He glared at me.

I glared at him.

"Then I don't know where we go," he said and a piece of me cried for him. "All I know is that I never meant to hurt you and I don't want it to happen again."

Some of my anger dissolved. I'd wanted honesty and he'd given it to me. I could hold his feet to the fire over it, or I could appreciate that he cared enough to want to protect me. "Let's go home, Graham. Disney can wait. Or I can go on my own."

"I'll take you to Disney, Peanut. Just not tomorrow."

"It'll be okay. Either way, *we'll* be okay." It wasn't the conversation a woman yearns to hear from the man she loves, but it was the best either of us could do in that moment.

We separated after the tour, showered, changed and headed back to the airport. The jovial mood of the day before was gone. I was tense. Graham was tense. I didn't want to say anything that would make things worse and Graham seemed to feel the same way.

Several hours later he dropped me off at my house and spent a few minutes talking to my dad before telling me he'd call me soon and leaving. My father gave me a long searching look then asked how I was.

I shook my head sadly and let my father rock me against his chest. Soon I'd be in Washington proving to people twice my age that I was capable of comprehending any project they assigned me. Then convince them that I could return to Denver and advance that project forward. They'd test me intensively but I was confident that I could impress them. In the safety of my father's arms, however, I let myself admit that there were still a great many things I didn't understand.

Like life.

And love.

Or how to be strong enough to let go of Graham if that ended up being what was best for both of us.

CHAPTER 28

Graham

I was as healthy as a stallion in his prime.

At least, that's the way I preferred to view the results of my Wildcats physical. It was a hell of a lot better than the doctor who examined me put it when he'd proclaimed me to be "as healthy as a horse."

Ty and I had spent the morning getting our paperwork in for our check-ups, and the last several days had been spent trying to iron out my contract.

We had a few months until training camp, but there was a hell of a lot of things to do to get ready for intensive training. And it all had to be done before every day was taken up by working my ass off physically, trying to live up to the millions of dollars given to me in my contract.

Truthfully, I still wasn't used to having money. Ty and I still ate the way we did in college. But I tried to keep my options healthy, even if my wide receiver loved mom-and-pop, greasy spoon restaurants.

"Best burger in Denver," Ty said after he'd chewed through more than half of a triple burger at one of our local meeting places.

I smirked at him as I plowed through a huge omelet with veggies and steak. No way was I wasting calories on a burger with processed cheese and crappy buns. I ate plenty of healthy carbs and protein, and I was going to have to ramp up my calorie intake in preparation for more intense off-season workouts, but no way in hell was I going to eat as poorly as I did in college. Even if the restaurant we were in reminded me of the cheap places I'd haunted in college.

"I wouldn't know," I rumbled as I devoured the rest of the veggies and eggs on my plate.

"Dude, you have to live a little," Ty said, and then proceeded to consume every fry on his plate.

"I live just fine," I informed him as I dropped my fork on my empty plate.

Ty and I had developed a relationship I appreciated. Not only was he an amazing football player, he was a pretty decent guy.

Every time we met up for off-season practice, I felt more and more comfortable with him, and surprisingly, I no longer thought about my words when we were talking. He'd told me enough about his own failures and mistakes that I didn't mind revealing my own.

"I know you like food," he mused. "So it isn't that you don't like to eat."

I leaned back against the worn leather of our booth. "I'm a professional athlete. Most of the time, I prefer to eat healthy."

"You eat every few hours," he observed.

"It keeps me from having energy spikes," I explained.

"Does it help?" he asked curiously.

I had to remind myself that Ty was a rookie, and was just out of college ball. Most college guys weren't as picky about their diet. I knew I hadn't been. "It helps. It's not that I don't want to eat stuff that isn't exactly part of my diet, but I'm saving it for restaurants with better food."

I was hoping that Lauren would go try out some of the best restaurants in the city with me, but we hadn't gotten the time to do it yet.

She'd been gone to DC for seven days, three hours, and a handful of minutes. And I felt every damn moment of her absence since the day I'd dropped her off at the airport.

"Now that you're making the big bucks?" Ty joked.

"I got a good contract," I confirmed. "And yours is a hell of a lot better than I got in my rookie year."

"I need to get this right," Ty confessed. "I'm out to prove myself. Show the Cats that they didn't make a mistake."

He was nervous. I already knew he was sweating the start of the season as much as I was. "I'm with you," I said. "I have a lot to prove for the money they gave me, and I want to earn my bonuses."

"It's not just the Cats," he admitted. "Some of it is personal."

I wanted to ask him why, but I sensed from his expression that he didn't want to talk about it, so I didn't pry. "Just go out there and do what you do in practice, and you'll be fine. You're the best receiver I've ever had."

Ty was lightning fast, and he could pull a ball in even if the throw wasn't completely accurate. He adjusted instinctively, and that wasn't a talent a guy could really learn. A receiver had it or they didn't.

"Yeah. You toss a decent ball, so you'll make me look good," he said with a laugh.

Funny thing about Ty...he might be cocky at times, but he still lacked confidence in himself.

"Lauren is going to help me with my accuracy," I shared. "I dislocated my shoulder at the end of last season, and my aim is slightly off now."

Ty looked confused. "She knows football?"

I shook my head. "She knows as much as a regular fan, but it's her brain power that's going to help me get even better. She's gifted in physics. After watching some of my tapes of last year's games, she thinks she can help me adjust my throws to accommodate the differences since my shoulder injury."

Ty hesitated before he asked, "Do you think she can help me? I'm up for all the help I can get, and I could use your dietary advice. I want every edge I can get."

I appreciated the fact that Ty was willing to take help. I'd been an asshole in my rookie year, positive I knew everything there was to know. And I'd been so damn wrong.

I shrugged. "I know she'd try."

"I've been in touch with some of the other guys on offense, and most of them would like to come out and toss some balls."

I hesitated. Although I wanted to do some unofficial practice with the other critical members of the offense, a few of them weren't exactly friends. I'd met some of them during my college years, and I hadn't exactly made a good impression.

"Most of them don't like me," I warned Ty.

He shook his head. "They don't know you, dude. Not really."

"I did what I had to do to bust their balls during college and last year in New England."

"You want this offense to be the best in the league?" Ty asked, staring at me as though he already knew the answer.

"You know I do," I snapped back.

"Then it's time to be a team player, dude. You don't have to kiss their ass. You just have to be able to judge their strengths and weaknesses."

I clenched my fists to my sides. "You don't understand," I said roughly. "I actually ran right over some of them to get to the Cats."

I wasn't proud of my history, but I knew some of my offensive members would just as soon bury me as play with me.

Ty leaned back and crossed his beefy arms across his chest. "Then explain it to me. Most of them are willing to come out and practice."

"I'm fucked up in the head," I said hoarsely. "Or at least I was before I got treatment."

Ty frowned. "Depression?"

I shook my head slowly. "Bipolar."

"Fuck, dude. I just learned to respect you even more than I already do."

I scowled at him. "Why? I just told you that I'm messed up."

"You had a hell of a lot more obstacles than I did," he said thoughtfully. "It's a tough disorder to get under control."

Ty wasn't looking at me like I was mental. In fact, his expression didn't change much at all. "It got out of control soon after I got into college ball. My roommates eventually had to take me into the hospital. I didn't know what the hell I was doing. It took until my senior year to get me stable."

"Do you miss it?" he asked carefully.

"What?"

"The manic phases. Do you miss them?"

I knew what he was asking. I was stabilized on medication, but I knew for some bipolar patients, the temptation of stopping their medications was nearly impossible to ignore. During a manic episode, I had felt like I could do anything. The high I'd had was addicting. I was king of the world, and there was nothing I couldn't do when I was manic. However, I wasn't in control of my actions most of the time. I was somebody else. Not to mention the fact that the mania had been closely followed by crippling bouts of bipolar depression.

"A little," I confessed. "Every once in a while, I wish I could feel like I did when I was manic, but I wasn't in control, and that was worse than the temptation to feel invincible again. My doctors tell me that since I caught it early, I wasn't as likely to go off meds. But I think it's the loss of control that really keeps me grounded. I don't want to go there again."

Some bipolar patients hated stability. They felt flat emotionally, so they opted for going through the highs and lows, even if they were out of their mind.

"Honestly, I never would have known if you hadn't told me," Ty observed. "Do you still have symptoms?"

For a moment, I'd forgotten that Ty was into mental illnesses. It had been his major in college, so he was obviously curious. Strangely, I didn't mind talking to him about it because there was no judgment in his questions.

I shrugged. "I have small highs and lows, but nothing major. They feel more like part of life."

"We all get that shit," Ty said calmly. "Yours might be a little different because of the disorder. But your focus is incredible."

"I've been working on it."

"It shows," Ty answered.

"But that doesn't mean that something can't happen. Something bad."

My illness was like walking on a very thin tightrope. At any time, I could topple off the line and shatter when I hit the ground.

"You can't focus on that, Graham," Ty insisted. "You've been doing good for a couple of years. Yeah, you have a tough disorder, but you should be pretty damn happy with how far you've come. I have a cousin who is bipolar, and she goes off her meds at least once a month. She craves those highs. She's never been stable for long."

"I want to be successful," I confessed. "I want that more than I want to be high."

"You chose your course and you stuck to it until you were able to function."

"It was like being in hell," I said hoarsely. I'd never been able to forget those years of being out of control, unable to play good football consistently.

"But you fought your way back to Earth. Never forget that. If, at any time, you need my help, I'm there," Ty offered.

I had to swallow the lump that formed in my throat. Nobody had ever offered to help me. Maybe because I'd never wanted to risk telling anybody. "Thanks," I said in a husky tone. "I have good doctors right now, and I'm in counseling. But I'll take you up on that offer if I ever slip."

It felt so damn good to know I had support if I needed it. It was something I'd never really experienced before.

Ty nodded. "Good," he answered. "How's the counseling?"

I scowled. "Like being raked over a hot bed of coals. I hate having shit dragged out of me that I'd prefer not to remember."

Ty chuckled. "It's good for you. And hey...you have Lauren to support you, right? She knows?"

I nodded sharply. "She knows. But I fucked up with her so much that she doesn't trust me. Not that I blame her."

Ty had been a good listener, and he knew where I was right now with Lauren. "What do you want from her?" Ty questioned.

The tension in my body eased, and my fists relaxed beneath the table. I slumped back on the bench seat, feeling defeated. "I don't know."

"Bullshit. I think you know," Ty countered.

"Lauren is part of my soul," I said, knowing what I told Ty was the truth. "She's been there for me for so long that I can't lose her."

"I think you're in love with her," Ty challenged.

"I can't have that," I said angrily. "I can't. Not with her. She deserves a guy who can treat her like the fucking amazing woman she is. She doesn't need to be sitting on a bomb that could explode at any time. She should be with somebody who doesn't run the risk of having bipolar kids someday. And I've done some pretty shitty things to her."

"Maybe," Ty analyzed. "But no relationship is perfect. And are you willing to give her up knowing that she could end up with somebody far worse than you? You've done some pretty nice things for her, too. And yeah, you screwed up, but everything you've ever done was out of fear, not because you're an asshole."

"I *am* an asshole," I argued.

"We all are at times," Ty told me. He hesitated before he asked, "So are you up to meeting some of our teammates?"

"I have to go pick up Lauren." Thank fuck her plane was coming in later today. "Go ahead and set it up."

Ty grinned. "You won't be sorry. The more off-season practice we get, the better."

I slid out of the booth and stood. "I hope you're right," I grumbled as I grabbed my jacket.

"I'm pretty much *always* right," he said cockily. "But I wouldn't mind if you worked with me on my diet, and I'll take whatever advice I can get from Lauren."

"She's off-limits for anything *except* advice," I warned him as I put on my leather jacket.

He shot me a knowing smirk, but he didn't comment. I could see the satisfied look on my wide receiver's face as I grabbed my car keys and went out the door to go get Lauren.

CHAPTER 29

Graham

FOUR MONTHS AGO....

"Daddy thinks we should marry, Graham," Hope said casually, as though she was considering whether or not to purchase a new pair of shoes.

Her words came close to making me choke on my protein drink.

We were in Hope's expensive condo, and I was getting ready to start winding down from my season. We still had a few football games to play, but we were out of the playoffs. I suppose I should feel guilty about how my team did, but the defense sucked. I might have played my heart out, but I couldn't save a team who couldn't keep other teams from getting into the red zone.

"Why does he think that?" I asked, still stunned by her comment.

Hope and I hadn't really spoken for the last few hours. I'd just turned off the TV. I'd been watching last week's game, trying to figure out who I could chew out for fucking things up on the field.

And Hope had been frantically working on her social and work schedules on her phone.

She finally looked up and smiled. Just like always, her smile didn't quite reach her eyes. But who in the hell cared, right? She was still beautiful.

Hope said, "Daddy says you'll be a star football player next year because of the way you played this season."

I already knew that. I was either going to end up as the starter for New England, or I was going to take another lucrative contract that came my way. I'd already heard that other teams were sniffing around at the possibility of taking me as a starter, so I'd probably have a pretty big decision to make once I knew all of the offers.

Did I want to marry Hope? Wouldn't I be crazy if I didn't?

She was everything a guy could want from the woman who would be by his side for the rest of his life. Okay, maybe we didn't do much together, and maybe sometimes I felt like I was an appointment to her instead of a date, but we both had busy careers. We were both driven. Hope was in high demand as a supermodel and a filthy rich man's only daughter, and I was still trying to carve out my place in the league.

And...Hope was safe. She'd been around me enough that I'd had to tell her that I was bipolar. But unlike sharing it with Jack and Lauren, I hadn't been worried about telling Hope. I'd already known that she wouldn't really give a damn. Illnesses weren't really her priority, unless she was at a charity ball or something.

Why wouldn't I want to marry her? I studied business in college. Hope's dad had some connections I'd never have, and I wanted to start my own business once I was too old to play football.

The whole arrangement would be perfect for my career, and Hope's.

"Okay," I finally said huskily.

Hope hopped up from her chair across the room. "Great. I'll get the invitations out, and I'll send you links to the ring of my dreams. Don't feel like you need to formally propose. I already found a ring I adore, and I can't wait to get it on my finger. I'll be the envy of all my friends."

I started hoping to hell I did get a great contract. I wasn't poor, but I knew Hope's taste for the finer things, and my current salary wasn't that great. She'd grown up with the best of everything. So I knew the price of the ring was going to be steep.

Hope continued, "I hope you stay here on the East Coast. If you don't, I'll just have to visit you occasionally. It wouldn't look right if we weren't pictured together. I know you're going to have to do what's best for your career, and I have to do what's good for me."

I nearly flinched. We were going to be married, but living across the country from each other if I didn't end up here? Hope did travel a lot, but I assumed she'd make her home base with me. Apparently...not. Her whole social life was in Boston, and she spent a lot of time schmoozing with her dad. But I admired her drive to make connections, so I guess I was going to have to accept the fact that she wouldn't be living with me while I was attached to a team elsewhere.

But I could be with her for some of the off-season, and like she said, she could come to me when she wanted. It wasn't like either of us would have to be pinching a penny.

"Sounds good," I told her.

"Daddy is going to want us to spend the holidays with him this year if we're engaged," Hope mused. "We can get a rush on the ring so I have it by Christmas. It will be so fun to show it off in holiday pictures. And I have to get the invitations out. We can have the ceremony before you start next year."

That worked for me. Once I started training, then training camp, and finally the football season, I could hardly breathe, and my ass was dragging.

I was bone deep exhausted right now from the season. I'd been pushing myself to the limit, and even though I was in the best physical condition I could be in, there was a limit to what a body could take.

Hope leaned down and pecked me on the cheek. "I'm so excited, Graham. I'm going to start working on everything right away. I'll take care of everything so you don't have to. It's going to be the wedding of my dreams."

She was dismissing me. It wasn't like I didn't get the fact that she wanted to be alone to plan things. More than likely, she'd be on the phone the minute I left.

I got off the couch and stood up. "Don't you want to celebrate?" I asked, shooting her a look that had most women wrapped around my cock pretty quickly.

I hadn't gotten laid in months. Hope and I had agreed to be exclusive six months ago, and we didn't see anybody else.

She tapped my shoulder, which was more of a brush-off than not. "You're exhausted and so am I. I just got back from Paris, and you've been playing so hard. Let's make a date for after you finish the season."

I knew what that meant. She wanted to schedule time to have sex. "Put me on your calendar," I grumbled.

I was used to her response. Neither of us really had time for spontaneous sex. But I was willing to *make* time. Obviously, Hope was not.

"What about the holidays? Should I tell Daddy to expect us?"

Okay, I was bummed about that. I tried to get back to Denver every year near the holidays to see Jack and Lauren, but marriage was all about compromise, right? Besides, I was really hoping the Wildcats would make me a great offer, and I could get back to Colorado permanently. They needed a good quarterback, and I could be back home again.

"I'll go to your dad's for the holidays if you join me for my trip in Aspen," I bargained.

Hope pulled a face. "I'm not a skier, but I'll go. Aspen is a place to see and be seen. We'll get some great photos for the social pages there."

"You'll love it there," I told her as I made my way to the door. "It will just be you, me, Jack and Lauren."

I didn't care if Aspen was a place for the rich and famous. To me, it was a special place with Jack and Lauren, and we were going to go in style this year if I got the contract I wanted. Finally, I'd be able to pay them back for all the years that they'd paid for a place for us there in the past.

"Is this the guy who came to visit over the summer?" Hope asked.

Jack had come for a job interview here on the East Coast over the summer, and Hope had briefly chatted with both Jack and Lauren via Skype several times. Jack's interview hadn't panned out into a job, but we'd had a great time while he'd been here.

It bummed me out a little that Hope didn't seem to remember either one of the two most important people in my life, but I put it down to her busy schedule. She met so many people that she couldn't possibly remember them all.

"Yeah, that's him," I finally answered. "And you've chatted with Lauren on Skype."

Lauren and I hadn't touched base as often as we did when I was in college, but we still talked on the phone, by text, or on video chat once in a while.

"Oh, yes," Hope said like a light bulb had just turned on in her head. "The chubby girl with glasses."

I didn't consider Lauren overweight at all. In fact, she had curves that would make any guy take notice. And her glasses were just...Lauren. She'd worn them for as long as I could remember, even though she rarely cleaned them well. I'd always thought they were adorable on her. Now that she was all grown up, they made her look like a sexy wise owl, and it was a good look on her.

Oh, well. Maybe Lauren did look overweight to a supermodel who was so thin I could pretty much feel all her bones.

"I suppose they're both tolerable," Hope said. "Jack was nice to me, but he asks some intrusive questions."

I grinned at her. "He's always been pretty blunt. He usually calls it like he sees it." It was one of the things I liked about him.

"I remember him asking me if I liked being a super-model," she said.

I'd never asked Hope that because I knew her profession was like part of her personality. She thrived on attention. "What did you tell him?"

"I told him I loved it," she answered. "But for some reason, he didn't seem to believe me."

I kissed her lightly on the lips as I got ready to leave. "That's just Jack. We've always been really close, and we don't bullshit each other."

Maybe I had kept some things from my two best friends, but Jack was pretty much an open book. I admired that.

Hope smiled, but her expression was brittle. "Well, if you come to Daddy's over Christmas, I'll do my best with your friends."

What more could I ask for? I couldn't expect her to be as thrilled about seeing Lauren and Jack as I was.

"Send me our dates," I said as I walked out the door.

"I will," Hope agreed before she closed the door behind me.

As I made my way out of the building, I was content.

I was marrying a beautiful supermodel that most men would love to have on their arm. Hope was ambitious, and I knew she'd be cordial to my friends. She rarely snubbed anybody because she might need them for something in the future. She didn't believe in burning any bridges if she could help it. And she was sophisticated enough to impress anybody.

Everything is coming together for me.

I was going to be a star quarterback, and I'd have my pick of teams to sign up with for the following season.

And I was going to marry the perfect woman. I'd have a wife who could open even more doors for me in the future.

But I don't...love her.

I slammed that particular fact out of my mind the moment it popped into it.

As I got into my vehicle, I reminded myself that I didn't love anybody.

Never had.

Never would.

It was enough that Hope would accept me as her husband.

It *had to be* enough.

I wasn't capable of anything else.

CHAPTER 30

Graham

"Oh, my God. This is amazing," Lauren moaned, sounding like she was having one of the best orgasms she'd ever experienced.

I was almost jealous, even though *I'd* been the one to drag her off to one of the better restaurants in the Denver area.

After picking her up at the airport, I'd decided to persuade her to try one of the less dressier places that was still on the top list of restaurants in the city.

Judging by the expression on her face, she wasn't regretting it.

She'd opted for carbonara, and I'd decided on one of the signature steaks with sides.

The food was great, but I couldn't help but be fascinated by Lauren's ecstatic expression.

We both loved good food, but she'd been reluctant about the prices.

I hoped she got used to eating in places like this one. "I want to take you out to a nicer place Friday," I told her.

"Where?" she said as her eyes popped open after she'd closed them to taste her meal.

I mentioned a place a lot more expensive than our current eatery.

"Graham, that restaurant is so pricy," she scolded.

"I'm more than capable of paying," I said calmly.

Yeah, I had to remind myself that I was now a millionaire, even though I still couldn't get used to looking at my bank balance. And I hadn't even gotten my football salary yet. Most of my riches were portions of my endorsements.

Turned out, endorsing boxer shorts and other products earned a hell of a lot of money. Way more money than I'd ever seen at one time, and more on the way.

She rolled her eyes at me. "I know that. I just don't want you to spend it on me."

"There's nobody else I want to spoil," I pointed out. "You know how hard things were for me. I want to share the spoils of my labor. Come on, Lauren. It's not going to break me. Besides, I *need* good food."

"I don't need it," she argued. "I'll probably gain weight."

Lauren had always been self-conscious about her curvy body, and the way she filled out a pair of jeans. Hell, I'd never complain about having that soft, beautiful body against mine. Any guy who didn't adore every inch of her was crazy.

I shook my head, not willing to think about Lauren with any other guy but me.

"So you gain a couple of pounds," I answered. "It's not a big deal."

She put another bite into her mouth and closed her eyes again.

My dick got hard just from looking at her, but I couldn't seem to make myself look away. Lauren was the most beautiful woman I'd ever seen. Every reaction was genuine, and I wished I would have just taken her out instead of leaving her at the cabin after the best sex I'd ever had. What in the fuck had I been thinking?

In truth, I'd been fucking terrified. My night with Lauren had been like a hard slug in the face the morning after, and I'd bolted instead of being there for her.

"*My ass* is a *big* deal," she said when she'd recovered from her tasting climax. "I need to drop some pounds."

I hated the vulnerability in her tone. "You don't need to do a damn thing," I rumbled. "You're fucking perfect."

She raised a brow. "My butt is too big, my hips are carrying way too much padding, and my belly could use some toning, too. Or maybe I'm just too short for my weight."

She was mocking herself, and I hated it. "Perfect," I said grumpily. Fuck knew I wanted her body enough to know that she was everything I needed right now.

I fucking craved having her surrounding my cock again. I needed that wet heat more than I needed to breathe, so her self-deprecation was unacceptable.

"If you keep saying that I'm perfect, I might start believing it," she teased, and then licked the carbonara sauce off her fork.

That brief flick of her tongue made me bite back a groan. My mind was running rampant, and I'd never known what a sexual tease fine dining could be.

Or maybe it was only this way with *her.*

With Lauren, *everything* was becoming a cock tease.

That was why I'd needed to get the hell out of Florida with her. The pain of not having my dick buried deep inside her was downright agonizing.

"Believe it," I told her huskily, my cock hard enough to cut diamonds underneath the table.

I tore my eyes away from her face and focused on my steak.

"How was the physical?" she asked.

"I'm a stallion," I said in a cocky tone as I grinned at her. "A very healthy one."

She nodded and swallowed hard. "I already know that."

Lauren wanted me just as much as I wanted her. I knew the combination was dangerous, but I was getting sick of playing it safe.

I was in a really fucked-up situation.

I needed to fuck her.

And I didn't want to lose her friendship.

They were pretty much two emotions that I just couldn't seem to make come together in my head.

The emotions Lauren stirred up in me were in direct conflict with each other, but I had no idea how to fix it.

She'd always been my Peanut, and I adored her.

But my cock desperately wanted her, too.

"I'm sorry I left you at the cabin," I blurted out. "I think you deserve a real apology. I was scared."

My heart was nearly pounding out of my chest, but I was going to have to face those fears and be truthful with Lauren from now on if I wanted to fix things.

Her expression softened as she gazed at me. "I know you didn't mean it, but it hurt."

"I know. It was a shitty thing to do. But I wasn't prepared for what happened between us. Hell, I'd just been dumped by Hope."

She chewed and swallowed before she answered. "Is it wrong if I say that I was glad you didn't marry her?"

I raised an eyebrow. "Not if it's true. We're always honest with each other. Well, most of the time, anyway."

Even though my emotions were messed up, Lauren had always known me as well as Jack had, and I was pretty sure she sensed that I wasn't in love with Hope.

Eventually, my thing with Hope wouldn't have been enough. I could recognize the stark difference between what I had with Lauren and what I had with Hope after what happened with Lauren at the cabin. "I'm glad we didn't get married, too," I confessed. "I talked to my counselor about her, and I get that my relationship with her wasn't healthy. We would have ended up resenting each other eventually."

"That's insightful," she said carefully. "You don't talk much about your counseling."

I winced. "I haven't mentioned it because it's not something I exactly enjoy. No sense in torturing myself more than once."

"But it will help you heal," she observed.

"I guess I'm not there yet," I complained. "Bringing up old memories hurts like hell."

"I'm proud of you," she said quietly. "It takes a lot of courage to go and face all of those things in your past. I'm not surprised that it's painful."

My heart swelled at her approval, just like it always did. "I want to live strong," I explained. "And counseling is part of that plan, even though I feel like I'm being drawn and quartered most of the time."

She laughed, and the musical sound cut through me like a knife. I liked it when she was happy.

She paused her orgasmic meal to reach for her glass of wine. "I know. I've been there. It's never easy to pour your guts out to a stranger, but it helped me grow. If Kelley hadn't been there for me, things would have been a lot more difficult. She's been a good friend."

I hadn't met Kelley personally, but I was hoping I would one day. She'd helped Lauren through some difficult times, and she'd picked her up after I'd quit on Lauren by leaving the cabin without a word.

Even though Lauren still had her vulnerabilities, she *had* changed over the years. "The things you did on our list took a lot of courage," I praised her, still not quite used to the fact that she'd become a risk-taker.

She'd showed me all her pictures of doing those things, but I still had a hard time imagining Peanut jumping out of a plane or scuba diving, not to mention some of the other crazy things she'd done.

Lauren was cautious by nature, and analytical, so she'd had to go against her learned behavior to make those leaps. But she'd done it.

"I calculated the risks, and every item was less dangerous than driving a car."

I smiled. Maybe she *hadn't exactly* gone against her nature. She'd just found a way to justify doing them. But she'd still been so damn brave.

"Maybe," I answered as I devoured the food on my plate. "But they're a lot scarier than driving."

Most women wouldn't even have attempted most of the things on our list, much less doing them alone. Except, I hadn't planned on her going alone, and I hadn't meant for her to do everything on the list.

It was probably good that I *hadn't* known. I was pretty sure I wouldn't have been able to let her do those things alone.

"I'm sorry you had to do it by yourself." I reached for my water, wishing to hell I hadn't been such a jackass.

I was learning to control my temper through counseling, and how to appropriately deal with the things I'd done wrong. Apologizing to Lauren had been the first step, but I planned on making several leaps to gain her trust again.

She needed me to be consistent, and I vowed that I'd be there for her, no matter how damn hard it might be. No more taking the coward's way out for me.

Lauren sipped her wine for a moment, and then put her glass down as she said, "I'm not sorry," she told me. "I think I needed to do those things on my own just to prove to myself that I could. I actually want to do several of them again."

I didn't need to ask what things she wanted to continue. I'd do any of them with her. "Can I keep you company when you do?"

"I'll think about it," she teased.

I grinned at her. "You do that."

Since I was still ironing out my final contract, I'd need to make sure I wasn't excluded from doing the things I wanted to do with Lauren. I'd have to agree to some stuff. But my agent could negotiate.

The conversation moved to lighter topics, and I didn't stop smiling until we'd finished the meal.

I ordered dessert after Lauren had refused. But she ate most of the decadent torte when I'd offered to share, just like I knew she would.

CHAPTER 31

Graham

"I got the job in Denver," Lauren informed me proudly as I walked her to the door of her father's house.

Our drive home from the restaurant had been mostly quiet except for our groaning about eating too much, and the discussion about the food that both of us had thoroughly enjoyed.

In all the confusion of seeing her again, we hadn't actually talked about her week in DC except for some of the tourist things she'd done. I'd known she'd been hoping to get into a full-time gig in Denver with a think-tank because she was meeting up with some of the head members of the project during her week in DC.

"That's great," I said enthusiastically. The last thing I wanted was for her to move away. Her leaving for a position was completely unacceptable. "Are you happy?"

She stopped at the door and leaned against the brick surface of the house. "I am. I think I have a lot to offer on this project, and it's a challenge."

For Lauren, challenges were rare. She was too damn smart to have to work very hard to solve most intellectual problems. "When do you start?"

"I have a couple of weeks. I have to get through all the paperwork and other requirements to start."

Her excited smile was all I needed to see. "You'll do great."

She sighed. "I didn't get the job I wanted with younger people. Most of them are way older than I am."

"Does that bother you? I know you wanted to be with some people your age."

Hell, I'd prefer that everyone she worked with was old enough to be her grandparents, but I also wanted to see her enjoy what she was doing.

Truth was, there weren't many people like Lauren, so surrounding herself with peers her age was pretty much impossible.

Her brows drew together, and I knew her brain was reasoning things out before she said, "Not really. It's the position and the work that really counts, and it's an important think-tank."

"I know you wanted to hang with a younger crowd," I told her. "But you're special, Lauren. There aren't many people as smart as you are at your age."

"I've accepted that," she said.

"How do you feel about hanging out with a bunch of dumb jocks?"

She punched me on the shoulder playfully. "You are not a dumb jock. You have a college degree."

"All of us do," I informed her. "Everybody starts in college. And you're a big reason why I actually have that degree."

I'd gotten a text at dinner from Ty. He'd set up a practice for tomorrow with some of the offensive guys.

"When?"

"Tomorrow. I know it's short notice," I said apologetically.

"I can do it. I did some analysis and diagrams after I watched videos of your games. I'm hoping they help."

The fact that Lauren had worked so hard to help me made my damn heart ache. She had such a giving nature, and it still baffled me, even after all the years we'd known each other. Life hadn't always been kind to *her*, yet she never stopped doing everything she could to help people. "I know they will," I assured her. "A few other guys will be there from the offense. We're doing some off-season practices."

"Will I be a distraction?" she asked, her tone concerned.

I plucked the glasses from her face and opened my jacket to clean them with the softer cotton of my shirt.

"You're *always* a distraction for me," I answered as I dropped her eyewear back on her face.

She blinked behind the newly-cleaned glass lenses. "That's not good."

No, it probably *wasn't* ideal, but I could never fucking concentrate with her around. Not anymore.

I shrugged. "I'm getting used to it. You're too damn gorgeous to ignore."

"Don't be absurd," she said as she looked away, her face flushing.

"You're blushing," I said with surprise.

"It's chilly out here," she denied.

I moved closer to her and tilted her face up. "It's not the cold, and you're definitely blushing."

For some reason, it tickled the hell out of me to see her flustered.

She looked at me with a dubious expression. "That's what happens when guys throw out false compliments."

My temper flared just a little. It made me crazy when Lauren couldn't see herself the way I did.

My dick was rock-hard. And every instinct I had was fucking screaming at me to bury myself inside the softness of her body. I already knew how it would feel. Nothing would ever erase the ecstasy of sinking my cock deep inside her warm, welcoming pussy.

"I'd better go," I grumbled.

"Don't," she requested. "What did I do wrong? You're upset."

I slapped my hands on the brick beside her head, trapping her inside both my arms. "Is it so hard to believe that I want you so goddamn much that I can't be this close to you and not want to fuck you until you start screaming my name? I have to be with you, but once I am, I'm screwed because I can't stop thinking about how much I want to bend you over the nearest object and fuck you until we're both satisfied."

I heard her breath catch, and she stared up at me with confusion. "I don't know what you really want. Is it friendship or something else?"

"Then let me make myself perfectly clear," I grunted as I lowered my head to kiss her.

The moment my mouth landed on hers, I felt completely lost. She tasted sweet and tart, an addictive flavor that made it damn near impossible to give up.

Her arms wrapped around my neck, and I felt her body tilt into mine.

My arms snaked around her body in a possessive hold as I nipped and licked at her mouth. "Mine," I growled. "You've always been mine, Lauren."

In that moment, I knew she was never meant to be with anybody else but me. I sensed it in a way that was a little eerie, but not terrifying.

It was a come-to-Jesus experience that I should have had several years ago, but I hadn't been willing to even contemplate the idea of Lauren and I together. Now, it seemed like the most natural thing in the world. The realization didn't come softly. It had roared over me like a Mack truck, but maybe that was what I needed. I'd been so damn stupid that I needed a slam to the head.

Before she could answer, I silenced her with another kiss, one even more powerful than the last. My hands moved down her body and cupped her luscious ass, then lifted her body until she could feel just how hard my dick was for her.

"Graham," she said on a sigh as I released her lips. "I ache."

"Me, too," I said as I pulled her tightly against me, needing to feel the connection with her. "This is why I had to leave Florida. I couldn't be with you and not want this."

"I want it, too. But I'm scared," she whispered into my ear.

Her words sliced through my heart. I'd done this to her. I'd made her wary because I'd been terrified myself. "I'm sorry," I said huskily as I backed away. Having her trust me was way more important than getting laid. I needed her faith in me. It was the reason I'd kept going when everything was messed up in my life, and that steadfastness had helped me fight back against my obstacles.

"Nothing I say is ever a false compliment. Do you have that straight in your much larger than average brain?" I asked hoarsely.

"Brain size doesn't necessarily result in higher intelligence," she said automatically.

"You know what I mean," I said, not giving her more time to rattle off mind boggling statistics. "Tell me that you understand that I think you're beautiful," I insisted.

She nodded slowly. "I understand. I don't exactly comprehend your reasoning because I'm not what society finds aesthetically pleasing for the most part. I guess you're an exception."

I leaned forward and kissed her on the forehead. God, she was so damn cute when she was flustered. If I'd screwed up her logic, then it was a win, even though I thought she needed to see herself like I did.

"Tomorrow?" I asked.

"Text me the place and time, and I'll be there," she agreed.

"What about Friday?" If she was in an agreeable mood, I'd get whatever I could. When she started thinking, I knew I was in trouble.

"Okay," she said, her voice uncharacteristically docile.

I nodded toward the door. "Go while I'm still feeling noble."

She scurried to the door and opened it, then slipped inside.

I waited until I saw the light go on upstairs before I took my ass back to the car and headed for home.

CHAPTER 32

Lauren

There was an awkwardness to pacing back and forth in my childhood bedroom while imagining a very different ending to my evening. Graham wanted me as much as I wanted him.

Mine. His sultry claim still warmed me.

I wanted to be his—so badly I was willing to do almost anything. I didn't like what that said about me. After our trip to Florida, he'd texted me a few times to ask if I was okay. Picked me up from the airport. Fed me. Looked at me the way I'd always dreamed he would. No pressure. No promises. Could I accept that? No, I had to throw myself at his feet and reveal that I'd been studying old video footage of him and offer to help him one more time. I would have been less ambivalent about accepting his invitation to spend time with his team if I hadn't pretty much cornered him into asking me to. I may as well have just got a tattoo on my forehead that announced I was still helplessly, hopelessly in love with him. *Obsess much?*

Knowing that he wanted a repeat of Aspen should have made me feel better. I remembered the awe I'd felt the first time I'd realized I could turn him on. There was no longer a need to surreptitiously brush my foot over his dick for confirmation. Graham had declared his attraction to me.

He was also pairing actions with his expressed feelings. Not only was he taking me out on what felt like actual dates, but he was also inviting me into his professional world. I knew how protective he was of that part of his life.

I met the eyes of Max, the teddy bear Graham had given me when I was a kid. Max and I had been through a lot together, and I was embarrassed to admit to myself that Max was still one of my dearest possessions, even as an adult. Graham had given me the bear because he knew that I was having a hard time adjusting to my special school, and told me that Max would watch over me whenever Graham couldn't—I wouldn't be alone. I'd hidden that bear in my backpack for a whole year while I'd attended the school for the gifted. Graham had been someone who had always known better than anyone that I needed reassurance despite the brave face I mustered when I needed to.

Graham was a good man, a good friend and so much a part of me that I didn't know the right next step to take. Life with Graham would have its challenges. His condition could be managed with treatment, but it couldn't be cured. One day it might rear its head again and throw our life into chaos.

Was he worth the risk?

Absolutely, unequivocally, yes.

That certainty didn't lessen my confusion, though.

If Graham breaks my heart again, it's on me this time. No one made me sleep with him. No one would blame me for telling him we need to take a break from each other. He's all passion and no promises—beyond friendship—and sex.

A knock on my door announced my father. "You okay?"

I almost said I was, but I shrugged since I had just a moment ago been pouring my thoughts out to an inanimate object because

I'd been pouring my feelings out to Max since I was child. Maybe I needed the insight of an actual person this time.

My father came in and took a seat on the chair at my old desk. "Graham?"

I nodded and sat on the foot of my bed. "I want to say no—but yes."

"You two have been spending time together. I thought things were going better."

"I know I'm intense, Dad—"

My father chuckled while nodding, then stopped when he realized how serious I was. "It's part of your beauty, Lauren. It's why the world will benefit from you being in it."

"I don't know about all that, but I do try to be the best person I can be. I don't always know what that should look like, though."

"We're still talking about Graham, right?"

"Yes and no. It's really about me. Things that don't bother other people drive me insane. But then I can forgive some people again and again. Does that make me a loving person or a doormat?"

My father leaned forward and a flash of anger lit his eyes. "It depends on what you're forgiving."

"Graham doesn't know how he feels about me. One minute we're friends. The next he thinks he wants more. Then he pulls back again because he doesn't want to hurt me. It's confusing and I keep telling myself I should be angrier than I am."

Relief flooded my father's expression. "Ah, young love."

I blinked quickly. "Love? I wish it were that, Dad. I'm afraid, for him at least, it's just a good case of friends who find each other attractive." I hugged myself. "It's different for me, though."

My father nodded slowly. "I know, sweetie. I saw that one coming for a long time."

"You did?" My eyes flew to his then I looked away—suddenly embarrassed that my feelings were that obvious.

He moved over to sit next to me and gave my back a pat. "Loving someone isn't anything to be ashamed of. And even though this feels like it'll kill you, it won't. You're young. You've got plenty of heartbreak ahead of you."

I half smiled, half sobbed. "Thanks for the pep talk, Dad."

He stood and walked to my door. "You're a beautiful young woman, Lauren, and guys are pigs—don't forget it. You're old enough for this talk. Sex is different for men. They don't need to care to want it."

My chest tightened painfully and tears filled my eyes. "Graham cares."

"Do you have any questions about birth control or condoms?" my father asked, looking as uncomfortable as I felt with the question.

"Dad, I've already had sex. This is about—"

"Stop," my father barked, surprising me. "If you want to date him, don't tell me anything that will make me punch him when I see him next."

"Sorry," I said. That wasn't what I wanted to come from our conversation at all. The idea that time might not be linear, which allowed for the possibility that man might one day be able to manipulate it, brought me comfort because if given the option I would go back and not have this conversation. "He's a good man, Dad. He just might not be mine. Which may not end up being such a bad thing. I don't exactly look like a pro-football player's wife. Not the ones I see on TV."

"What God didn't give you in beauty he made up for in brains and heart," my father said confidently. "Any man who chooses silicone implants over character is a fool."

"So I'm ugly but nice?" I asked.

My father looked pained. "Not ugly, just—you don't do yourself up like some women. That's all I'm trying to say. Your beauty is a natural one. I'm just saying that if you dress like a man all the time that might be why Graham keeps thinking of you as his friend. God, I wish your mother were still here. I'm not good at this stuff."

"You did fine, Dad. Thanks." I wiped a stray tear from my cheek. The talk had actually made me feel a little better. I understood what my father was trying to say and hadn't thought about how much not having a mother had affected me.

He walked out into the hallway then turned. "You were only about as tall as my knee when I knew you'd run circles around me and Jack intellectually. You see the world differently than we do, Lauren, but that's not a bad thing. I can't tell you what's in Graham's heart, but I know what's in yours. Be you, Lauren, no matter what happens with him. Don't try to become someone you think he'd want. Celebrate the gifts you have and someday you'll find someone who will love you for them."

I smiled. "I will."

He cleared his throat. "And always, always use a condom. Birth control pills don't prevent STDs."

I cringed inwardly. "I know, Dad. Thanks. Good night."

He closed my door and I turned on my desktop computer. My father's words echoed through me. I needed to be me no matter what Graham wanted. Realizing that didn't help me when it came to figuring out how he felt about me, but it did help me decide how I wanted to present myself to his teammates the next day.

For the next few hours, I researched the hell out of whatever I could find online about the Wildcats and what kind of technology they were already using to support their training. Then I sent an email to Anders, a computer programmer friend of mine who loved a good challenge. I wanted a program that was 3-D and could isolate certain movements in a video then allow me to write directly on the video as well as demonstrate gyroscopic procession and how sometimes less spin would produce greater yardage. I knew he could get his hands on any program out there and with a little tweaking could make it do what I imagined. I threw in the caveat of having it done that night and waited.

A short while later he emailed me back in an encoded message that he'd acquired a copy of the program they used but preferred a different program that could already do most of what I wanted. He asked me what it was for. When I told him, he said it would take a few hours longer, but he'd do up something I wouldn't get arrested for using.

I laughed, thanked him, and wrote, "Smart friends don't get smart friends thrown in jail."

I wasn't surprised when he didn't respond. Anders didn't have a sense of humor and, knowing him, he was already working on my request. He was painfully introverted, but we had become *sort of friends* after he'd read my undergrad dissertation. He'd read everyone's in his graduating class for entertainment. He was an odd duck, but then, so was I. On paper he would have been a perfect match for me, but there had never been so much as a spark of interest between us.

Before going to sleep I dug through my closet and pulled out every dress I owned. Some were too tight. Some looked too formal for a football field. I found a floral sleeveless dress that fit me perfectly. It was casual, but feminine. I remembered being with Kelley when I'd purchased it. She'd said the color brought out my eyes.

I spun in front of the mirror in my room. The skirt didn't fly up so it would be safe to wear even in wind. My eyes shone with excitement as I wondered if Graham would like it. I told myself it didn't matter if he did because I felt pretty in it. *Friend or lover—this is me.* I reached for the glasses I'd taken off for a moment and put them on again. *Actually, this is me.*

I spun again. I'd always felt more comfortable in slacks than dresses, but I wanted to wear one now. I would soon be working with men who smelled like the moth balls they used to protect their clothing. If I had to spend the time optimizing the natural skills of modern day gladiators I was damn well going to look good while doing it.

Graham texted me with directions to where he and his team-mates would be practicing early the next morning. I asked him if there was a large TV or screen available so I could share something with everyone at once.

He texted back:

What do you want to share?

I answered:

It's a surprise.

Graham: *Don't do anything special. They'll be happy with any insight. I'm hoping you have an idea for me, but really I just want to see you again.*

He couldn't have said anything more perfect or motivational. He wanted *me*. Well, I'd bring him exactly that. The Wildcats were about to have their socks knocked off. *And so are you, Graham.*

Lauren: *Good night, Graham.*

Graham: *Night, Peanut.*

I fell asleep smiling.

CHAPTER 33

Lauren

I bounced out of bed the next morning. My friend had
sent over a program that did everything I needed it to.
I'd already tried it out on my laptop using footage from
the last game the Wildcats had played. I used it to suggest some
throwing techniques that might improve Graham's accuracy. I
also cross referenced the current team to the previous year and
hunted down footage on any new recruits then wrote some cal-
culations that might help them.

I showered, donned the dress I'd chosen the night before,
applied a light layer of makeup, and pulled my hair up into a
loose ponytail, smiling at my reflection when I was done. I would
never be like the models on the magazine covers, but I decided
right then and there to celebrate what I'd been given. Yes, my
hips were wide and my face had a youthful roundness to it, but
was there only one definition of beautiful? Maybe, just maybe, I
could be my own kind.

My father looked up from his coffee as I entered the kitchen
and he smiled. "Going to see Graham today?"

"And some of his teammates."

My father frowned. "Be careful. Remember, no matter how big a guy is a kick to his nuts will drop him to the ground."

I kissed him on the cheek, grabbed a piece of toast off his plate and a bottle of water from the counter. "I'm sure that won't be necessary." I motioned to my computer I had slung over my shoulder. "I'm going to do a presentation on how they can improve their game."

He nodded, then added, "If they're wearing a protective cup—a poke to the eyes also works." He jabbed two fingers through the air to demonstrate.

"You actually sound worried."

He waved in my general direction.

I chuckled. "It's quite modest, Dad. And you're the one who suggested I wear a dress."

He frowned again. "I don't know what I was thinking. Go back to your room, put on jeans and one of those baggy shirts you always wear. You are not allowed to grow up overnight."

"It's still me, Dad," I promised then cocked my head to one side. "And I'm taking this whole conversation as a compliment."

He nodded. "Just be careful."

I gave him a kiss on the cheek and walked away feeling pretty good about myself. My father wasn't normally overly protective, but as I looked back I realized he'd never needed to be. That had always been the job of Jack and Graham. Had I shaken his faith in both? I hoped not.

We were all growing up and making mistakes along the way. Kelley assured me that was normal. I liked that—normal. I didn't want to think about how long it had taken to see myself that way. I didn't want to ruin how good it felt to simply feel comfortable in my own skin.

Graham met me in front of the players' practice field. His eyes widened as he took in my new look. "Holy shit, Lauren, you look amazing—"

I blushed and looked at him from beneath my lashes. "Good morning, Graham." Considering his attire of athletic pants and a T-shirt, I would normally have felt overdressed and self-conscious, but the heat in his gaze told me I'd chosen the right outfit. I didn't want to be *one of the guys*. Not with him.

I tried to keep my composure as my gaze slid over him again. How had he jokingly described himself? As a stallion in his prime? Yes, I could see that. Everywhere I looked he was bulging with muscle and some impossible to ignore excitement to see me. My body was just as thrilled to be near him, but thankfully the female body concealed it better.

"Should I give you two a minute?" a male voice said from beside him. Only then did I realize we were no longer alone. The other man could have been Graham's age or a little younger, and was just as beefed up and similarly dressed. Although I appreciated his physique because I knew the hard work that went into maintaining it, I felt none of the attraction I felt for Graham. I did, however, like the friendliness of his tone and how relaxed Graham remained in his presence. The man's name was Tyler Miller. I recognized his face from the videos I'd seen of him. He was the wide receiver Graham really liked.

"No wonder you felt you had to stake your claim." He held out his hand. "Graham talks about you all the time but he failed to mention that you're gorgeous. I'm Ty."

I blushed again, enjoying the moment even though he probably would have said the same to any woman. I shook Ty's hand as I said, "I'm so excited you're here. I used your last incomplete pass to demo what the software I brought with me is capable of. I'd like to start my presentation with that play if it's okay with you. Then I put together some clips of Graham and several other players on the team along with a few suggestions for each."

Ty's eyebrows rose and fell and he let out an impressed whistle. "Sure. That sounds amazing. And so much more than I expected."

Graham wrapped his arm around my waist. "Not me. She's brilliant. Prepare to be impressed."

"I already am," Ty said kindly.

Graham's arm tightened around my waist and I looked up at him. He was irritated. No. Jealous? My gaze went from him to Ty and back. I could have told him that he had zero reason to worry since there had only ever been one man who made me feel the way he did, but I decided to not make it that easy for him.

I had done the ridiculous on the ride over and listened to a podcast on how to snag a man's heart. It actually hadn't been as bad as I'd expected it to be.

Be yourself—check.

Be a challenge—epic fail.

According to the podcaster, who had used her marriage and anecdotal stories of helping her friends find love, rather than citing a degree on the subject, men valued a woman more if they felt they had won her. I had never been one to play games, but her philosophy matched a common belief that people tended to value something more if they had to work for it.

I was entering into uncharted territory. The idea of flirting with another man to wake Graham up held no appeal for me. I did, however, see that I could be a little less like a puppy running to meet him at the door whenever I saw him. *Be a challenge.* Okay, here goes.

I stepped away from Graham and patted my computer bag. "Can you show me where I'll set up? How many should I expect?" I squared my shoulders and used the professional tone I usually reserved for my older colleagues when I needed to be taken seriously.

Graham rubbed his chin as he watched me adopt that role.

Ty waved for us to follow him. "Why don't I introduce you to the guys first, then we'll lure them to the school. Graham arranged to get a classroom for you."

Unofficial practices were being held on any available field. This one just happened to be attached to a high school.

"Four men from the offense are here," Ty explained as we made our way to where the other men were standing. "Two are excited to talk strategy but the other two aren't as enthusiastic."

Graham jumped in. "They'd better be smart enough to know not to start any shit. Who has an issue with Lauren being here?" His muscles flexed beneath his shirt as he moved.

Ty said, "Gareon and Bruce. Treyvon and Dexter are fine with it."

Graham's hands fisted at his sides. "I should have known. Bruce loves to stir shit and Gareon always follows his lead. I've shut them both down in the past and I'll do it again if they so much as look at her wrong. Why did they fucking even come?"

Oh, no. The last thing I wanted to do was cause a problem for Graham with his team.

Ty put his hands up in front of him. "Calm down, Graham. No one is going to disrespect your girlfriend. They're here to throw some balls around and see you. This is about getting the offense to gel, not fight. At the end of the day, how you feel about each other affects if we win or lose. Whatever history you have with them—let it go. It's a new team, a new game."

Graham nodded and his hands relaxed. "You're right."

We stepped out onto the players' field and I was glad I'd worn flats. I was trotting along to keep up with Graham and Ty while trying not to let myself give in to a rising wave of worry. Four men were already on the field tossing footballs back and forth. They stopped when they saw us and headed in our direction. Graham lengthened his stride and I quickened mine until Ty shook his head at me and said softly, "He needs to handle this on his own."

I stopped and clutched my computer bag. Graham didn't look the least bit intimidated by the four hulking men who stood before him like a human wall. I watched, waited, and prayed. Just as Ty had said two looked less than pleased by not only my presence but with Graham as well. I couldn't hear what they were saying, but the conversation looked civil enough.

A moment later, Graham turned and they all began walking toward us. Ty said, "You've got this, Lauren. Beneath all that muscle, they are just men who want to be the best athletes they can be. They have just as much riding on making this work as Graham does."

I smiled up at him in gratitude. "Thank you. That helps."

Graham frowned at me and Ty again. Had we been alone I would have slugged him in the arm and told him he was being silly, but there was nothing I could do with the audience we had.

Each man introduced himself to me, two with the enthusiasm of children on the first day of school. I refused to let that bother me. I introduced myself and said, "I'm excited by the opportunity to apply what I know about physics to see if my video simulations reflect real world application of my theories."

Gareon shook his head. "Shame I can't stay. I have too much shit to do. I'm game to toss around a ball on another day, though."

Bruce chimed in, "Me, too. I did too well last year to want anything messing with my head."

"Too well? If your quarterback hadn't gotten injured and taken the blame for all your bad receptions you would have probably been benched," I said.

"That's not true," Bruce countered, his temper flaring.

Graham moved to stand at my side. He looked like he was about to say something but I silently pleaded with him not to. Experience had taught me that if I wanted these men to respect me I would have to prove myself—and that was not something that intimidated me anymore.

"The numbers are uncontestable." I quoted his stats from last year compared to the year before.

"Who the fuck do you think you are?" Bruce snapped.

"That's a lot of defensiveness for someone who plays offense," Ty joked in an attempt to lighten the tension. It failed.

"Careful, Bruce," Graham said in a cold, tight tone.

"I think I'm the person who can show you how to position your body better to improve your personal stats. Give me five minutes of your time and if you're not impressed, I'll leave."

"Five minutes?" Gareon mocked. "I guess I can spare that. Go for your Hail Mary."

I smiled with confidence as Graham led us into the school and to the classroom he'd set up before I'd arrived. Five minutes wasn't much, but if I cued the clips up differently each man there would at least have heard a suggestion on how they could improve their game. Ty had given me an insight on what Graham's teammates wanted as we'd walked to the classroom. I wish Graham were as easy to understand. I glanced at Graham as I quickly set up the equipment, and saw that he was still tense and I winked.

A slow smile spread across his face. He leaned in. "I—" He stopped as if realizing that anything he might have said to me would have been heard by everyone there. "I can't wait to hear your presentation."

It was soon show time. I stood in the front of a small theater I'd created with my laptop beside me and the program projected onto a large screen in front of us. I brought up the clip of Ty's incomplete pass, broke every part of it down, then used mathematical equations to explicate why it had been impossible for Ty to catch the ball. There were five pairs of blank stares until I ran the 3-D simulations of how changing position even slightly mattered, and demonstrated how that changed the sticking ability of the ball. I did the same with tweaking how each throw should be met with a different type of catch to increase the likelihood of the receiver retaining the ball.

When I played the clip of Gareon followed by my suggestion, he stood up and walked closer to the screen. "Play it again."

I did.

"You're right," he said and gave me an odd look. "If I had shifted even slightly I wouldn't have lost the football."

I nodded. "And since Graham's injury, he's throwing lower spirals. With minor modifications you could use this to your benefit." I charted out the downward parabolic path. "If you know what angle it'll come to you at, you can adjust accordingly."

Graham walked up and joined Gareon. "I could increase my reach as well."

Treyvon and Dexter joined them. Treyvon said, "Can you show my clip again?"

I ran it again.

"And mine," Dexter requested.

I showed his next.

"I need to try this," Gareon announced.

Graham gave him a slap on the back. "Let's do it."

Ty walked over to me and nodded toward Graham. "You're good for him."

A giddiness brought a goofy smile to my face as I realized I'd done it—I'd won them over. "I know. He's been good for me, too."

"I hope you two work out," Ty said sincerely.

"Me, too," I said and laid my hand on his arm. Ty seemed to genuinely care about Graham and knowing what I now did about Graham's childhood, I knew how important their bond was. I wished it could have been Jack there, cheering Graham on, commiserating with him when things went badly then kicking his ass to try harder, but that was on Jack. And what mattered was that it had not stopped Graham from being capable of other friendships. I had begun to think Graham would never be able to forgive Jack, but seeing him building new bonds with men he had clearly had issues with previously gave me hope.

I closed my laptop and slung the bag on my shoulder. Graham waited for me just inside the door. The backs, the tight end, and the Cats' other wide receiver filed out and Ty waved that they'd see me outside before he closed the door behind him.

Graham lifted my computer bag off my shoulder and laid it against the wall. "Thank you for today." Although his words were simple enough, his mood was more complicated. Instead of looking pleased with me, he looked—torn, frustrated—hungry.

"You're welcome," I said breathlessly as he backed me up against the wall. He filled my vision and sent my senses into overload. Science be damned, how could being with him feel as good as it did if we weren't meant to be together?

He dug one hand into my hair and closed his other over my ass, pulling me flush against him while tilting my head back. His hardening cock nudged against my stomach. "You're mine, Lauren."

I opened my mouth to ask him what that meant, but my question was lost to a toe curling, plundering kiss that wiped all coherent thought clear out of me. Nothing mattered beyond his lips, his tongue, the feel of his hands. I wanted more, so much more. I wrapped my arms around his neck and gave myself over to the pleasure.

He ripped his mouth from mine, his breath ragged and hot on my cheek. "I want you right here, but I can't do that to you. I didn't think I was the jealous type, but every time you smiled at Ty—every touch I saw you give him—it shredded me inside. Don't leave me, Lauren."

I wanted to tell him that I never would, but that was no longer true. "Then don't hurt me again, Graham. Don't shut me out. If I really am yours, then be mine. Be someone I can believe in."

He tucked my head under his chin and hugged me to his chest. I felt, as well as heard, the fast beat of his heart. "I will be. I swear I will."

I nodded against him and wrapped my arms around him, holding him as tightly as he was holding me. Would we make it? Could he be the man I needed him to be? I still wasn't sure, but knowing that he wanted to be was almost as good as a declaration of love from him.

Almost.

But then, Graham had never told me that he loved me, not even when I was a kid. He wasn't comfortable with expressing himself that way.

If I measured the success of the day by how hard to get I'd played, I'd failed miserably. I decided, however, to stop trying to calculate our trajectory and allow myself to enjoy where I was—in the arms of the man I'd adored as long as I could remember.

We stepped back from each other and he cleaned my glasses on his shirt the way he'd done a thousand times before. Some things had changed between us, but others hadn't at all. Our relationship wasn't a traditional one but maybe, just maybe, that was what made it beautiful.

I stayed long enough that day to see the players testing my theories and adopting a few of them. Graham tried throwing lower and farther by adding the additional spin I'd suggested. The others were tweaking how they positioned themselves for different throws. It was fascinating to watch, but I waved that I was leaving. Graham was getting along with the others and I had done what I'd come to do.

Graham jogged over to me. "I'll walk you to your car."

I hated to take him away from the others. "That's okay."

He touched my cheek gently. "See you tomorrow?"

"Tomorrow?" I asked, unable to concentrate when his attention was focused on me that way.

"Our date."

"Oh, yes."

"I can't wait to get you alone."

My mouth opened and closed but nothing came out. I could have reminded him again that alone or not we needed to move ahead slowly, but that conviction weakened whenever he was near. "See you tomorrow," I said, making a quick and somewhat awkward retreat.

CHAPTER 34

Graham

I was as nervous as a teenager on my first date.

And holy hell, it wasn't a comfortable state of mind for me.

I was a twenty-five-year-old guy who didn't do *dating*.

Hell, even my time with Hope had been an *appointment*.

I went to parties, and I got laid. I had no fucking idea how to really impress a woman. Maybe because I hadn't given a shit enough to try.

Until now.

I took one last look at my reflection. I wasn't dressed in a suit, not because I didn't think Lauren was worth dressing up for, but I wasn't a tie kind of guy. If I thought it would make her look at me like I was hers, I'd wear a tux and a million different ties of every color. But she'd hate it if she thought I wasn't enjoying dinner because I was being strangled by a shitload of accessories.

So I'd just decided to be the best *me* I could be.

My black jeans were brand-new, and the cream-colored sweater was appropriate because it was still a little cold in the evening in Colorado.

When I'd stopped at the mall earlier in the day, the clerk had helped me pick out the sweater I was wearing. Apparently, it looked good with my darker hair and complexion, at least that's what the woman had told me.

Honestly, all I wanted was for Lauren to think I was attractive. Maybe I'd screwed up by listening to a clerk who was old enough to be my grandmother.

Disgusted with myself, I turned away from the mirror and made my way to the kitchen as fast as my new pair of black oxfords could take me there.

I tugged on my black leather jacket, and grabbed my keys.

I hated being this uptight.

Lauren was my best friend, but it had somehow become critical that she thought I was dating material, too. The *friend* and the *fucking* thing had been messing with my mind again, but in my heart, I *knew* what I wanted.

As I got into my Range Rover, I admitted to myself that I wanted more than a friend and a fuck from Lauren.

I wanted it all, which was a problem since I didn't really do dates. And I definitely didn't know jack-shit about romance.

I grinned as I sat the gifts that I'd bought for Lauren down on the freshly vacuumed seat. My Range Rover was as clean as the day I bought it since I'd gotten off my ass and cleaned it earlier in the day.

As I did the drive to Lauren's house, I grimaced as I thought about the day before. I'd been so fucking proud of my Peanut and her fearless approach to my teammates. But then, I'd already known she was brilliant. The biggest eye-opener was the way I felt seeing her talking to any guy she wasn't related to, except me.

I didn't want any other male even touching her or being the recipient of one of her beautiful smiles. It pissed me off, especially considering I couldn't really claim her as my woman.

That ends now. Tonight.

A few years ago, my upward mobility had meant everything to me, and I'd mapped out the perfect plan while I was getting my bipolar condition stabilized. I'd thought Hope would be a great addition to those plans. In some ways, I really needed to thank Jack for ending that engagement. If he hadn't, I'd be looking at walking down the aisle in another month with the wrong woman.

Now, I wanted more.

Lauren had always been the woman I *needed,* but I never imagined I could actually *have* her by my side.

Sure, I was still concerned about my worthiness, but I wasn't going to let that stop me. I'd come to a concrete decision, and I knew it was right.

Nobody was ever going to care as much about Lauren as I did, and there was no way in hell I was going to let her go because I didn't try. I wasn't a quitter, and I refused to let myself be defined by my mental illness.

There would always be fears associated with my bipolar disorder. My future of having kids someday was uncertain since the illness was hereditary, and yeah, I could end up in a hospital bed babbling about things that made no sense if I slipped out of my stable state, but wasn't it better to just live my life if or until that happened, knowing I'd have somebody around who genuinely cared about me to help me get through the experience?

Hell, I'd be there for Lauren no matter what happened to her. She could have delusions about being the Queen of England and start dancing around on tables naked, but I'd know who was *really* inside her mind and her body. It wouldn't change the way I felt about her. However, I would have to cover her body and drag her off the table. Nobody was going to see her naked except me.

So if I felt that way about her, was it such a long shot that she could have those same emotions?

I couldn't really remember a time in my life where Lauren wasn't part of my history and my future. *Okay. Yeah.* Our relationship was changing. My dick adored her now that she was an adult, and I wanted carnal knowledge of every inch of her curvy body. The possessive, caveman stuff had surprised me, but maybe it shouldn't have. I'd always seen myself as Lauren's protector, but she didn't need that anymore. She was brilliant, and she could handle herself against any reasonable adversary. So those feelings had turned into a need to claim her as mine.

A fucking unrelenting instinct that was killing me.

Maybe it was a relationship that made no sense on the surface. The jock and the genius?

Problem was, I saw so much more when I looked at Lauren than her intelligence. I always had. I saw *her*. The whole person.

The little girl who had always felt different, but had an endless compassion for other people around her.

The teenager who had made me laugh because she had a sense of the ridiculous, and could make jokes about it.

And now, the adult beautiful woman who I craved like an addictive drug.

Oh hell, I'm fucked.

I should have known I was screwed from the moment Lauren's foot had brushed over my erection at the cabin in Aspen. I wish I had stopped to think about what was happening then, but I hadn't. First, I'd let my dick brain take control. Then, I'd freaked, afraid that I'd do something to hurt Lauren, so I'd run away like a coward to protect her from me. I hadn't consciously recognized that I was doing something that would completely erode a trust we'd built for well over a decade of friendship.

I'd already beaten myself up a million times for losing her trust.

I was ready to prove to her that I could be there for her when she needed me.

Showing her how I felt was so damn necessary that I was nervous. I could dwell on what would happen if I couldn't. Or not.

I'd decided not to accept defeat because that was pretty much my nature, and I needed Lauren too badly to take anything less than her surrender.

I wanted us all wrapped up in each other, entwined, preferably naked, until we didn't know where one of us started and the other began.

I groaned in the dark interior of my vehicle as I turned off the freeway, cursing myself as I imagined getting Lauren naked.

"Don't go there right now," I rumbled aloud.

Yeah, I planned on getting her in bed before the night was over, but I wanted her to know I was going to be there when she woke up in the morning.

I killed the engine as I pulled into Lauren's driveway.

Before I could think too much, I snatched the gifts on the seat beside me and hopped out of my vehicle.

I *could* make Lauren trust me again.

I *could* spoil her like she deserved to be spoiled.

I rang the doorbell, and Lauren's dad opened the door seconds later, as though he'd been waiting for me to get there.

He stepped aside and let me in with a wary expression on his face. I wasn't used to that.

I'd always liked Lauren and Jack's father, Ben. He'd treated me like a second son when I was younger, something I'd never experienced in my many foster homes. I realized now that I'd pushed him away somewhat, just like I'd kept everybody else at a distance when I was a kid. But I didn't need that protective defense anymore.

I shook his hand and he slapped me on the back. I hadn't seen him in a while, and I recognized the fact that I'd missed him.

"Good to see you again, sir," I said as I let go of his hand.

"Lauren is upstairs," Ben said. "But she'll be down shortly. Call me Ben. I feel old when you call me 'sir.'"

I stood in a kitchen that hadn't changed much over the years as I agreed readily, "Ben."

"You clean up good," he told me. "Where are you two off to?"

I hated the edginess I was feeling when Ben looked at me. But then, he seemed to be looking at me as a prospective boyfriend instead of a friend of Jack's.

I told him where we were going for dinner.

He whistled. "Nice place. I wanted to take Lauren there for her birthday, but it was a little too rich for my blood."

I shrugged. "I can afford it, and Lauren deserves the best I can give her."

I made a mental note to take Ben and Lauren out to some places that had been previously out of reach. What was the point of having money if I couldn't use a little of it to have fun with the people I cared about?

"You've done good, kid," Ben said. "You got condoms?"

I squirmed, feeling just a little bit guilty that I saw Ben's girl as the woman who haunted every sexual fantasy I had. "I think we're good," I said quickly.

I'd kind of forgotten how direct Lauren's dad could be. But we hadn't exactly talked about sex when I was younger.

He motioned to the kitchen table and I sat down in a chair.

As he took a seat across from me, he said, "Don't mess with her head, Graham. She's too good for that."

I started feeling like we were speaking the same language now. "I know," I confessed. "All I want to do is make her happy."

"You love her?" Ben asked directly.

I nodded my head immediately. "I do. But I messed up once."

His solemn face lit up in a smile. "If your heart is in the right place, everything will work out. You and Lauren always seemed to fit."

"Don't you think that's strange?" I asked curiously. "We're so different in so many ways."

"Doesn't matter," he denied. "The important thing is that you always saw *her.*"

"I'll take care of her the way she deserves," I vowed.

"Dad? Are you grilling Graham?" Lauren's voice spoke from the entrance to the kitchen.

Ben and I both stood up like we were being caught in the act of doing something wrong.

"Just catching up," Ben denied as he winked at me.

Lauren rolled her eyes in exasperation, but she looked fondly at her only parent as she said, "It's just dinner. And it's Graham."

My heart started to accelerate like I was doing a training run as I looked at her.

Jesus! She was gorgeous.

She made me grateful that I'd made the effort to clean up. But my attempts were put to shame by her black cocktail dress. It was deceptively simple, but the silky material seemed to hug her every curve. I was mesmerized by the view from the back as she went to drop a brief kiss on her father's cheek.

"I won't be out late," she informed him.

"You will," I contradicted. "Don't plan on seeing her until tomorrow," I informed her father.

Ben looked at me with a resigned expression.

Lauren glanced at me with surprise, but she didn't speak.

"You'll need a jacket," I told her. "It's not cold, but it's not exactly warm, either."

She picked up a light coat that was on the back of the chair in the kitchen.

I took it from her and held it out for her as she slipped her arms into it.

"What's this?" she asked as she picked up the gifts I'd left on the table.

The blueberry muffins were self-explanatory. It was her favorite, and I'd gotten them fresh-baked at a shop in the mall.

But I did smile as I saw her looking at them like they were golden.

She finally set the muffins down and picked up the other package.

"It's no big deal. Something you can open later."

I knew that wrapping paper wasn't going to last more than thirty seconds. Lauren wasn't a woman who could ignore something mysterious, even if it wasn't all that exciting.

She tore off the paper, and then flipped open the box.

The sweatshirt was Wildcats blue, and I watched her face as she saw what was written on the front.

The Quarterback is Mine.

I shrugged as I mumbled, "Just something you can wear to the games. I'll get you an official jersey when they come out." Of course, she'd be sporting my name and number on that beautiful body of hers.

She hugged it to her for a moment as she said, "I love it."

"That thing is bound to keep other women away," Ben warned.

"That's the idea," I told him honestly. "I don't want any other woman."

I wasn't about to hide the fact that I was determined to make Lauren mine, not even to her dad.

He nodded like he approved as he said, "You two kids have fun. I'll see you tomorrow."

"Dad," Lauren said in an admonishing voice.

I nodded back, knowing Ben and I had reached an understanding. If I took care of his little girl, I had his approval.

If not, he was going to take me on, no matter how much younger and stronger I might be. I respected that.

I planned to cherish Lauren forever, so I had no problem with the agreement.

Lauren took my hand and tugged me toward the door. "See you later, Dad."

"The convenience store right down the street sells condoms," he mentioned.

I grinned as Lauren's face flushed with embarrassment. I couldn't help it.

We got as far as the Range Rover before we both lost it and started to laugh.

CHAPTER 35

Graham

The restaurant had been everything I'd hoped it would be, and I'd thoroughly enjoyed watching the looks of ecstasy on Lauren's face throughout each course.

However, my patience was starting to wear pretty thin.

I had a love/hate relationship with the way Lauren enjoyed her food.

I loved seeing her happy.

But I hated watching the aroused look on her face when she tasted everything on the table.

It made for a painfully hard meal, even though the food and service had been outstanding.

"I'm done," Lauren said sadly as she placed her linen napkin on her plate carefully. "This is the most decadent thing I've ever done."

I watched her as she reached for her wineglass, silently swearing to myself that Lauren and I would share every wicked thing we could find in the future. "It was good," I answered.

Her brows drew together in the *Lauren* way I fucking adored. "Good?" she questioned. "Graham, it was extraordinary. The food, the wine, the table linens, the service. This whole restaurant is fantastic. And I doubt I would have experienced it if not for you. Thank you."

We both loved good food, so I grinned at her. "There are a lot more places I want to go."

She looked around the elegant interior of the restaurant. "I'll run out of dresses. It's not like I own a whole closet full of nice outfits."

"Does it matter?" I asked. "Denver has a lot of great places that are casual, or I could give you my credit card to buy more dresses and clothes." Fuck! That sounded like a good idea. I liked the idea of taking care of her, and now I had the money to buy her anything her heart desired without it even making a dent in my new net worth.

Most good eateries had always been out of my reach when we were younger.

"It doesn't really matter where we go as long as I'm with you," she answered in a sincere tone.

It didn't escape me that she totally ignored my offer of new clothes. Peanut was stubborn, but I wouldn't have her be any other way. I had a lot of faith in my persuasive abilities, and I'd learned how to get around her stubbornness most of the time.

"But good food doesn't hurt," I teased.

Lauren sighed. "You aren't going to be good for my diet."

"I'll be available to help you work off the calories," I offered huskily.

Her beautiful eyes locked with mine, and I saw the same damn longing I knew I was showing to her when I looked at her. The gnawing sensation in my gut grew agonizing the longer she stared at me.

"Did you mean it?" she asked in a breathless tone. "What's on the shirt you gave me, and what you said to Dad?"

I reached across the table and grasped her hand. "I did. I do. Maybe you won't believe me quite yet, but I'm not going anywhere, Lauren."

Her slightly haunted expression gutted me. But I'd given her enough mixed signals in the past to justify it. I wasn't going to lie to her ever again.

"I want you to be mine," she said hesitantly.

"I *am* yours," I said immediately, trying to tear down the last of the wall I'd built up between us with my stupidity.

We'd made fun conversation over dinner, just enjoying each other's company. But I was more than happy to spill my guts to her. I was ready.

My engorged cock twitched, and I admitted that my dick was more than eager to talk to her, too.

She scrunched her nose adorably as her thumb toyed with the top of my hand. "Is it weird that we feel this way after being friends for so long?"

"My dick realized that it wasn't strange long before my brain did," I confessed. "But this is right, Peanut. I think we both know that."

"I feel like I've been waiting forever for you to notice me, but then you got together with Hope..."

I could hear the anguish in her tone, and it nearly killed me that I'd been so damn stupid.

I stroked a thumb over her wrist. "I'm a work in progress, Peanut," I admitted. "It's not easy to be with somebody who is bipolar. There's always that fear of the disorder taking control. Hope didn't want kids, and neither one of us expected much from each other. But I *did* expect her not to screw other guys. I guess I thought Hope and I were perfect for each other because we were both ambivalent."

"You deserve so much more than that, Graham," she replied softly.

I raised an eyebrow. "So what do I do now that I know the only one who can give me what I want is you?"

"Sex?" she questioned.

I shook my head slowly. "If that's what you think, then I'm not doing a very good job of expressing myself. I want everything, Peanut. I admit, I'd like nothing more than to tease you until you're half-crazy with desire, and then bury myself inside you until we're both satisfied. But that's not going to be enough for me. I need *us*. Maybe it's too soon to want that, but I can't watch you be with anybody else but me."

"It killed me to see you with Hope," she answered. "I never admitted that to myself consciously because I knew it would hurt too much."

Our waiter left the bill on the table quietly, and I let go of Lauren's hand to take care of it.

"I would have felt the same way if you were with somebody else," I confessed. "But you and me...I just couldn't conceive it because I didn't want anybody I cared about having to live with my disorder. It's not for the faint of heart," I joked.

"But bipolar doesn't define who you are as a person. That's completely unique."

I grinned at her as I fished for my wallet. "I think I just had that conversation with myself."

"Do you believe it?"

"Yeah. I think maybe I finally do. I just need a woman who can accept the risk." There was only one woman I needed to take me on, and I was looking at her.

"I can," she said firmly. "I know *you*."

The tension I hadn't realized existed released from my body. "You're probably the only person who really does," I replied hoarsely, fumbling in my wallet until I found my credit card and tossed it on the check.

I lost a few other items in the process.

"What's this?" Lauren asked as she helped me pick up the items that had fallen from my wallet.

"That's priceless," I said, snatching the object from her hand.

"It's a four-leafed clover," she observed. "It looks like it's preserved in resin."

"It's *your* four-leafed clover," I explained. "The same one you gave me before I left for college. I haven't been separated from it since you found it for me."

I smoothed a hand over the plastic cover, trying to make sure it was intact. I'd gotten it preserved right after Lauren had given it to me. It was preserved and mounted on a heavy piece of white cardboard, and covered in a sturdy plastic. I'd been thinking about a more permanent place to put it because it was starting to look a little tattered.

Lauren took it back into her hand and ran a finger down the clear cover. "You saved it?"

"You sound surprised," I answered. "What's the probability of finding one of those?"

"One in ten thousand," she recited immediately.

"I knew you hunted hard for that. It meant a lot to me. I kind of clung to it while I was in the hospital in college. That four-leafed clover and you helped me hang on to my sanity. Every time I wanted to give up, all I had to think about was your tenacity when you were looking for one special clover among thousands of them. It made me stronger."

"If I would have known what you were going through, I would have searched for more," she said.

I snatched the good luck charm back, making sure it went into my wallet. "I didn't need more. I had this one. It was more than enough."

Lauren gazed at me, but she didn't say anything. I had no idea what was going on in her head. She looked like she was thinking about something, and I didn't like the melancholy look on her face.

The waiter who had quietly dropped my check had taken it from the table, and was on his way back to return my card, so I stood up. "Thanks for the great service," I said, putting my card back in my wallet.

We exchanged a few niceties, and he departed with a smile.

When I walked to Lauren's side, I could tell she was still thinking about something, and she didn't look happy. "Hey, no frowning tonight," I said sternly as I grasped her hand and pulled her to her feet.

"I wasn't sad," she said as she grabbed her coat. "I just don't know what to say."

"That would be a first," I teased.

I'd stepped outside and was holding the door open for her before I could see the tears in her eyes with the help of the illuminated exterior of the restaurant.

"Are you okay?" I walked her to the parking lot and was opening the door when she flung her soft, gorgeous body into my arms.

I had to choke back a groan when I tightened my arms around her.

She felt so damn good.

And holding her felt so damn right.

"I hate what happened to you, Graham. You had so many obstacles already that it just isn't fair that you were alone when you needed somebody the most," Lauren said in a muffled voice against my shoulder.

I smiled against her silky hair. I loved the female in my arms so damn much that when she hurt, I hurt with her, but I didn't want her to be unhappy about the past. "If I've learned anything... it's that life often isn't fair, sweetheart."

"Life sucks," she murmured.

"Not right now," I told her as I rubbed a hand up and down her back. "In fact, other than the fact that you're crying, I think it's pretty damn perfect."

I had a boner the size of New York City, but I wouldn't trade the past for my present. If every minute of my shitty past had led me to Lauren, I'd do it all over again.

"Do you mean that?" she said with a sniffle.

I stepped back so I could see her face, and answer her eye-to-eye. "I'm happy where I am right now, Lauren. I'm in a good place, and I have the career I've always wanted. All I need now is you."

Her face looked tormented as she said, "I love you, Graham. Maybe I always have."

"Mine!" I growled. A fierce possessiveness I'd never experienced before Lauren made my chest ache like I was having a heart attack.

Her words conjured up every damn fantasy I'd had since I'd been with her in Aspen. "I love you, too, baby," I said, forcing the words past the huge lump in my throat.

She cried harder. "You've never said that to me before."

For me, it was a monumental moment. "I've never said those words to *anybody.* I should have said them to you a long time ago. I've always loved you back, Peanut, even though it was in a different way when we were kids."

"And now?" she asked hesitantly.

"Now I love you like the woman I can't live without. I love you with all my heart."

It didn't matter that we were in a public parking lot. I fucking *needed* to be inside her.

I pushed her back against the Range Rover, trapped her with my body, and I kissed her, not caring if I ever stopped.

She responded, her arms wrapping around my neck as I did what I'd wanted to do the whole damn night.

CHAPTER 36

Lauren

*I*t wasn't my first time in his arms, but knowing that he loved me changed everything. Every doubt. Every fear fell away beneath wave after wave of joy. Yes, my body craved him, but my soul was cheering it on.

I pulled back slightly only because I didn't want the first time we *made love* to be in public. His hands ran down my back, cupping my ass so I was pressed intimately against his cock.

"What's wrong?" he asked, looking as dazed as I felt.

"How fast can you drive to your place?" I joked.

Comprehension lit his eyes. "Legally?" he joked and helped me into the Range Rover before jogging over to his side and climbing in. He closed the door and pulled me to him for another deep kiss that left us both shaken and breathing heavily. "I have an apartment. I know I do. And I know how to get there, but when you look at me that way I can't remember my own damn name. God, I want to fuck you right here."

His love made me bold. I ran my hand up his thigh and caressed his cock through his jeans. "I want it all, Graham, so much more than we could do in a parking lot." I unsnapped the top of his jeans and slid his zipper down. "But if it's okay with you I'll start while you drive."

He groaned and took my hand in his. "Lauren, I want to do this right. I can wait."

I leaned closer and brushed my lips across his. "Love doesn't come with a playbook. There is no right or wrong way as long as we both enjoy it and right now I want to try something I've never done. Now shut up and drive."

He let my hand go, started the car and laughed. A deep excited flush darkened his neck and spread across his face. "Anything for you, Peanut." He shifted his hips and his open jeans loosened.

We shared the kind of smile only lovers do. I tucked my hand down the front of his navy-blue boxer shorts and freed him. I'd read my share of spicy romances and felt confident with my knowledge of male anatomy and probable erogenous zones. All I was debating was the best angle.

He pulled out onto the road while I was still working through different scenarios in my head. It was difficult to form a single coherent thought with his cock growing beneath my hand. "Do people usually secure their seat belt while doing this?"

He groaned. "I don't know," he answered. I could have challenged that. Of the two of us he was definitely more experienced, but he didn't look like he could concentrate on much more than driving at that moment.

I loved the possessive hand he dug into my hair. We stopped at a red light and I thought he might direct me downward, but instead he claimed my mouth again, his hand tightened in my hair until it was pleasurably painful. When he raised his head he said, "Holy fuck, Lauren, I want this time to be slow and perfect for you. How am I going to do that if I'm already out of my mind?"

"It's already perfect," I said. Seat belt or not. I lowered my head, taking him deeply into my mouth. This wasn't about my pleasure or his, it was about ours. With him I was free and unafraid to explore my sexuality. A car honked behind us, announcing that the light had changed and the Range Rover jerked forward. I slammed against Graham's chest and our connection was momentarily broken.

"Sorry," he muttered.

"It's okay." His cock glistened beneath the street lights we passed. Proud. Gorgeous. Mine. "How am I doing?"

He chuckled. "Everything you do is fucking incredible."

I raced my tongue around the tip of his huge cock, then down around the length of it then started sucking and pumping my head up and down. His thigh was rock-hard beneath the hand I used to steady myself. Up and down, deeper and deeper. I got lost in my own crazy rhythm. I forgot where I was. I forgot everything beyond the taste of him, the guttural sounds of pleasure I was wringing from his lips, and the way my own sex was throbbing and craving his touch.

When we reached the second light he ran one hand up my leg, under my dress to just over the crotch of my panties. His fingers pushed the material aside and dipped inside me, one and then another. He curled them within me and I gasped as he located a spot that had me whimpering with pleasure. He moved his fingers in and out, returning again and again to that spot until I was wet and squirming against his hand. He dragged his fingers out and forward and started circling and rubbing my clit.

His touch was rough, demanding, but no more than I wanted it to be. I cupped his balls with my hand and licked him from them to his tip and back. His fingers swiped back and forth with precision and I moved against them, raising my head just long enough to whisper my demand. "Put them inside me again." He did and I cried out. Never. Never had I wanted a cock like I wanted his.

I raised my head and began to dig wildly through his pockets for a condom. He turned sharply and headed down a dark street between two buildings. I found the condom and held it up victoriously. He withdrew his hands long enough to park the car and throw his seat back. Without hesitation, I shimmied out of my underwear, sheathing him as I climbed onto his lap, facing him. "I love you so much," I ground out as I lowered myself onto him.

"I love you, too, baby," he thrust upward into me. His mouth met mine again and we kissed wildly, pounded against each other feverishly, as if it were the first as well as the last time even though this time it was neither.

He unzipped the back of my dress, then pushed it off my shoulders and down around my waist. He was beyond teasing. He nipped. He claimed. I hung on, offering all of me to him, feeling safe even while I lost control because I was with my best friend as well as the man who was promising me forever.

He raised his face and held mine between his hands. "Say you're mine, Lauren."

"I'm yours, Graham. All yours."

"And I'm yours, Peanut." He rewarded me with a series of upward thrusts so powerful, so hard and fast that I called out his name as I gave myself over to a mind shattering orgasm.

He began to jackhammer up into me and it sent fire spiraling through me. Could I have quantified it as a second orgasm, I was beyond caring. All I knew was we fit together as well physically as we always had emotionally.

I spasmed against him. He grunted and swore as he came inside me. We shuddered in unison then collapsed against each other.

It was only then that, although I was bare to the waist, I noticed he was still fully dressed. I laid my face against his shoulder and sighed. "Nice sweater."

He kissed my forehead. "The lady at the store said you'd like it, but she didn't say how much."

With him still inside me I straightened on his lap and gazed into his eyes. "What lady?"

He smiled tenderly and caressed my cheek. "She was about a hundred years old."

"Good," I joked. "Those are the only women I want to see you with."

His expression turned serious. "I don't need anyone else, Lauren."

"I was only joking," I said and cringed at how defensive I sounded. The sex had been perfect. He'd said he loved me. What more did I want?

As he always had been able to, Graham sensed the change in my mood. He kissed me gently then eased me off him. "Let's go home."

His home? My home? Was the night over? I didn't want it to be, but I also didn't want to cling to him if he needed space. "Okay," I said.

"You didn't have any plans for tomorrow, did you?" he asked after he'd cleaned himself off, refastened his jeans and pulled the car back onto the road.

"No," I said, telling myself that he might always need time to process changes in our relationship and part of loving him was being able to honor that. What I really wanted to do, though, was shake him and demand to know what everything we'd said to each other meant in practical terms. "Why?"

He took one of my hands in his and kissed it. "Because I doubt either of us will have much energy after tonight."

My breath caught in my throat. "Oh yes?"

He took one of my fingers between his teeth and nipped it gently. "This was amazing, but we're nowhere near done. I'm going to fuck every inch of you, slowly, over and over. Then I want to wake up and have you all over again. How does that sound?"

"Like you need to drive faster," I said with a smile.

The lusty grin he gave me was matched with an increase of speed that had me reaching for my seat belt. He gave me a wild ride back to his place, and then another one just inside the door of his apartment.

CHAPTER 37

Lauren

I woke the next morning with a moan of contentment and a smile on my face. Flashes of the night before danced behind my still closed eyelids. Wild, carnal sex. Tender, sweet sex. He'd given me both in abundance. I licked my lips loving that the taste of him was still with me.

Breakfast. I'd need sustenance before another marathon of sex. I rolled onto my side and threw my arm out, seeking him. My eyes flew open when I felt only an empty bed beside me.

No. I refused to panic. This was different. I had no reason to doubt Graham. He'd said he loved me. He said he was mine. What kind of relationship would we have if I lost my shit every time he was out of my sight? Love was based on trust, wasn't it? I needed to trust him.

I listened for the sound of him in the adjoining bathroom.

Nothing.

I held my breath and listened for any indication that he was in the apartment.

Nothing.

I sat up, hugged my suddenly uncertain stomach, and whipped my legs around. Naked, I gave in to my fear and sprinted from room to room. I counseled myself to stay calm. I reminded myself of every time he'd been there for me, every promise he'd kept.

But I couldn't stop the memories of the last time I'd believed in him and woken up alone. I tried to distinguish how this time was different, but reason fell as doubt set in.

He'd once said he didn't know how to love. What if this was what he'd meant? What if he could say all the right words and still repeat the cycle of leaving me?

It wasn't the same. This time, if he left me without a word, if he refused to take my calls or see me, my heart would break in a way I wasn't sure would ever heal.

His keys were gone.

His phone was gone.

No note.

The room spun slightly and my legs went weak beneath me. My clothing was folded up neatly on the table beside the couch. To make it easier for me to get dressed and leave before he returned?

My stomach heaved. I ran to the bathroom and stood over the toilet, wishing I could retch and get it over with.

That was when I heard the door of the apartment open and close, followed by the sound of his car remote being tossed on a table. I was a jumble of relief, anger, fear and shame.

"Hey," he said softly from the door of the bathroom.

I straightened and stood there shaking. "I thought you were gone."

He stepped forward and pulled me into his arms. "After last night, I woke up hungry and thought you might be, too. I decided to surprise you with muffins but realized I didn't have the mix. There's a store two minutes away. I thought I'd be back before you woke."

I told myself I wouldn't cry. I was done crying. I chastised myself for overreacting and tried to compose myself, but I couldn't. Raw and unsure, I wanted to be better than I was in that moment. I wanted to tell him that the past was done and gone.

I couldn't, though. I couldn't stop shaking. I raised my fists between us, and pummeled them on his chest. Not to hurt him because I didn't want to hurt *him*. I did it because I didn't have the words to express how angry I was with *myself*. We had come so far. He was offering me everything. What if I was the one who ruined it this time? What if while he had spent so much time worrying about his diagnosis and how that would affect me, he hadn't considered my challenges?

I was still my own worst enemy.

He hugged me and murmured, "It's okay, Peanut. I'm here. I'm not going anywhere." And he kept hugging my tense frame until eventually I laid my head on his chest and closed my eyes.

"I'm sorry," I croaked.

He kissed my temple. "I love you, Lauren."

"I know." I could have lied to him then, but I needed my friend as much as I needed my lover. "I love you, too. You should be able to go out to the store without worrying that I'll lose my mind." I searched his face for any sign that I was driving him away.

His arms tightened around me. "It's okay. We're okay. I shouldn't have left. I should have considered how you might feel if you woke without me and waited."

Tears filled my eyes but I sniffed and blinked them back. "Last night was perfect and I—"

He smiled down at me, but I knew I'd hurt him. "I don't need perfect, Lauren. I need you."

I sniffed again and chuckled only because of the way he'd said it. "Thanks?"

He growled and kissed me then. Somewhere in the passion I found my footing again. When he raised his head, desire was clouding what had already been a difficult conversation. "Trust takes time and I shook yours. I'm willing to prove to you that I'm not going anywhere this time."

I caressed one of his cheeks and let his words wash over me. "I want to tell you that you already have."

He kissed me briefly. "I'd rather you tell me the truth—always."

I nodded. "I love you so much, Graham. I don't want to imagine my life without you in it, but I panicked when I woke up alone. I hate that I did. I'm embarrassed and angry with myself."

He tipped my chin up. "Be angry with me instead. I put that doubt in you."

My heart ached for him. "You've been through so much. I understand why—"

He ran a thumb over my lips. "You need to promise me something right now."

I would have promised him almost anything just then, but I didn't say it. I simply waited.

He said, "Don't cut me excuses. I don't want or need them. I may need your support one day, but I know you will be there for me. I need to know that I'm that for you. If I fall short, you kick my ass until I get it right. We clear?"

I swallowed hard. Graham could have gotten defensive or told me how he thought I should feel, but then he wouldn't have been the man I'd spent my whole life loving. He saw me, even the sides of me that I wasn't proud of, and he accepted them. "Okay."

He swung me up into his arms as if I were the size zero woman I'd never be. "Good, then how about we cook breakfast together?"

I wrapped my arms around his neck. "I'd like that."

A lusty smile returned to his face. "But stay naked. It's my favorite look on you."

He placed me down on my feet just inside his kitchen. I waved at his fully clothed body. "Then you strip as well," I challenged.

His eyebrows wiggled then while holding my gaze he began to slowly remove all of his clothing. By the time he was fully naked, his cock waved fully erect at me and I had trouble remembering what had brought us to the kitchen.

With his hands on my hips, he lifted me onto the counter and spread my legs for him. I leaned back, loving the way he cupped my sex and leaned closer. "Relax and let this one be all about you, Peanut." With one sure move he pulled a chair over and sat between my legs. He pulled me forward until I hung off the edge a bit, parted my sex with his fingers, then blew his hot breath against it before swiping his tongue down the length of me.

There were still things I didn't know—like how many times I needed to wake up beside him before waking without him wouldn't topple me—but I did know that none of those thoughts belonged in that moment. I gripped the back of his head, guided his tongue to my clit, and thankfully didn't have a damn thought outside of how good it felt.

CHAPTER 38

Graham

It had taken me a month to convince Lauren that she needed to move in with me, but it was worth every moment of that time spent convincing her she could trust me.

Was she there yet? Did she have complete faith in me?

I had no idea, but if it took years, I'd happily give her all the time she needed until she was ready to marry me.

As long as she was mine in the meantime.

I'd used the excuse that her think-tank job was a lot closer to my condo, but I knew that wasn't why we wanted to be together.

For me, nothing felt quite right without Lauren around. I fucking loved being with her, and I wanted to see her gorgeous face every night when she arrived home from work.

And I made damn sure she went to work every morning smiling.

"Take your hand off my nachos," I growled to Ty.

Lauren laughed as all three of us sat around the table in my condo having a birthday celebration. Since Lauren's birthday was two days after mine, we'd picked the day in between our birthdays to celebrate both of them. Now that Lauren was settled in with me, it made sense to have a small party in the condo.

Ty had invited himself.

And Lauren had asked Kelley to stop over. We hadn't seen Kelley yet, but Ty already had his hands all over the food.

"I don't get a chance at junk food very often anymore," Ty protested. "Not now that I'm following your diet. But it helps me to avoid energy spikes, so I'm rolling with it. But today is a cheat day."

I glared at him, daring him to touch the heaping plate of nachos in front of us. He had a decent burger, minus fries, but Lauren had made the nachos for me because she knew I missed them.

"Eat the chicken wings," I suggested.

He reached for the plate again. "Not the same. Lauren didn't make them."

"Suck it up," I demanded as I snatched the plate and put it safely in front of me.

Lauren was an amazing cook, even though she didn't like doing it that often, and I was okay with that. We generally did something simple when she got home from work, or she had to put up with something I made.

Things would shift when I started training camp in a couple of weeks. I knew I'd be dragging ass home every day instead of working more casual practices with my offense. But we'd figure things out as we went along with our careers. Lauren and I were good at adapting to different situations. Things just seemed to flow into place without us really noticing the difference. I knew most of our silent communication was due to the fact that we'd known each other for so long.

Lauren seemed to know what I needed even before I did.

And I sensed what she wanted the most.

We were still getting used to the fact that we loved each other so much that we had initiated every surface in my condo by having sex on it.

The intensity of our relationship just seemed to keep getting stronger.

And our love just kept on growing.

But I wasn't afraid of those emotions anymore. In fact, I was grateful that everything had happened the way it did. I hadn't completely forgiven Jack, but I'd told Lauren to invite him over. I might have to grind my teeth for a while, but he was Lauren's brother. There was no way I could continue to hold a grudge. Maybe we'd never have the same kind of friendship we'd had before, but for Lauren, I'd tolerate the bastard.

The doorbell rang just as I tore into my nachos, and Lauren sprang to her feet. "I'll get it."

She looked at me hesitantly.

I met her eyes and nodded, letting her know I was okay with whoever walked through the door if she was good with who was outside it. The condo was *our* place now, and I didn't want her to ever feel uncomfortable with inviting anybody she wanted into our home.

She gave me an encouraging smile that melted my damn heart before she hustled to the door.

As long as it wasn't some dude who looked at her like he wanted to fuck her, I was determined to be nice to any of her guests.

Ty looked at me as he took a break from inhaling his burger. "You okay with Jack being here? I did slug the guy pretty hard."

Honestly, I was glad that Ty had put Jack on his ass. It might've created less tension between me and Jack. "He deserved it," I said unapologetically.

"He's definitely not going to like me," Ty warned.

I shrugged. "Doesn't matter." I liked Ty, and I knew Jack, even though we didn't spend any time together anymore. "He's not the type to hold a grudge. I think he knows he deserved it, too."

"I can't see you being with anybody but Lauren," Ty observed.

I grinned at him. "Me, neither. But I have no problem making Jack squirm, so no worries."

Ty had been the type of male friend I'd never had in my life, the type of guy who either liked somebody or he didn't. There was no bullshit with him. He either accepted somebody unconditionally, or he steered away from them. We got along with all of the rest of the offense, and I'd actually gotten to like some of them during our practices. Our offense was starting to gel, but Ty was the only one I'd let completely into my life.

I heard two distinctive male voices joining with Lauren's, and stopped shoveling food in my face to stand up and greet my guests.

Ben walked through the entrance to the kitchen first, followed closely by Jack.

I was happy to welcome Lauren's dad.

Jack was a little bit harder to get excited about.

Ben and I had come to an unspoken agreement: I'd treat Lauren with love and respect, and he'd trust me with his daughter enough to stop warning us both about condoms.

It worked.

I greeted Ben with a handshake, and then looked at Jack.

It was painful to see the friend who had betrayed me. But I also saw good memories when I saw his face, times when we'd stood by each other no matter what. Jack was part of my past, and he'd be part of my future. I wasn't sure when all of the betrayal stuff would go away, but I was grateful for the fact that I had Lauren now. I hung onto that fact as I finally offered him my hand.

"Jack," I acknowledged out loud. "Glad you're here."

"Thanks for inviting me," he said quietly.

"I didn't," I stated bluntly as we quickly shook hands. "Lauren asked you to come, and I love your sister more than I dislike you."

Jack grinned, a mischievous look that I'd seen so many times before. "I guess that's something," he answered.

I introduced Ty, and then I watched as the two men seemed to size each other up.

Jack offered his hand to Ty. "You have a mean right hook."

Ty accepted Jack's greeting grudgingly. "My dad was a boxer." Ty's warning to Jack was pretty clear, although it looked like he was willing to get along with whoever we welcomed into our home.

As I watched the exchange between my former friend and my new one, I wondered if there would come a day when we could all forgive and forget.

Ty might be tolerating Jack, but he'd be the first one to stand up and defend anybody he cared about. That was one of the things I liked about him. There was very little that wasn't black and white with Ty.

"I wonder what happened to Kelley," Lauren said with a frown as we all got ourselves seated back at the table.

I could tell she was worried. Kelley had just moved back to Denver from California. I hadn't gotten the opportunity to meet Lauren's friend yet, and Lauren hadn't seen Kelley since she'd arrived in the city the day before. "Text her?" I suggested.

Lauren dashed to get her phone in the living room, and she came back with a look I knew well on her face. She was upset. "What's wrong?" I asked as I got up and went to her side.

I could hear Ben asking Ty about his football career, but I was focused on the unhappy look on Lauren's face.

"Her rental car broke down," she informed me. "She texted that she's going to be late."

"I can go pick her up," I offered.

"I'll go," Ty said enthusiastically as he got eagerly to his feet.

I smirked at Ty. I was pretty sure Lauren's dad had started his lecture about using condoms with my friend, and I couldn't blame him for wanting to avoid that subject. I guess I needed to give him a break.

Lauren texted back and forth with her friend, making arrangements for Ty to pick Kelley up while Ty—the sneaky bastard—managed to swipe some of my nachos.

"Move it," I told him as I pushed him toward the door.

Ty was still chewing as he got Kelley's cell number and the information from Lauren.

"I'll bring her back safe," Ty assured Lauren with a smile.

I gritted my teeth as Lauren put a hand on Ty's arm and thanked him before he left.

Lauren's sweet nature was something I'd have to get used to, but I didn't have to like seeing her close to another guy, even a friend.

I was pretty sure Ty loved every moment of Lauren's attention. He seemed to get off on seeing me off-balance when it came to my girlfriend. I wasn't sure whether he was a sadist, or he just wanted to help me feel more comfortable with her showing innocent affection for other men.

I knew he was safe. Rationally, I knew he wasn't lusting after my woman.

But it still pissed me off.

"I'll wait until you get back to bring out the cake," she shouted at Ty as he left the condo.

I wrapped my arm around Lauren's waist, just wanting to feel her beside me. She melted into my body like she belonged there, which she did.

"I love you," she murmured in a low voice meant only for me.

My heart stuttered as I tightened my arm around her. She knew I had possessive instincts, and her first inclination was to reassure me that she'd always be mine. "I love you, Peanut," I said huskily in her ear. "But I wish you'd stop touching other guys."

She laughed, a carefree sound that calmed my ass down in a hurry.

Lauren wasn't laughing at me; she was trying to make me laugh at myself.

It worked.

As I looked at her radiant expression, I grinned back at her.

What was a little discomfort when I had a woman like Lauren? Compared to what I had with her, it was pretty much nothing at all.

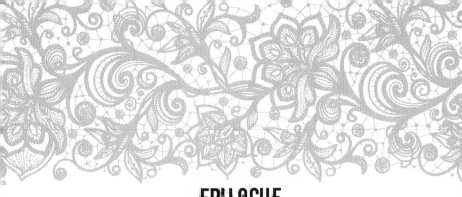

EPILOGUE

Lauren

SEVEN MONTHS LATER...

The crowd was deafening as the Wildcats offense rolled back onto the field.

"Please let Graham and Ty win this game," I whispered to myself, knowing nobody could hear me over the roar in the stadium.

I was a wreck. The score was tied, and there were only a few minutes left on the clock.

I was on my feet with the rest of the crowd, and Kelley was next to me, looking as cold as I felt. Granted, it could have been colder. It was pretty much the average temperature in Denver in January, but after being exposed to the elements for over two hours, I was starting to feel the cold wind.

"I'm freezing my ass off," Kelley yelled.

I looked at the pretty brunette next to me and smiled. "Welcome to Colorado in the winter," I told her in a voice loud enough for her to hear as I watched the team set up for the snap.

Kelley swore that she hated football, but I'd watched her during the game, and I'd noticed every time she flinched while she was watching Ty taking a hit.

Something had happened between her and Ty when he'd gone to pick her up during our birthday party months ago, but she'd never told me what happened. She'd told me that Ty wasn't significant enough to talk about.

Knowing Kelley as well as I did, I instantly knew there was something she wasn't telling me. But she hadn't cracked over the months, saying over and over again that Ty didn't matter.

I was starting to think that she protested way too much for a woman who didn't care about Graham's best friend.

As far as I knew, she'd never seen him again outside of the few meetings they'd had at our condo after the birthday party.

What was it about Ty that she disliked so much?

Personally, I adored Ty, so I couldn't imagine what had fueled Kelley's irritation with him.

During their brief meetings at the condo, they'd both ignored each other, a fact that hadn't escaped me or Graham.

I cheered as the running back escaped a tackle and gained more yardage. I'd helped him work on that spin to throw off the other team's defense, and it had worked.

"Come on, Graham!" a male voice called from the other side of me.

I looked fondly at Jack, who was on the opposite side of me, and my father who was next to him.

We were all here to cheer Graham and the team on.

My heart was in my throat as I watched Ty break away and run down the field. He and Graham were setting up for a long pass, and the clock was ticking down way too fast.

I watched as Graham confidently released the football, and it sailed toward Ty.

"And Miller goes in for the touchdown!" Jack hollered.

They did it. They did it.

There was almost no time left on the clock and Ty had caught Graham's ball perfectly and fought his way into the end zone.

The Wildcats had won the divisional championship game.

"They're going to the Super bowl!" I yelled like every other fan in the stadium.

Jack swooped me up and twirled me around. "I knew he could do it," my brother said excitedly.

Jack was one of Graham's biggest supporters. I wouldn't say he and Graham had recovered the friendship they'd had in the past, but I had hope that someday they might. It had been a slow process, but they were closer than they'd been seven months ago, so I had hope.

Even Kelley seemed caught up in the moment, and she hugged me as she bounced up and down.

I'd make her a Wildcats fan eventually. It had been her idea to come to the finals, something she'd never suggested before because she swore she disliked football. But I certainly wouldn't have known by the look on her face at the moment.

The extra point was made, and the game ended.

The crowd was still rowdy as I said, "We need a warm building and some hot chocolate."

I'd seen everything I'd wanted to see.

Graham and his offense had gelled, and they'd pulled out the win against a formidable rival team. I swiped a tear from my cheek as I looked out toward the field before I went inside.

I couldn't see Graham because of the horde of fans that were celebrating.

But I could *feel* him.

My eyes were on the big screen, and I could see his face turned toward the stands.

I love you, Graham. You're such an amazing man.

My heart swelled with pride as I saw him finally turn away and address a reporter.

After this game, I knew I wouldn't see him for several hours. He'd be tied up in statements and interviews. But he'd come home to me, just like he had every single day during the intense months of training camp and the season.

The public could have him for now, but he was coming home to me.

No more uncertainty, and no more doubts. I'd finally gotten out of my own way and recognized the fact that Graham would always be mine, whether he was with me or not.

"You okay?" my dad asked as he put a hand on my shoulder.

I nodded quickly, knowing my father could see my tears. "I'm good. I'm just happy."

I hugged him to reassure him that I was much better than okay.

"You got yourself a good man, Lauren," he said as he let me out of a bear hug.

I could see Kelley making her way inside with Jack not far behind her. "He's had such a long road to get here, Dad. He's worked so hard."

If I thought too long about how much Graham had struggled to get his head above water, I knew it would break my heart.

"He's home now, honey," my dad pointed out. "And he's happy. Some people spend a lifetime looking for what he has now. The hard work has all paid off."

I nodded and smiled as I put my hands in my pockets to get them warm, and then turned toward the heat of the indoors.

We found Jack and Kelley inside, both of them in line to get a warm drink.

Dad and I stopped next to them.

When Kelley had relocated, I'd hoped that Jack and Kelley might hook up, but they'd never shown any interest in being anything more than friends.

We got our hot chocolate and took some available seats in the building to get warm before we made the trek to the car.

I was just sitting down when my cell phone rang. There was no doubt in my mind who it was. Graham called me the minute he could get a second alone, which was usually near the locker room after he'd taken a shower.

A quick glance at my caller ID confirmed my conclusion.

"You were phenomenal," I said into the phone. "But did you have to keep me in suspense until the last minute?"

"I had no choice," Graham shot back. "They were a tough team."

"I'm so happy for you," I told him as I pulled off the lid on my cup.

"I don't know if this ever would have happened if it wasn't for you," he stated huskily.

"Oh, no. I am not taking any credit. This was all you, Graham. And you earned it." I hesitated before adding, "I love you."

"I love you, too, Peanut. I'll see you soon. Thanks for sticking by me all season."

"I always will. I knew you'd win today, Graham, do you know how?"

"How?" he asked in that bemused tone that always warmed my heart.

"The same way I knew I'd make it down the black diamond ski run as long as I had you at my side. Being with you has taught me to believe in things I can't see—I simply know them." His silence didn't scare me as it once would have. I understood now that he was often quiet when he was his most emotional. "Give Ty a hug for me."

"No hugging," Graham grumbled, but his voice was deeper than normal.

I laughed, delighted that he was still the man I loved, even after becoming part of a championship team.

We hung up after a quick exchange, both of us more than ready to celebrate and to work off steam when he got home later.

Or at least that was Graham's excuse for turning into an unstoppable, horny male when he finished a game.

I wasn't sure what drove him every other day because he was pretty much insatiable all the time.

Not that I was about to complain.

I took a sip of my hot drink after I'd dropped my phone back into my pocket. Jack, Kelley, and my dad were in an intense conversation right next to me, but all I could think about was Graham.

I stood up and fumbled to shed my jacket, warmer now that I'd been inside for a half hour. I smiled as I saw my shirt, the one that Graham had given me before training camp had even started.

The Quarterback is Mine.

Maybe I hadn't quite believed it when I'd gotten the shirt from Graham, but I knew it now. I trusted him more than anybody else in the world, and no matter what our challenges were in the future, the words on the shirt would always be true.

Graham Morgan, QB number twelve, was irrevocably, completely and always would be...mine.

It hadn't taken a genius to figure out what we meant to each other, but all of my analysis had never worked when it came to Graham. I didn't need my high IQ or my reasoning ability. I'd just had to follow my heart.

~ The End ~

JAN'S AUTHOR ACKNOWLEDGMENTS

My deepest thanks to Barbara Riste, MBA MA LCP for helping me try to get into the head of a man with bipolar disorder. Your insight and suggested reading material was invaluable to me on my journey with Graham.

And as always, thank you to my husband, my KA team, and my wonderful street team, Jan's Gems. Your support means everything to me.

And Ruthie, you already know I adore you. Thanks for making this project amazing.

xxxx Jan (J.S. Scott)

Please visit me at:

http://www.authorjsscott.com
http://www.facebook.com/authorjsscott
https://www.instagram.com/authorj.s.scott

You can write to me at
jsscott_author@hotmail.com

You can also tweet
@AuthorJSScott

Please sign up for my Newsletter for updates,
new releases and exclusive excerpts.

Books by J. S. Scott:

The Billionaire's Obsession Series:

The Billionaire's Obsession
Heart of The Billionaire
The Billionaire's Salvation
The Billionaire's Game
Billionaire Undone
Billionaire Unmasked
Billionaire Untamed
Billionaire Unbound
Billionaire Undaunted
Billionaire Unknown
Billionaire Unveiled
Billionaire Unloved

The Sinclairs:

The Billionaire's Christmas
No Ordinary Billionaire
The Forbidden Billionaire
The Billionaire's Touch
The Billionaire's Voice
The Billionaire Takes All
The Billionaire's Secrets

The Walker Brothers:

Release!
Player!
Damaged!

A Dark Horse Novel:

Bound
Hacked

The Vampire Coalition Series:

The Vampire Coalition: The Complete Collection
Ethan's Mate
Rory's Mate
Nathan's Mate
Liam's Mate
Daric's Mate

The Sentinel Demons:

The Sentinel Demons: The Complete Collection
A Dangerous Bargain
A Dangerous Hunger
A Dangerous Fury
A Dangerous Demon King

The Curve Collection: Big Girls And Bad Boys
The Changeling Encounters Collection

Let's stay in touch!

www.ruthcardello.com

Sign up for my newsletter and receive a free ebook.

Follow me on:

GoodReads
https://www.goodreads.com/author/show/
4820876.Ruth_Cardello

Facebook
https://www.facebook.com/ruthcardello

Bookbub
https://www.bookbub.com/authors/ruth-cardello

Twitter
https://twitter.com/RuthieCardello

91943615R00154

Made in the USA
Middletown, DE
04 October 2018